THE CYBORG'S WARNING

BOOK 2

Benoit Lanteigne

80 Mapleton Rd, Unit 11-80
Moncton, New-Brunswick, Canada
E1C 7W8

Benoit Lanteigne

80 Mapleton Rd, Unit 11-80
Moncton, New-Brunswick, Canada
E1C 7W8

https://thecyborgscrusade.com

Book Layout © 2016 BookDesignTemplates.com
Edited by Eliza Dee, Clio Editing
Book Cover Design by 100 Covers

The Cyborg's Warning / Benoit Lanteigne. -- 1st ed.
ISBN 978-1-7779002-8-1

CONTENTS

Do you want a free short story that serves as a prequel to The Cyborg's Crusade? Then, join the cyborg's fan club on my website,

https://thecyborgscrusade.com/fanclub.html

The next book, The Cyborg's Riddle, is available for preorder and releases on January 8, 2024.

Beyond Repair

Chapter 1

Tigal 23, 2133, on the Nirnivian calendar

The truck's air conditioning chose the perfect time to break. As that thought entered Isham's mind, he wiped off sweat from his brow. Ostark's temperature tended to push the upper limit of the thermometer, and according to the radio, this was the hottest day of the year so far. That explained why he'd fired off a series of curses when the AC had stopped pushing a cold breeze halfway through his trip. It wasn't like he could roll down the window. This particular truck lacked the common feature. Even if it hadn't, using it would have been against the rules. Suppressing a sigh, Isham glanced at one of the several armored vehicles escorting him. Those poor fellows probably had it worse, so he'd manage.

Few drivers dared to deliver military equipment to outskirt outposts. When his friends had learned he accepted such contracts, they'd tried their best to dissuade him and questioned his sanity. BBR often attacked these kinds of convoys. The isolated roads leading to their destinations proved excellent for ambushes. The army's efforts to stop the terrorists yielded little result. Pressed for a reason to take such a risk, Isham had explained he did so for his daughter. The job paid a bundle and had ended up being his lone option when it came to providing a decent education for Anna in the future.

Most considered him either stupid or too brave for his own good. The truth was, neither word applied. Isham understood the danger, barring the former. As for the latter, courage failed to contribute to his decision. In fact, fear gripped him every step of the way. He scanned the road ahead with a fervent focus, dreading any sign of an upcoming raid. Whenever he noticed a movement in the bushes, it almost triggered a panic attack. Monetary benefit was his sole motivation, and as soon as he'd accumulated enough funds, he'd...

Wait... what the freak? A kid had dashed into his trajectory. They'd collided in an instant. Why was a child in this desolated part of the country? No one lived here. Panicked, Isham slammed on the brakes, swerved and crashed into a nearby military vehicle.

The resulting bang accompanied by the sound of crushed metal assailed Isham's ears. The bulletproof windshield shattered. Glass shards rained on him, cutting his flesh as his body rocked and tumbled. His brow hit the steering wheel, and a blunt pain tore him apart. Thanks to his slow speed, the injuries proved less severe than they might have been. Blood dripped into Isham's eyes, but he ignored that fact and kicked his door open. Though every muscle ached and begged for him to stop, he rushed toward the child. Isham froze once he found her and, understanding what he witnessed, he screamed. On the soil rested a bloodied Anna. Completely immobile. No pulse. Dead. Tears streamed down his cheeks as another shout escaped Isham's lips and he hugged the cadaver. Crimson stains covered him.

How? How could this happen? Why would any kid, let alone Anna, be here? They lived miles away, and this zone was uninhabited. It made no sense. Around Isham, chaos erupted. The Ostarkiran soldiers escorting him ran in random directions, yelling. At least one of them rolled on the ground for no apparent reason, bawling about bugs. Gunfire echoed through the area. Isham ignored it all. Nothing mattered without Anna. He strengthened his grip and cried. Time lost its meaning. It might have been minutes or even hours later when a soldier grabbed him from behind, brandishing a knife. The assailant mumbled something about Isham being a dirty terrorist. Then he plunged the blade toward Isham's neck. Any resistance would only delay him joining Anna in death, so Isham didn't even try to free himself as the edge slashed his throat.

***

Under different circumstances, it might have been an idyllic scene. Back leaning against a tree of many in the forest, Wrathchild took a deep breath. Fresh air tinged by a sweet vanilla-like aroma coming from the Pris filled her lungs. She spotted its distinctive blue foliage, the only one among the surrounding flora and contemplated her luck. Prises were a rare sight. The land of Ostark and Nirnivia offered a hostile environment for their kind. Despite knowing this, their ancestors had planted some, and a few survived to this day.

Upon a branch above Wrathchild stood a pissack watching the BBR troops with suspicion. As a kid, she'd adored the furry rodents like many children. Back then, Auntie Bonny, a term of affection rather than a blood relation, often got such animals to feed on nuts she held in her hand. Had Wrathchild possessed some, she would've tried her luck, but alas...

In the sky, Wrathchild noted several birds flying and chirping random songs. The sun shone, perhaps with too much strength. They endured an intense heat. Not that the fact surprised them. When visiting Ostark, better be prepared for high temperatures. Still, she enjoyed the atmosphere, at least until the rumbling motors echoed, burying the sounds of nature.

Wrathchild swallowed hard as her companions sprang into motion. Most grasped their binoculars and pointed them toward the closest road. Diabo, in particular, showed great enthusiasm. Most leaders commanded at a distance, but he never did. Often, the crimson beast led his men into battle, putting himself at risk. Paradoxically, she deemed this behavior both commendable and reckless.

The surrounding vegetation shielded the group from their prey's eyes, or so they hoped. Not that it mattered all that much. A smirk appeared on Diabo's lips, and he signaled Allison, the stray jacket-wearing woman.

Unlike her peers, Wrathchild failed to reach for her binoculars. She knew what to expect and saw no point in viewing the resulting carnage. Soon, terrified screams accompanied by Diabo's ever-widening smile confirmed her prediction, and she resisted a shiver. The cacophony lasted for about five minutes and then it stopped. A frown appearing on her brow, Melissa grasped her binoculars at last. The Ostarkiran soldiers stared at each other, most sitting or lying on the ground. Though shaken and wondering what had happened, they were calmer than anticipated. Suppressing a nervous expletive, Wrathchild glanced at Allison. The three-eyed blond woman collapsed to her knees and cried.

Diabo also focused on Allison. He glared at her and stepped forward until he towered above the diminutive figure and brandished a menacing index finger. The girl whimpered in advance. "Damn it, Allison!" He clenched his fist. "Why did you stop?"

"Please don't make me do this anymore. It's painful... please, no more fear... I don't like fear. Please. It hurts so much!"

Though the tree provided a comfortable support she'd rather not forsake, Wrathchild left it behind and walked toward Diabo at a brisk pace. "Boss"—in less than a second, he turned his neck and looked at her, the sheer rage filling his yellow irises causing her to pause and avert her gaze— "maybe finish job ourselves? They're disoriented. Little danger."

She was in pain. Allison mind reader. Not good one. Only see fears. Plus no control; forces visions on others without wanting to. Diabo thought was powerful weapon. Found way force her. Messes her up. Feared died if pushed too hard.

—Thoughts of Wrathchild, Hocmar 28, 2134, on the Nirnivian calendar

Diabo glared at her while stroking his chin as if he debated how to handle her intervention. Wrathchild stayed immobile, wishing to avoid escalating the situation, but prepared herself to reach for her sword just in case. There wouldn't be any logic in attacking his own follower, but with him, one had to be careful.

"What's wrong, Wrathchild? Sympathy fer a gun?" Laughter escaped his lips. Upon hearing his hilarity, Wrathchild's muscles relaxed. "Shit, I ain't letting 'em go that easy. We're damn lucky Doctor Death ain't found a way o' stopping our little toy yet. It can happen anytime. I'm gonna have my fun till then. 'Sides, gotta put Allison back in her place, don't ya think?"

As he spoke, Diabo picked a remote control attached to his belt. Poor Allison whimpered, and Wrathchild turned her head away. Both understood what came next. Undeterred, the red monster pushed a few buttons without a trace of hesitation. Despite her reticence, Wrathchild peeked at Allison, praying she'd survive. The device wasn't meant to kill the living weapon, but its usage always worried her. A buzzing sound cut through the air, and Allison went stiff as a broom. Her eyes opened wide and her mouth gaped as she propelled her skull backward.

"Arrrgghhhh! Nooooo! Aaaaaah!"

Uncontrollable sobs were heard as she crumpled sideways and twisted in contorted shapes. While she convulsed, she held her temples as if a splitting headache overcame her. Wrathchild gritted her teeth. In a moment of pity, she peeped at Diabo, still clutching her blade. Soon, she rejected the notion. Defying her leader here would only lead to her demise, leaving Allison to her fate. Negotiation lacked any chances of success. And so she did nothing and cursed her name for her decision.

The Ostarkiran soldiers' desperate screams returned. Again, Diabo observed the massacre through his binoculars. Several minutes passed before he began stretching as if preparing for physical activities. "Well, boys, I wanna have some fun. Feel free to join in!"

On that note, he rushed toward the enemies like he did when he judged their numbers had thinned enough. The other goons soon followed, except Wrathchild, who lingered behind. Once alone, she approached Allison, crouched next to her and caressed her cheek.

Conflicted. Should leave with Allison. Take her away. Save her. Could survive? Probably not. Sick, need medical attention. Couldn't keep alive without help. Not until left neutral zone. Didn't matter. Couldn't betray Diabo. Too weak.

—Thoughts of Wrathchild, Hocmar 28, 2134, on the Nirnivian calendar

Another stroke and Wrathchild mumbled, "Sorry..." Then she unsheathed her sword and dashed after her comrades. No point wasting ammo on disabled targets. Absorbed by the imaginary terrors, the remaining Ostarkiran troop didn't notice the BBR assailants advancing on them. Most writhed on the ground or ran around in confused patterns. As she progressed, Wrathchild finished them with her blade. Most of her colleagues used knives for the same purpose. Diabo, on the other hand, slaughtered them with his bare hands, unleashing an unrelenting rage, punching the soldiers until a bloody mess remained or strangling them. Wrathchild had witnessed her share of violence, but she shuddered at the enjoyment he displayed.

As she accomplished her macabre task, Wrathchild pondered what visions assailed her foes. The loss of loved ones? A degrading fatal disease? A swarm of bugs feasting on their flesh? So many possible phobias. Then a bullet flew near her face, interrupting her reverie. Alerted, Wrathchild spun toward the source. A confused Ostarkiran soldier sprinted at her, shooting. Thank God his fright rendered his aim awful. Surrounded by projectiles, Wrathchild engaged her super speed, drew her gun and fired right into the man's forehead. A second later, another bang echoed from her side. Undaunted, she whirled and deflected the projectile with her blade. A mere instant after, she jumped at the aggressor and decapitated him.

Apparently out of harm's way, Wrathchild took a few deep breaths and relaxed. Once the adrenaline spike diminished, she surveyed the area. It seemed they had eliminated every enemy. Diabo walked toward the truck they meant to intercept. What was that in his hand? Was it... a severed spine? Shocked, Wrathchild covered her mouth with her fingers and gagged. That went quite far even by his standards. As she chased the disgusting vision from her mind, she joined the others at the transport. Once close enough, she heard a BBR goon ask, "What's in there anyway, boss?"

Diabo shrugged. "Don't know, really. Should have some nice supplies fer us, whatever it is. If not, who cares? We got to kill some scumbags."

Chapter 2

As expected, when Wrathchild arrived, she found Allison strapped to a sophisticated stretcher and stuck in a state resembling a coma. The three-eyed girl stayed immobile except for the rhythmic rising and lowering of her chest. At least that showed she lived. Once standing beside Allison, Wrathchild removed the wet compress resting on her forehead. The telepath twisted as much as her restraints allowed and mumbled an inaudible complaint. With a sad smile, Wrathchild grabbed a fresh pad, dipped it in a nearby bucket and used it to replace the old one. The deed done, she caressed Allison's arm.

"Gonna be okay, kid. Gonna be fine."

Thanks to an advanced piece of technology, Diabo controlled Allison's telepathy. A push of a button forced her to unleash her power on their enemies. The same equipment prevented her from rebelling against BBR, an act she'd no doubt attempt if given the option. Such brain manipulations brought consequences; the whole ordeal proved exhausting for the young woman, and she would be out cold for days, or even weeks. In Wrathchild's opinion, the side effects worsened each time. She lacked the medical knowledge to confirm her suspicions, but she feared if they kept abusing Allison's abilities, she'd die soon.

Taking care of Allison when those breakdowns occurred wasn't part of Wrathchild's job. In fact, sometimes she noticed Diabo staring at her, wondering why she bothered nursing a "gun." Though she might've imagined it, she suspected he disapproved of her compassion, but he didn't stop her, so she continued. She'd always shared a connection with the poor soul. No idea why, so she assumed guilt.

After Allison calmed down, Wrathchild patted her hair. Her fingers brushed against cold metal and, sweeping aside a lock, she peeped at the electronic crown fixed on the telepath. Out of reflex, she then reached for the same apparatus attached to her own skull. While identical from a technical perspective, they served opposite goals. For Wrathchild, the crown equaled liberation. She suffered from a mutation that rendered her metabolism hyper fast. In her natural state, she moved with incredible speed, and she spoke at such a pace that her speech ended up unintelligible. Back then, she had relied on drugs to alleviate her symptoms. However, they caused nasty side effects. The medicine slowed her down so much she felt dumb and unable to think properly. She also endured nausea and other minor ailments. Thank God, one day the crown replaced the pills: another gift from that bastard Torkin. For all his evil, he had helped her more than anyone.

With her new toy, she tamed her abilities. She could suppress her swiftness and even amplify it to make her quicker than ever. Her mastery evolved until she managed to adjust the velocity of specific limbs independently. While impressive, she failed to master a single aspect of her physiology: her mind. Wrathchild's thoughts rushed through her head without respite, causing inferior concentration. The mere act of forming complete sentences challenged her. Her brain wanted her to form them faster than even her inner voice could, let alone her mouth. Because of this, Wrathchild often dropped words in order to keep up. This explained the broken speech pattern some found so annoying.

While the electro-crown proved a blessing for Wrathchild, it was nothing less than a curse for Allison. Despite her appearance and talents, Allison didn't suffer from a mutation. Rather, she came from a species of mind readers. Or so everyone assumed; it was hard to tell with visitors. She had never joined BBR, as Diabo had decided her unique skill provided an ideal living weapon. BBR had captured and enslaved her using a customized electro-crown that delivers incredible pain when she disobeys him. At first, she'd resisted and sometimes she still tried, but in the end, the torture always won.

Chose to be here. Not Allison. Wasn't me kidnap her, but don't kid myself; guilty anyway. Let Diabo do it.
—Thoughts of Wrathchild, Hocmar 28, 2134, on the Nirnivian calendar

Moral dilemma aside, Allison had turned out to be a great asset for BBR. In the instant it took to blink, she reduced an enemy platoon into a bunch of whimpering cowards. This raised a major question: why hadn't BBR destroyed the Ostarkiran forces already? A simple answer existed: limitations. Allison's telepathy was limited to a radius of thirty meters and she couldn't subdue more than a few hundred people at the same time. Also, in her natural state, Allison's capabilities lacked the strength required for Diabo's purposes. Plague and the scientists under his command had increased her power via genetic modifications, but now she could only use her abilities for thirty-seven minutes a day, assuming she did so without resistance—fifteen minutes if coerced by the electro-crown. Though important restrictions, they weren't the main reason Ostark still thrived. No, that was because Doctor Death had foreseen the danger she represented.

When the mechanical man had first appeared in Ostark, he'd demonstrated his worth and President Laforge had hired him as an adviser. Right from the start, the cyborg warned that the Nirnivian telepath might become a dreadful menace. He suggested a theoretical countermeasure: the telesthesia blockers. With the assistance of an elite research team, Doctor Death developed a prototype. They were immense devices the size of a medium building and blocked Allison's telepathy, rendering her useless. Before Diabo abducted her, telesthesia blockers protected every facility of remote importance to the Ostarkiran military.

The telesthesia blockers made Doctor Death inaccessible. Diabo would love nothing more than to mount an assassination attempt with Allison at the forefront. The mechanical man knew they valued him as a target and hid in secret locations. This complicated matters, yet he wasn't as sheltered as Rose. He sometimes emerged for cabinet meetings, speeches or medical procedures. The terrorists attempted to attack him during these events, but since the president never appeared outside of a telesthesia blocker's range, why bother bringing Allison? Instead, for the most part, her assaults ravaged transport trucks delivering equipment to remote facilities. On occasion, their destination obliged them to follow isolated routes devoid of a telesthesia blocker's influence. Whenever BBR identified such cargo, they struck, assassinating the escorting troops and stealing the load. This offered two rewards: demoralization of the Ostarkirans and much-needed extra supplies for BBR.

At least, the Ostarkirans failed to develop compact telesthesia blockers. If they had, Allison would be completely worthless. Then again, Wrathchild remembered that implied the telepath would be free. Perhaps this would have been a better alternative after all.

Chapter 3

Tigal 24, 2133, on the Nirnivian calendar

To his frustration, James woke up around four in the morning. Tiredness still assailed him, yet he sensed he wouldn't fall asleep again. Despite his pessimism, he still attempted to do so, tossing and turning for a while. Soon, it became clear his original cynicism had proved warranted. With a sigh, James crawled out of bed and reached for the light. Being accustomed to the darkness, his poor eyes resented the brightness, resulting in a squint. He shielded them with his hand, to little effect, but his pupils adapted and the pain subsided. There remained the question of what to do...

The chamber offered few entertainment possibilities. James considered visiting the rec room and sampling nighttime Nirnivian TV, but upon further consideration, he chose otherwise. Somehow, sneaking around Valardir at such an hour seemed like a bad idea. The guards might be startled by his unexpected presence, and an accident could happen so quickly. He did have access to books, but since he had attempted reading them before, James realized they consisted of dense historical texts. An unfamiliarity with Nirnivia and a lack of vocabulary meant he failed to comprehend the documents.

Though not intending to, James started rummaging through the refrigerator. In truth, he wasn't hungry. It was simply something do to. Food as a diversion wasn't far from eating your emotions. Perhaps it was worse, he couldn't decide. Not that it mattered. The fruits and processed meat available provoked little desire, and he closed the fridge without grabbing a snack.

For a moment, James remained standing, scratching his head. What if he returned to his mattress after all? It'd be pointless, but no better alternative presented itself. Then a thought entered his mind, and James walked to the desk, opened a drawer and grabbed a pen and his journal. Thus equipped,

James sat on the bed and plucked the picture of Nadia from his wallet, then fixated on the blank page.

I began a journal a couple of days before. Since I was so bored, I figured it'd give me something to do. Besides, Nadia always told me writing down what happened to her helped her gain perspective about her life. I'd already developed a habit of talking to her picture about my day, so I just scribbled the key points. Thing is, because I was stuck alone so often, there wasn't much perspective to gain.

—Thoughts of James Hunter, Hocmar 28, 2134, on the Nirnivian calendar

How long he struggled with his diary, James couldn't guess, but when the phone rang, he had accomplished negligible progress. The ringing startled him, and he gasped as he dropped the jotter. Out of instinct, James glanced at the clock. Not even six yet. He received few calls, all from Rose, and he doubted the prophet would contact him so early unless an emergency had arisen. The second that thought entered his brain, a surge of adrenaline rushed through his veins and he ran toward the phone. Covered in sweat, he picked up the receiver. A monotonous synthesized voice greeted him.

"Hello, Mr. Hunter, I must apologize for the intrusion. I hope I did not wake you. Am I right in assuming you are currently alone? We have some important matters to discuss; however, if this is an inconvenient time, our conversation can be delayed." Whoever contacted James modified his voice. His tone lacked any natural qualities, yet somehow it felt familiar.

"Who... who are you?" As James said that, the screen mounted on the phone's cradle turned on. The monitor displayed an image, fuzzy beyond recognition, but it soon cleared up, revealing the mysterious interlocutor. James swallowed hard. A vision of horror stared back at him. Devoid of any hair and scarred, the man looked as if he had suffered severe burns in the past. No mouth remained; a crudely sewn speaker replaced it. An electronic right eye shone with a faint blue light. James had witnessed this gruesome figure on TV soon after his arrival. He could never forget.

"How embarrassing, I did not introduce myself. I am the president of a country called Ostark. I am certain you have heard of me by now."

As I gazed at the mutilated man, panic grew inside me. I didn't know much about him, but everything they'd told me indicated he was dangerous. Doctor Death wasn't as scary as Diabo, but he had this creepiness to him. Diabo looked like a savage monster willing to tear you apart. This was different. He was obviously a normal person, but so ravaged it seemed impossible he could be alive.

—Thoughts of James Hunter, Hocmar 28, 2134, on the Nirnivian calendar

"Um, yeah, I know who you are. You're Doctor Death," James said in a whisper. Should he hang up? Should he scream for help? Should he listen?

"That is the name my enemies use to slander me. It is not of my choosing." Until then, the cybernetic man's robotic eye displayed a smiley, but it turned upside down. "I do not blame you for your distrust. I am sure Ms. Rose Ricdeau and her followers told you plenty of lies about me, and unfortunately, I currently cannot refute their claims. I come with a warning. Ms. Rose Ricdeau is not what she seems. She is a beautiful woman who can be charming beyond reason, but she is also very dangerous. Should you make one wrong move, she will stab you in the back without hesitation."

The conversation was unbearable. He was a mess; his disfigured face had to be the most unpleasant sight I had ever endured. I wondered what the hell had happened to him. If that's possible, his voice was even worse. Completely monotone... I almost ripped my ears off. And yet, part of me wanted to listen to him. It's like a horrible car crash. You try to look away, but somehow, you just can't.

—Thoughts of James Hunter, Hocmar 28, 2134, on the Nirnivian calendar

"Why should I believe you?" He groaned. "Rose has been nothing but kind to me. I'd be dead without her. She saved my life twice and gave me a new home."

The cyborg nodded. "I understand that, from your point of view, Rose has been most cordial. Unfortunately, you did not appear in Ostark, so I could not provide any assistance. Here, you would have been treated as an honored guest. Surely you would not have been thrown in jail like a common criminal."

"That was a simple misunderstanding."

"Perhaps. Even so, the fact remains that you were imprisoned for several hours. In my humble opinion, you are far too forgiving toward the Nirnivians' transgressions. Nevertheless, I merely desired to issue a warning. I understand there is no reason to believe me. I am a perfect stranger, and I realize my appearance does not inspire trust. However, think about it. I have nothing to gain from you. My only concern is your well-being. I implore you: watch your back. Be observant, and you will notice details that show that I speak the truth."

The talk made me uncomfortable. It was obvious he wanted to drive a wedge between me and Rose. Besides, if I was caught talking to him, I'd be in trouble. I had to get rid of him.

—Thoughts of James Hunter, Hocmar 28, 2134, on the Nirnivian calendar

"Shut up! Just leave me alone!"

"Unfortunately, I cannot comply. You see, I must do all I can to assure your safety. My moral code leaves me no choice. As such, there is one last thing I must mention—"

James had had enough. That face... that voice... he couldn't stand it any longer. It had to stop. While gritting his teeth, he slammed the receiver down, terminating the communication. Then he sat down on his bed, trembling. He took a few deep breaths as sweat dripped down his brow. After a couple of seconds, he glanced at the phone, expecting it to ring again. Thank God it didn't.

Once my nerves calmed down a bit, I figured I had to tell someone what happened right away. There were probably cameras in my room, so they'd find out Doctor Death contacted me. If I didn't raise the alarm, it'd be suspicious, so I went to Rose. I was so scared, I forgot how early it was.

—Thoughts of James Hunter, Hocmar 28, 2134, on the Nirnivian calendar

***

A resounding clicking sound tickled the mechanical man's ear as James Hunter hung up on him. Filled with calm, he studied the receiver in his hand for a moment before putting it down. Though an apparent failure, the first contact had gone better than he'd dared hope. He'd half-expected James to end the call the instant his face had appeared on the phone's screen, but against the odds, he had accomplished his goal. Regardless of whether James admitted it or not, he'd planted a seed of doubt and it would grow. Since he spoke the truth, no other alternative existed. Sooner or later, the new visitor from Earth would notice disconcerting details about his hosts and he'd remember the president's warning. He had mastered patience as a virtue during his youth, so he'd wait until James became ready to listen to him. For now, he returned to his Alcharia virus studies.

As the cyborg reached for a test tube, he froze. That gaze he felt. No question, the bastard paid him a visit again. Then the familiar diabolical cackle echoed, followed by, "So it begins, eh? 'Bout time we get some fun 'round here!" As he'd trained himself to, the Doctor ignored the laughing fool and his presence vanished, allowing him to return to his work in peace.

Chapter 4

As she suppressed a yawn, Wrathchild dipped the rag in the bucket, then squeezed it to remove the excess water. The correct moisture attained, she grabbed the mirror shard resting on what passed as her dresser. She pressed the cloth against her face and shuddered at the cold touch. Hot water might be superior for hygiene purposes, but it proved a rationed resource among BBR's ranks. At any rate, she cleaned her visage as best she could, attacking the spots of dirt she noted on her reflection.

An ache spread through Wrathchild's shoulder during a strident scrubbing motion, and she winced. After a moan, she massaged the sore muscle. Little effect rewarded the gesture. She opened a drawer and rummaged through its contents until she discovered the desired bottle. With a sigh, she squeezed lotion on her fingers and applied it to the tender area. Though cold at first, the cream soon heated up to the point that she grimaced. Still, she kept smearing it, but not too much. BBR lacked easy access to medication, this one included. She had to ration it.

Once satisfied, Wrathchild put back the balm in its designated spot and noted the wrinkles on her wrist. Frowning, she picked up her mirror again and studied her face, particularly the corners of her eyes. She also checked her hairs and acknowledged the multiplying gray strands. In fairness, she looked like an attractive middle-aged woman. Great, except she was twenty-three. Part of the blame lay with the fact that she took poor care of her appearance, yet it failed as a complete explanation.

No doubt Plague would've used the opportunity to warn Wrathchild she should be more careful with her powers. She exhaled at the thought. Yes, Plague had a point, but the nature of BBR denied her that possibility. Most of her comrades deemed her mutation amazing and envied her skills. Maybe they'd reconsider if they were aware of the price she'd paid.

Since birth, she had enjoyed an ultra-fast metabolism, and that implied rapid aging. Most doctors gave her a life expectancy of sixty to sixty-fix years, which paled in comparison to the ninety-eight allotted to a normal Gorumar. The crown fixed on her skull allowed her to control her speed, but it didn't stop her body's deterioration. Worse, it exacerbated it. When she used the crown to accelerate, it took its toll. At this rate, Plague estimated she'd be lucky to reach forty, and he might be right. The wrinkles and gray hairs multiplied. More and more, she endured intense soreness after battles, even if she escaped unscathed. Sometimes she wallowed in pain for days. But what was the alternative? Death on the battlefield? That wouldn't help her prolong her existence. She worried about her condition, not so much for herself but for the others. How long before she'd become a useless wreck? Those fears entered her mind more often lately. She endeavored to chase them away, but with less and less success. Those aware of her ailments shared her concerns but, Plague excluded, they preferred not voicing them. She groaned. The lone solution she found was leaving BBR, and that wasn't an option. She had nowhere else to go. She'd burned all her bridges. And so what? Like it or not, she'd never abandon Diabo.

Chapter 5

White as a sheet and trembling, James stared at the beeper on Rose's door. A soldier patrolling the area glanced at him in the distance. James assumed he thought it strange someone would visit "Her Holiness" at this hour. Still, he chose not to interfere, though he lingered nearby and observed the situation cross-armed. The prophet was often awake this early, and James deduced that explained the lack of intervention from the guard.

After a few deep breaths, James pushed the button and waited. No reply. She might have left for training already, but just in case, he gave it another try. The attempt failed to produce results, so in a last-ditch effort, he activated the interphone. "Um, Rose... it's James. Are you there? It's important."

Alas, the door remained closed. Right when James considered leaving, however, it slid open, revealing the winged woman not in her expected white dress, but rather pajamas. Her messy red hair and bloodshot eyes suggested he'd interrupted her much-needed sleep, and he blushed at his faux pas.

"Hunter? What's going on?" Despite her best effort to conceal it, he detected the annoyance in her voice.

Guilt-ridden, James scratched his head. "Oh, sorry... um... I didn't mean to wake you up." He laughed nervously. "You're usually up before now."

A nod came from Rose. "There was an emergency yesterday. I worked late. I managed to clear my morning so I could rest." She crossed her arms, implying she wished to avoid small talk and get to the point. "So, what's going on?"

"I'm sorry! I di... didn't... Rose, he called me! That guy... you know!"

Rose frowned. "Huh? What are you talking about?"

"That cyborg guy..." A second passed as he attempted to recall the name. At last, he snapped his fingers. "Doctor Death! He called me! On my phone!"

Suddenly, it was like Rose had drunk ten cups of coffee. All signs of drowsiness disappeared. Her eyes went from almost closed to wide open, her slumped posture straightened and she grimaced in terror.

—Thoughts of James Hunter, Hocmar 28, 2134, on the Nirnivian calendar

"Come in! Quickly!" With surprising strength, she pulled him inside. A gulp escaped James's mouth, and he found himself sealed within Rose's chamber. "How did that happen?" she shouted as she glared at him furiously. Terrified by her reaction, James swallowed hard and recoiled. "This is Valardir! He can't..." Then Rose started pacing, her fingers pressed to her temples. "How did that happen?"

That's when I realized I'd misread her. Rose didn't mean to yell at me. She wasn't angry, she was afraid. Given this man had tormented her for years, the fear seemed justified.

—Thoughts of James Hunter, Hocmar 28, 2134, on the Nirnivian calendar

"I don't know how." James exhaled. "My phone rang, and it was him."

The alleged Melkar rubbed her brow and continued marching. While it might have been his imagination, he saw a few tears drop on her cheeks. "I'm so sorry, Hunter,

I shouldn't have screamed like that. You did well to tell me: it's an important security issue." As she pondered the situation, Rose reached for her doll on the bed and caressed her hair. As before, the misshapen toy gave James a shiver. "Now, the big question is, why contact you of all people? No matter how he managed to do this, it must have been complicated. Why go through all that just to speak to you? Maybe he hoped to get some information, but we made sure you know nothing of value, and he's more than smart enough to realize that."

"I was wondering the same thing! Especially since he didn't ask anything. Um, I swear I didn't tell him anything important."

"Don't worry, I believe you." With a compassionate smile, Rose approached him and patted his shoulder. By all appearance, she meant to calm him, but James sensed a tremor in her touch, confirming she hadn't recovered from the shock. "You poor thing, this was a hard morning, wasn't it?"

"Yeah, that guy is freaky."

Rose agreed by acquiescing. "Listen, Hunter, everything he does has a purpose. For the life of me, I have no idea why he called you, but he had a reason. It would be good to figure out what it was. Hunter, do you remember what he said?"

James recalled the conversion in as many details as possible. It had been short and inconsequential. "I think so. He didn't say much. I, uh, hung up before he could. Sorry."

"No, no, on the contrary, that's great. You didn't give him what he wanted. But can you tell me what happened before you hung up?"

"He said you weren't who you seemed, that you were dangerous, and that someday, if I wasn't careful, you'd stab me in the back."

"Yeah, well, I'm used to him slandering me." Rose sighed. "It almost sounds like he's trying to start a fight between us for whatever reason." Rose brought her hand to her forehead again. "Ow, it's too early to think."

"Hey, for what it's worth, I didn't believe a word he said. I've been around you enough to know you're a good friend."

Rose giggled in appreciation. "Thanks! Remember that when I stab you in the back." A wink confirmed her jest.

It was only a joke, but it still made my skin crawl.
—Thoughts of James Hunter, Hocmar 28, 2134, on the Nirnivian calendar

"Okay, Hunter, give me a minute and I'll handle this. I look horrible; better turn off the video." Rose dropped her doll, picked up her phone and dialed a number.

***

With a sigh, Jonathan loosened the last screw. Right on cue, the motion detector he was dismantling came apart, and he peeked at the insides. Such a delicate piece of equipment. Annoyed yet persistent, he studied the technical manual that detailed the gizmo's specifications. At the same time, he inspected the gadget's innards, hoping he'd notice a problem that explained their poor performance. His chances of success proved low. First, he lacked the necessary expertise. Second, every sensor was affected, and he doubted they all suffered from the same defect, though it wasn't quite impossible.

Soon after he began, sweat dripped into Jonathan's eyes, obscuring his vision. He let out a grunt and wiped the perspiration with his sleeve. The intense heat suggested a problem with climate control, but he'd ignore it for now. With a groan, Jonathan loosened the tie he wore over his plain white shirt, flicked a strand of hair that had escaped from his ponytail out of his view, and concentrated on his work.

About fifteen minutes later, the door's beeper sounded, interrupting Jonathan's toiling. When he opened the door, he discovered his friend, Brian. The moment he entered the office, Brian glanced at the dismantled apparatus sitting on Jonathan's desk and offered an impressed whistle. "You're actually doing it? Wow!"

A shrug came from Jonathan. "Don't have any other ideas, so..."

"Fair enough." Then Brian noticed the mat stuck in the corner. Disheveled blankets covered it, and he guessed the meaning. "Wait..." He stared at Jonathan, blinked twice and frowned. "You slept here?" He forced a chuckle. "That's ridiculous."

Jonathan dismissed Brian's concern with a wave. "It's fine, Madison is visiting her mother with Paul. The house is empty, so I figured why not?"

"Sure, but still..."

Before Brian finished his thought, the phone rang. Without missing a beat, Jonathan picked up the receiver. "Hi, this is Jonathan Rivers from the computer technical service."

A sweet and beautiful female voice tainted by a hint of nervousness replied to him. Jonathan almost gasped out of surprise. While he had never spoken with Rose Ricdeau, he recognized her voice in an instant. "Hi, Mr. Rivers, I apologize for calling you this early."

Mouth gaping, Jonathan adjusted his glasses and looked at Brian. "That's all right, Your Holiness, that's why we're here. What can I do for you?"

Shocked, Brian stepped back. Once he recovered, he fired an "are you shitting me?" glance at Jonathan, who pressed the speakerphone button. "Mr. Rivers, have you heard about our human visitor, Mr. Hunter?"

A derisive smirk formed on Jonathan's lips. "Of course, everyone's heard about him."

Brian advanced toward Jonathan with a warning gesture. As a reply, his head bobbed in the direction of the phone's blackened monitor. Rose had disabled video output, so she couldn't see his expression. Relieved, Brian exhaled and then waggled a menacing index finger. Jonathan joined his fingers in the OK sign to reassure him. His good pal understood his disbelief in religion. Often, Jonathan lamented the folly of the public for worshiping a simple mutant as a prophet. He claimed their fanaticism to be dangerous and even suggested perhaps Rose manipulated them on purpose in the past. Given that he was aware of Jonathan's temper, Brian must've feared he'd show less than respect for Rose now that he was talking to her.

"The guy upset the whole country, and we're feeding him with our taxes. That was your idea, right?" This particular sentence caused Brian to facepalm, and Jonathan told himself he should be more diplomatic. "It's great how you're helping those in need." In silence, he added, *With our money.*

"I assure you money from taxes isn't used on him, but we have other matters to discuss." Rose groaned. "Mr. Hunter received a disturbing phone call this morning."

Jonathan scowled. "Some jerk is messing with him? No problem, I'll track him down. Should only take a minute."

"That won't be necessary; I already know who it was." She paused for a whimper. "Mr. Rivers, the one who called him was Doctor Death."

Stunned, Jonathan stopped breathing. His legs wavered and he almost collapsed. As for Brian, he grasped his temples with both hands and paced for a bit. Then he crumpled on the mat Jonathan had slept on and grew a shade paler. "That's impossible, Your Holiness. Someone's playing a joke on him."

"Maybe, but if so, it's not funny. We can't ignore this either way, Mr. Rivers."

Unfortunately, Jonathan agreed. Best-case scenario, there was a prankster in their midst. A limited threat, but such behavior might stir panic and had to be dealt with. Worst case, Doctor Death had infiltrated Valardir and a heap of trouble besieged them. The transmitters appeared like phones, but they weren't. They utilized the facility's internal network, rendering communication with the outside impossible. If the cyborg could call into the facility, it likely meant he had gained access to a lot more. Even in the most optimistic outcome, he had accessed a ton of restricted info. Jonathan and his colleagues would be blamed; there was little doubt about that.

"Of course, Your Holiness."

"Any idea how we can prevent this from happening again?"

"I can't answer that yet, Your Holiness. We'll have to investigate, find out if and how our systems were compromised, then figure out a countermeasure."

"I expected as much, but I meant what can Mr. Hunter do to avoid these calls until then?"

"That won't be an issue. We'll confiscate his phone. I'll send someone right away."

"That's a little drastic. Is there any other option?"

"Well, patching whatever flaw the doctor exploited, but it'll be a while. For one thing, we've been ordered by the Commander to prioritize the new security measures above all else. I'm sure he'll change his mind when he learns about this, but it'll slow us down. Even then, we'll have to investigate. There's no telling how long that'll take. No offense intended, but I'm not comfortable with the freaking"—Jonathan bit his tongue at the last word that had slipped out, but Rose showed no reaction—"Ostarkiran president talking with the human."

"Me neither, and Hunter doesn't look like he'd enjoy repeating the experience." Rose sighed. "I have to agree. His phone must be removed. As for the Commander, don't bother with the official channels. I'll tell him myself. That should speed things up." She giggled. "There are advantages to being his daughter!"

"Yeah, I imagine."

"Thank you for your help, Mr. Rivers. And try to have a nice day despite everything."

"That'll be a challenge, but I'll do my best."

On that note, Rose hung up. Gritting his teeth, Jonathan shook his head in disgust. "What's up with her holier-than-thou attitude?"

A puzzled expression formed on Brian's face. "Huh? What do you mean?"

After a derisive snort, Jonathan replied while adopting a mocking high-pitched tone. "Oh, you guys are just techs, you're not worthy of speaking with the Commander. I'll handle it—me, the Melkar!"

"Oh, come on, she didn't mean it like that at all. She's trying to cut some red tape, and that'd be great. You're just acting offended because you don't like her. More than that, you only don't like her because she's the Melkar and you're an atheist. You don't know her."

"Yeah, and you and everyone in this freaking country don't know her either. You guys only like her because she's the Melkar. You're not any better than me there." He moaned. "But, whatever, you're right. I'm bitching because I'm tired and overworked, and now this Doctor Death thing will make it ten times worse. I need to vent on something and she's an easy target for me. Sorry about that." A short silence came as he rubbed his brow. "We're so screwed."

Brian concurred with a nod. "Probably." A sad smile as he pointed at Jonathan's mat. "We'll all have to bring our camping equipment."

"What's the point? Even if we fixed it miraculously fast, Ostark already infiltrated the system and that's on us."

Brian approached Jonathan and patted his shoulder. "We can still minimize the damage."

A snicker escaped Jonathan's throat. "Depends on how much damage there is."

***

"All right, that takes care of that," Rose said while hanging up. "Now, I'll have to contact Dad as soon as he arrives, and that'll get the ball rolling. Hopefully, the techs can find the problem and fix it." A scowl appeared on the alleged Melkar's brow. "I feel bad for them. They're already under pressure because of the updates to Valardir's security and"—Rose shook her head—"suffice to say, they don't need this." Her eyes closed. "None of us do... God only knows how much Doctor Death compromised our systems. We might be in grave danger." Then she opened her eyes again and glanced at James. "But I can't do a thing about it, so I'll have to rely on Jonathan and his colleagues. Oh, I'm afraid they'll take away your phone. It's not that we don't trust you, but NISDA won't be comfortable with Doctor Death talking to you."

"That's fine, I'm not comfortable with it either."

"I figured as much." There was a short pause as Rose rubbed her chin with her index finger. "I still don't understand why Doctor Death bothered calling you. By doing so, he showed us he'd infiltrated our systems. Surely it would've been to better to keep us in the dark for as long as possible." She waved away her own reflections. "Anyway, this whole ordeal has given me an adrenaline rush. I won't fall back to sleep now. How about we grab breakfast? Once we're done, Dad should be here."

"Yeah, sure, uh, that sounds great."

"Perfect! If you don't mind stepping out for a second so I can change." Rose gestured toward her pajamas. "If I showed up in public like this, Mom would lecture me for hours about how it isn't proper Melkar attire."

A chuckle came from James. "Hey, it's not really proper for anyone in public."

"Guess not."

"I'll wait in the hall, then." Rose nodded and James started walking away. Suddenly, he stopped and snapped his fingers. "Um, I remembered one thing. Doctor Death said he had something important to tell me, but I hung up before he did."

"That makes sense. What he was about to say must have been the real reason why he contacted you."

"Yeah..." Embarrassed, James scratched the back of his head. "I'm sorry, I should have handled this better. If I'd pretended to believe him and listened—"

"Hunter, stop that thought." A smile formed on Rose's face. "You're not a spy. Whatever he was about to tell you was to his advantage; knowing what it was wouldn't help. The Doctor is too smart to give us an edge like that. I don't mean to belittle you, but you're no match for him." The prophet frowned. "None of us are. If you try to trick him, you'll fail and he'll get what he wants. You did the right thing."

James acquiesced. "Good to know, thanks."

And that's how I lost my phone. I never got it back, but it didn't matter. Yeah, Rose called sometimes, but rarely, and she lived next door, so whatever. A bit more annoying and scary is that various officers questioned me about the "encounter" with the mechanical freak, including Mr. Ricdeau. At least they understood I hadn't done anything wrong and were friendly.

—Thoughts of James Hunter, Hocmar 28, 2134, on the Nirnivian calendar

Chapter 6

For Plague, the world always appeared in blurred shapes. When people first met him, they presumed he suffered from sickness. The bandages covering his face and the greenish skin that could be found underneath suggested as much, and in this case, appearances proved accurate. Once they grew accustomed to his zombie-like body and noticed his pure yellow bloodshot eyes devoid of irises, they then deduced he'd lost his vision. Here, however, the same appearances ended up deceiving them. Oh, he was beyond legally blind, no question there. Still, he perceived more than the solid blackness most assumed. Auras of colors and vague forms his sight detected, but he admitted they served little purpose.

Despite his condition, Plague reached for the glass of water resting on the table serving as his work area and caught it in one try. He drank a bit, moistening his dry throat. His thirst satisfied, he then grasped the twisting button on the radio receiver and turned it to the left. The relative feat he accomplished with ease thanks to the layout of his "office." With great care, he placed every object and tool in a precise manner. After he'd memorized the positioning, locating his possessions became simple enough. This forced strong emphasis on order, of course. If he mislaid a trinket, it might be lost forever, or at least until someone else found it for him.

The radio receivers emitted a senseless white noise that grew in pitch the more Plague rotated the dial. A round screen was mounted on the device, displaying a graph in black and green that described the frequencies he received. Alas, in this format, he couldn't use the information. Instead, the data was transferred to a brilliant apparatus that represented it via a tactile sensation. That allowed him to interpret the results, albeit at the price of having to remove his glove—a fact that concerned him. Thank God he worked alone; that reduced the risks involved. Then again, who knew when a visitor might show up?

No question, something strange was going on. Due to the nature of their organization, BBR was divided into a bunch of small cells spread across the neutral zone. Crucial members tended to be assigned to different groups. Because of this arrangement, NISDA or the Ostarkirans eradicating a camp implied minimal loss for the terrorists and, at most, the death of one important leader. This caused a problem for communication, though. Distance made meeting face-to-face a major inconvenience, not to mention far too slow. On the other hand, standard technology could be traced to reveal their locations. BBR had thus developed a form of radio transmission that was almost untraceable, difficult to decipher and virtually impossible to jam. The issue was that the technique reduced range, which they had solved by installing various amplifiers through the neutral zone. It worked wonders, and thanks to their minuscule size, their enemies rarely managed to destroy them.

While not clear what was going on, Plague observed weird signals traversing their amplifiers array. At first, he deduced the effect to be noise caused by interference. That happened on occasion. Still, he sensed something... wrong. Perhaps a lack of randomness, or rather a randomness that was too perfect. Upon further studies, he confirmed someone sent unauthorized messages through their array. It was impossible to tell who at this point. Maybe their own men or, more sinister, Nirnivia or Ostark. The sneakiness BBR had implemented in their own technology had bitten them on the ass. It was difficult to figure out the source and destination. Regardless, he'd have to find them both and reveal his conclusion to Diabo and Stalker. He could do it now, but he preferred having more information to relay before raising the alarm. The whole deal might be nothing, the goons sharing "entertainment." While that would indeed represent a futile usage of their precious resources, Diabo often overreacted and...

His transmitter beeped. After another cough, he answered.

"Sorry to bother you, sir. The boss wants to know when you'll deliver your progress report on Project Cyano. It's due today."

Plague suppressed a sigh. "Yes, tell him I'm sorry. Something came up. I'll call him in five minutes, ten tops."

"Thank you, sir."

The instant the communication terminated, Plague erupted into another coughing bout. The brief conversation ravaged his throat. Tired, he exhaled and returned to his business.

Chapter 7

No matter his opinion on the alleged Melkar, Jonathan had to admit she produced results. Less than two hours later, the Commander summoned him and his colleagues for a special meeting. The last time the technicians had filled the auditorium, a Perz named Nicky had replaced Constance Prim, who was on medical leave. Today, the familiar rounded shape of the blond Zarg woman returned behind the podium. However, she remained quiet for now, waiting in case latecomers showed up. Brian sat beside Jonathan, cross-armed and frowning. Normally, they'd use the moment to chat, but they understood their precarious position, and their concern extinguished any desire for a conversation. In fact, the room proved almost silent, except for the occasional whispers.

"Attention, everyone, we're about to begin." The few people talking hushed, and Constance nodded in appreciation. "Thank you. There have been rumors running amok about a recent development, and I'm sure you are most aware of them. You're probably wondering how much is true and what has been fabricated." She gulped. "Based on what I've heard, I'm afraid a lot of it is accurate. Around six in the morning, Doctor Death contacted James Hunter, the human living on level five with Her Holiness, through his phone."

She paused for emphasis, and nervous murmurs spread across the audience. Jonathan noticed several of his colleagues exchanging worried glances. As for himself, he didn't react, since he had known beforehand.

"This shouldn't be possible, and it's almost certain Valardir's security has been compromised. What we can't tell is to what degree. We found no evidence of a virus or access to classified information. Also, Mr. Hunter hasn't been arrested, though he will be interrogated, and unlike what some vile tongues imply, he didn't collaborate with Ostark. He reported the breach the instant it happened. There is no reason to think he is a spy." She moistened her lips. "Still, this is an unprecedented event, and the situation looks grim. Due to the nature of the incident, Commander Ricdeau decided he should speak to you in person, and so I will let him take my place."

Right on cue, Daniel Ricdeau emerged from a curtain positioned behind the scene. Applause resounded as he marched toward the mic at a determined pace. Despite his benevolent smile and wrinkled face, Jonathan sensed the strength and authority in every echoing step. Once he arrived, he shook Constance's hand and thanked her. Then she stepped aside, and he took her place on the podium. He waved at the crowd.

"Hello, everyone, and thank you for the warm welcome." A short laugh came from him. "At this rate, you'll make me blush." Daniel's expression grew a touch more serious. "I wish we were meeting under happier circumstances. We are currently facing a major crisis, and we need your help to get through it. We need to discover how Doctor Death infiltrated our phones and whether he accessed anything else. For now, we assume that's the case, and Valardir's computer systems are running in safe mode."

Jonathan swallowed hard at the mention. Since the planning of Valardir's construction, everyone had been aware of the risk of their system being compromised. Safe mode had been the answer. When it was activated, everything nonessential shut down. Classified information became inaccessible, even by NISDA. In short, it mitigated danger but caused two major issues. First, they never ran safe mode except in tests and practice exercises. Second, this meant Valardir's capabilities shrank exponentially. Basic functions would slow to a crawl, and it might last weeks or months. A less drastic option called "quite safe mode" also existed, but it seemed that, due to the potential catastrophic consequences, the bigwigs had gone straight for the big gun.

"This only happened hours ago, but there are already ramblings of demotions and firing." Daniel closed his eyes and shook his head. "It's Gorumars' nature to presume someone has to be blamed. Let me assure you, High Command has no intention of turning this into a witch hunt. I know better than anybody that we are fighting against a capable foe." The senior bit his lip. "I hate to admit it, but the truth is, we're lucky Valardir hasn't been hacked until today. You are the Nirnivian technological elite. NISDA has complete trust that you did an exemplary job and that this isn't the fault of anyone in particular. Now, it's possible we might find proof of gross negligence later on. If so, we'll have to investigate, but at the moment, High Command believes this is a blame-free incident. That being said, we're in a pickle and we need you. It's imperative we discover what Doctor Death did to our systems and what has been impacted ASAP. Finding out how is also a priority. And there's the question of the ongoing security enhancements. They are important too, especially when it comes to the current problems we're experiencing with the motion sensors. We can't afford delay on this matter."

With a sinking sensation weighting his heart, Jonathan raised his arm as if he asked permission to speak. Panicked, Brian whispered for him to stop, though Jonathan ignored his plea. The Commander spotted him and gestured toward him. "Yes, do you have a question?"

"Sir, I agree we have to fix the motion detectors, but you're asking for the impossible. I'd love to get everything done without delay, but we can't do either job properly if you rush us to that point."

Daniel chuckled. "Oh my, it seems I expressed myself with too much enthusiasm. Of course, a delay is unavoidable. What I mean is that we count on you to minimize it. High Command is confident you have the skills to do so. And, with any luck, maybe it won't be as bad as we think. You've performed miracles before, after all!" There was a short pause as he beamed at the crowd. "Besides, don't forget it's almost the end of the year. There'll be contract renegotiations soon, and your performance here is sure to have an impact."

A frown appeared on Jonathan's face. "Are you implying a possible pay cut?"

"Quite the contrary, my boy"—he laughed and dismissed the notion with a wave—"this is an opportunity for you to shine and prove you deserve better terms!"

While Jonathan gave the appearance of accepting this explanation, doubts lingered in his mind. The budget shrank every year, and an excuse to slash salaries might appeal to the bigwigs. Deep in thought, he contemplated the possibility as Daniel continued his speech. Soon, Brian leaned against him and whispered in his ear.

"You live dangerously, my friend! At least he doesn't look pissed."

Jonathan acquiesced and mouthed back, "He's friendlier than Tigh, I'll give him that."

Chapter 8

I didn't attend Rose's sermons often, but on that day, it felt essential. The whole ordeal with Doctor Death freaked me out. It didn't help that I had nothing to do except think about what had happened. After a while, I became overwhelmed and decided a walk in the corridor would occupy my mind. I passed by the chapel and, by coincidence, a guy entered. I saw through the opened door that Rose prepared to speak, so I went inside; not sure why, I guess hearing her familiar voice made me relax.

—Thoughts of James Hunter, Hocmar 28, 2134, on the Nirnivian calendar

"Oh, this is so cute, everyone!" Rose said after a giggle. "A seven-year-old girl is asking why I spend so much time answering questions people send instead of reading sacred texts like her priest does." The winged woman beamed and focused on the camera. "Well, you see, I've been doing this for over twenty years and I'm running out of material!" With difficulty, James contained a chortle for fear it might offend the audience. There was no need to worry, however, as everybody laughed, so he joined in. "No, seriously, religious literature is boundless. I could still find plenty to read, and most passages are so crucial that they deserve a revisit. Except, countless priests do just that. The contents of our sacred texts are widely available, so you can also study them by yourself if you wish. The real challenge is understanding them. They are beautifully written and filled with wisdom, but they are complex, and our simple minds cannot always comprehend them." She indulged in a short silence for emphasis.

"Even today, although they've been scrutinized for millennia, experts often disagree on their meaning. And so, by answering questions, I hope I can help decipher them. Now, I may be the Melkar, but that doesn't mean my interpretation is correct. It is important to remember that. It's easy to forget sometimes." Rose sighed and paused for a few seconds as if she recalled past events. "As the holy prophet, it is assumed I possess greater spiritual clarity than others, though I'm not convinced that is the case. Nevertheless, I think that by taking what you interpret from those texts, what I interpret, what your priest interprets, and what your parents and loved ones interpret, you might find the truth, or at least something that works for you. You have to decide what you believe in."

Most religious folks I've seen, both pastors and followers, acted like they couldn't be wrong, even when others who shared the same faith disagreed. To hear a person of such authority say that we had to choose our own path because she didn't have the answers was refreshing. Maybe I'd never met a good priest before Rose.

—Thoughts of James Hunter, Hocmar 28, 2134, on the Nirnivian calendar

At that instant, James heard the door slide open. Curious, he turned his head and spotted Daniel Ricdeau entering the room. The old man advanced at a deliberate pace, cautious to avoid making noise. He offered Rose a gesture of apology for intruding, though she didn't react due to her situation. Once Daniel reached James's bench, he slipped in.

"Hi there, my boy," the Commander whispered as he sat beside James. "I've been searching for you. A guard told me you were here. I'm surprised. I didn't expect you to be interested in our religion."

"Um, I like listening to her sometimes. She's a great speaker."

"That she is." Daniel moistened his lips. "I wanted to talk to you about Doctor Death's call. You're a nervous fellow, my boy, so I thought you'd worry about it. Let me reassure you: you did the right thing. There'll be increased surveillance around you, as you might notice, but we'll do our best to be discreet. It's for your protection, in case the Doctor has another trick up his sleeves. Everyone knows you can be trusted."

James nodded. "I understand."

Though I admit it still made me uneasy.

—Thoughts of James Hunter, Hocmar 28, 2134, on the Nirnivian calendar

With the message delivered, they both hushed and listened to Rose. "Here's a letter that deserves attention. People keep forgetting about this. The sender is a nine-year-old boy who wonders why Timagoron is so evil. A simple question. Many would give the equally simple answer that it's just how he is, but that's wrong." She scowled and closed her eyelids. "The truth is, Timagoron isn't evil." Rose's eyes reopened. "Oh, I'm sure most are shocked by my statement. Several priests use that simplification. I have too in the past. As an explanation, it's easy and convenient, but reality is never that straightforward, I'm afraid." The alleged prophet rubbed her chin as if deliberating her next words.

"From our limited perspective, Timagoron plays the role of the villain. He tries to erase us and send us into nothingness. And yet, he does what he thinks is best for the universe. According to Timagoron, Gorumars are a mistake—an unintended consequence caused by the division that created him and Ulgorack. Because of this, he believes we are corrupting Ulgoron's divine vision. It's not that he enjoys hurting us, but rather that he attempts to protect creation from our"—Rose performed finger quotes—"vile behavior. Timagoron might be mistaken. He might be committing atrocious acts, but this does not mean that he himself is evil."

"You know"—the senior leaned toward James and murmured in his ear—"seeing her live is much better than listening on the radio or TV. Before, Rose preached in the city. Sometimes she'd tour the country so everyone could meet her at least once." Evident disappointment tainted his voice. "Now she only addresses the public from inside Valardir. Only those with security clearance can attend. I myself can rarely come, but I'm still lucky. Most Nirnivians can't ever see her anymore."

"Um, why did she stop?"

Mr. Ricdeau waited for a moment before he replied. Darkness filled his visage as his mouth twisted in a contorted grimace. The expression suggested he recalled unpleasant memories. As the Commander reminisced, James caught a fragment of Rose's lecture.

"...goron thinks life's a mistake. I disagree. Who knows? Maybe he's right. And there are those who believe so—the Timanites."

"Well, my boy, Doctor Death pretty much forced her." He sighed. "When the war started, it was already more difficult because we had to consider Rose's safety. Still, some live appearances were possible until Doctor Death came to power. She became his target, and that changed the whole game. Doctor Death is a skilled surgeon, but he's also a genius tactician and a master hacker. Ever since he's been in charge, we can't hide anything from Ostark. They found out about Rose's schedule and sent men to capture her. Yet, somehow, all their attempts failed, luckily for us. It's like Doctor Death sent his mediocre troops instead of his best. I have no idea why he'd do that...

"Rose knew her people needed her. At first, she refused to go into hiding. We tried to be craftier. Things like spreading false information so the Ostarkirans couldn't locate her and reducing our dependency on computers. Despite our efforts, it soon became clear that live presentations were too dangerous for Rose and her followers. She agreed to do fewer of them and later gave them up completely. Now, she never leaves Valardir for security purposes. Doctor Death is too persistent, too efficient. We can't stop him." Even though the Commander whispered, his despair echoed through his words.

"Rose is quite safe, but there's a price. Isolation is hard on her. It's hard on the people too. They miss her guidance and tend to lose hope more easily. Doctor Death might not have gotten Rose, but he's winning the war." Daniel grunted. "And Rose's safety might be only temporary. This is our most secure facility, but I fear it isn't enough. Someday, Doctor Death will infiltrate this place. After what happened to you, it seems he may already be there, and if so, Rose will be at his mercy. NISDA has to strike back, but we are weak; they'd crush us."

"Um, I'm sorry." James bent his neck. "I wish I could help, but I'm just an average joe who isn't good at anything."

The old man tapped James's shoulder and smiled in a comforting manner. "Trust me, you help more than you think. I noticed she's been a little less depressed since you've been here and that's great. If the Melkar gave up, so would everyone else."

I already knew Rose was confined to Valardir, but somehow, after that discussion, I realized how difficult it must have been for her. She could never go outside anymore. She never felt the sun on her skin. In a way, she was a prisoner. Back then, I didn't leave the complex myself, but I was allowed to. That made a huge difference.

—Thoughts of James Hunter, Hocmar 28, 2134, on the Nirnivian calendar

Chapter 9

Tigal 30, 2133, on the Nirnivian calendar

The laptop set before Plague displayed an image of Stalker on the right and Diabo on the left. Not that he saw them. His clouded vision prevented visual confirmation. Only familiarity with the software granted him this knowledge. Or did it? A random thought came that an update might've changed the layout, and he'd never realize unless someone warned him.

After Plague had studied his previous discovery of illicit transmissions more, he'd decided he should share the information with the other founders. A meeting in person being dangerous, they each stayed in their own cell and talked through the same communication array he meant to discuss.

"Thanks for setting this up right away, guys, I appreciate it."

Stalker shrugged. "You're welcome."

As for Diabo, he remained silent, but Plague imagined him waving his hand for things to proceed faster. Though his boss was invisible, Plague understood his temperament well enough to predict the crimson beast fired a glare that implied delaying would be a grave mistake. Unwilling to draw Diabo's ire, Plague cleared his throat and said, "About a week ago, I noticed short and random signals going through our communication array. They're nothing like our usual transmissions, and they come in bursts."

The coarse voice of Diabo echoed. "So what? Better ain't tell me this 'bout freaking interference."

A chuckle came from Stalker. "Gimme a break, boss, he wouldn't raise the alarm over that."

"No, I wouldn't, and that's why it took a week before I reacted." Plague sighed. "At first, I thought it was interference. It happens from time to time, but... it doesn't fit." He snapped his fingers twice. "It's random, but not really. There's a method to the madness, but I can't figure it out. I'm pretty sure it's a legit communication, but it's unlike anything I've ever seen."

"So no way it's from BBR." Plague imagined Stalker shaking his head and clenching his fists. "Shit, Ostark or Nirnivia is using our own tech so it's impossible to track." A coughing bout overcame Plague. "Better get that checked out, man."

Plague reached for the glass of water beside his computer. After a sip, he dismissed Stalker's statement with a wave. "I'm fine. Nirnivia and Ostark can't trace us through it, but we control the array, so we have options. Doesn't mean it's easy. Ain't gonna lie, I can't find the destination for the life of me, but the source is somewhere in Nirnivia. Can't pinpoint it yet, but I'm getting there." He rubbed his chin. "There are three possible destinations: Nirnivia, Ostark and BBR itself. Logically, Nirnivia doesn't make any sense: they don't need to route through the neutral zone to talk to themselves. So, either Nirnivia has a spy among us and they're sending him instructions..."

Plague paused for a second, and Stalker used the opportunity to say, "I doubt it. Nirnivia is fighting us to keep up appearances with Ostark, but they ain't got no reason to be good at it."

"Yeah, I agree. And the conclusion is, it's an Ostarkiran spy hidden in Nirnivia. And frankly, that weird communication protocol is screaming Doctor Death. He's the only one I can think of who'd pull off a stunt like this."

A grunt from Diabo sent a shiver down Plague's spine. "So what? Ain't no goddamn concern to us. NISDA ain't no friend."

"Yeah, fair enough, except if Ostark beats them, our resistance is kaput. I'm no fan of the cowards at NISDA, but the Doctor's got them cornered. It might be in our best interest to let them know what's going on."

Stalker asked, "You think they can help us find the spy?"

Plague chuckled. "Nah, they're hopeless. Besides, they don't control the array, so they're at a disadvantage. Still, if they know, they might be able to protect themselves against the spy."

Plague visualized Stalker scratching his skull. "I dunno... would they listen to us?"

After a grunt, Plague acquiesced. "That's a fair question."

"Nah, they ain't gonna listen." A roar came from Diabo. "'Sides, NISDA gave up. They're in the Doc's pocket. Freaking traitors if ya ask me. Can't depend on those guys. I say Plague finds that spy and we'll take care o' him ourselves."

Deep down, Plague wondered about the wisdom of this plan. It supposed the search would end with success, for one thing. For another, NISDA would remain vulnerable for what could be months. He debated bringing up those arguments but decided not to. If he did, Diabo would blow a fuse and counter that he was in charge and they had to obey him. Given his stubbornness, they'd eventually give in. Despite this, the crimson beast would then be furious for days, resulting in painful interaction for Stalker and him. It just wasn't worth it.

"Fine. I'll keep you posted."

Chapter 10

After a moment of agonizing tension, the ball Janice targeted entered the pocket. Despite her unconditional victory, she beamed at James and lifted her hands in the air. Without delay, he smacked his palm against hers, thus granting the requested high five.

"Great match, buddy! You're getting better!"

"Uh, thanks." Blood rushed to his face, resulting in a blush. "You still won, though."

She shrugged. "Details, details... this was the closest one yet!" She pointed a nonchalant thumb at the table. "Wanna give it another go?"

Janice had a point. I had given her a bigger challenge than usual, at least in appearance. Deep down, I suspected she tried to let me win in an effort to help me forget about Doctor Death. In the end, my skills weren't up to it, and she couldn't lose in a convincing manner, so the plan failed. That's my assumption, anyway. Actually, I think Daniel sent Janice to check on me and make sure I wasn't panicking over the incident. Most of the time, we played after she finished her workday, but she showed up in the afternoon. I didn't feel she'd do that without her dad's blessing. Well, if that's the case, she did a good job. For one thing, she didn't mention Doctor Death, and that allowed me to get him out of my mind.

—Thoughts of James Hunter, Hocmar 28, 2134, on the Nirnivian calendar

"Yeah, sure!"

And so, they set up the board again. Once done, Janice was preparing her first shot when the rec room door slid open, breaking her concentration. She sighed and turned to catch a glimpse of the arrival. James followed her lead. A somewhat short yet large man marched inside. He wore the familiar NISDA uniform and sported the brush-style haircut favored among his colleagues. Not that James focused on these details. Instead, he tended to fixate on the scar descending along the soldier's visage. He tried not to, but the distinctive injury attracted his glance regardless. Searching his memory, James attempted to recall whether he'd encountered the man before, but he drew a blank, so he concluded they'd never met. He decided he'd remember the wound. Janice, however, recognized the visitor in an instant. A wide smile formed on her face, and she sprinted toward him. Once close, they exchanged an intricate handshake like James had seen special club members share in movies.

"Hey, Ricdeau, how have you been?"

She giggled. "Pretty good, I guess! How about you?"

"Ah, can't complain."

"Yeah, that new law is a pain in the butt." James frowned at the sentence, wondering if she was serious, but a second later, the duo burst into laughter and he forced a polite chuckle. Why such hilarity? The quip wasn't that funny. Perhaps the mention alluded to an inside joke. "It's been what, a year minimum?"

"Hey, don't blame me! You volunteering for a post out of nowhere didn't help." The male soldier smirked. "What was that about, anyway?"

Janice's lips contorted in a grimace and she averted her gaze. "Oh, I felt like taking a break from city life."

"Ah, okay, but the neutral zone's border? That's more like a break from society! I didn't picture you as the hermit type!" At that moment, his eyes widened and he stared at James in a manner suggesting he had failed to notice the third person present. "Am I interrupting something here?"

"Oh, right…" Appalled by her oversight, Janice slapped her brow. "I was so surprised, I forgot to introduce you guys." Grabbing the man's shoulder, she gestured at James and walked him forward. "That's my buddy, James! James, this is Gareth Stevenson. We were in the same squad during the war. He lives in a different city, so I didn't expect to see him today."

James managed a shy wave for the new acquaintance, who then offered a handshake. The grip possessed the expected strength, and James winced. "Yeah, unexpected business came up. I'll be around for a few months. Figured I'd visit Janice since I have the clearance."

We exchanged pleasantries, and he watched us finish our game. No surprise: Janice won, and she challenged Gareth. They played while they talked about old stories. I was out of place, but I stuck around anyway, barely paying attention to their conversation. They were neck and neck for the whole thing, but Gareth finally got his chance. One ball each, both well positioned, and it was his turn.

—Thoughts of James Hunter, Hocmar 28, 2134, on the Nirnivian calendar

Irises fixed on his target, Gareth aimed his cue. He drew it back, about to strike, but at the last second, he stood up from his crouch, forsaking his shot. With his index finger, he stroked along his ears before picking at his cuticles. Shocked, Janice's mouth gaped, and she stepped backward.

"Janice… do you think about back then sometimes?"

No need for more context. A somber expression tainted her features. "Yeah, we all do."

"Do you ever wish you could go back?" Janice tilted her head, scowling, but before she uttered a word, Gareth said, "It was a nightmare. I killed so many people. I watched friends die. I dream about it almost every night."

"Again, we all do."

"The thing is, it's like I belong there. I've lived in a world of fire for so long, what they call a normal life doesn't make much sense anymore. I'm always on edge, afraid an Ostarkiran is hiding in the shadows about to slit my throat with his knife. Nirnivia never won, Ostark didn't either. It just stopped. We didn't finish the job." His voice trembled. "That's the worst part. So much death and destruction, yet nothing was resolved. Jacky lost his leg. Natasha died in that suicide bombing. For what? So we could give up?" Gritting his teeth, Gareth pointed at the table. "It's like I forfeited when it's almost over. And I'm supposed to go on and eat some druikinaka for breakfast, goof off with my coworkers and have fun? It's crazy. During the war, I wanted it to end so badly, but now that it's over, I... kind of want to go back and make our friends' sacrifices count. Do you understand?"

"Yes..." Janice swallowed hard and patted his back. "I had a tough time getting used to the normal world too. I'm not sure I'm there yet either."

"You're good at hiding it."

She shrugged. "Some deal better with the trauma, but I'd say we're in the same boat." After lowering her head, Janice exhaled. "Trust me, the war messed me up plenty, and we're not alone."

"Sometimes I think about Renald—remember him?" Unable to speak, Janice nodded. "He never really made it back. Never could settle. One night, he strangled his wife, thinking she was an Ostarkiran. Thank God she survived, but that marriage was over; not that I blame her. Then he lost his job. He was too aggressive. Last I heard, he was homeless and living in the street. Sometimes, I..." Gareth paused and whimpered. "I wonder if I'm heading down the same path."

"Buddy, maybe you should tell this to a therapist."

"I did, still do. But they don't understand. Those guys are trained in psychology. They're experts in the theory, but they weren't there like you."

Janice rubbed Gareth's upper arm. "Buddy, you're dealing with serious issues, but I'd say it's to be expected for people who went through what we did. I don't think you'll end up like Renald. You're not that damaged. You wouldn't have lasted all these years if you were. But you must continue therap—"

It was getting way too personal. I had no business hearing this, so I left. I should've done it sooner. Janice had her hands full, so she didn't see me leave. I returned to my room, and about an hour later, she came and invited me for supper. She didn't mention her friend, but it was obvious it affected her.

—Thoughts of James Hunter, Hocmar 28, 2134, on the Nirnivian calendar

Chapter 11

Tigal 31, 2133, on the Nirnivian calendar

With a groan, Wrathchild grabbed the tattered rag resting among her tools and wiped the black stain on her face. She'd made a beginner's mistake during her bike's maintenance, resulting in the mess. After all the lessons she'd endured from that bastard Torkin back then, the faux pas annoyed her far more than it should. Given she lacked a mirror, she couldn't tell how successful her cleaning efforts were. If she had to guess, she'd go with hardly. Still, once she believed she had scrubbed enough, she stopped, intending to finish the job later. The deed done, she reached for her wrench and returned to her motorcycle. Metallic clinks echoed as she worked.

The task consumed Wrathchild to the point that she failed to notice the man watching in the distance. Of course, he specialized in remaining unseen. Detecting Stalker proved an accomplishment, even when he wanted you to. Wrathchild kept toiling on her bike, oblivious until he uttered a "Hey." Startled, her heart jumped and a rush of adrenaline overcame her. She wrapped her fingers around her sword's handle, ready to pounce. She was familiar with surprises. On the streets, she received plenty of them—most unpleasant. To survive, she couldn't hesitate when confronted with the unexpected; thus she lived in a state of constant readiness.

Blade unsheathed, she spotted the intruder and sighed as she recognized Stalker. Her muscles relaxed and she withdrew her weapon. The master of camouflage was almost a stranger. She barely knew him, but they had fought together. The fact that they resided in different cells partly explained the unfamiliarity. Yet, had they been roommates, the situation might have been the same. Stalker kept to himself—he didn't talk about private matters, especially not when it concerned his past. That was fine with Wrathchild. Though they shared an enemy, that didn't mean they had to be close friends.

Like the other BBR founders, Stalker's appearance was unconventional to say the least. His features reminded everyone of a predatory animal, and he blended in with the scenery. Despite this, some of his traits suggested a lost beauty robbed by Doctor Death's experiments. Even now, he possessed a certain charm. He didn't look like a normal person, but he was far more handsome than Plague or Diabo could ever wish to be.

"Hey, Stalker!" Wrathchild said. "Didn't see you."

"Yeah, I hear ya." Stalker stared at the bike, his expression filled with disdain. "Still working on that old thing, huh?"

"Yes." Wrathchild ignored the unflattering comment and declined to defend her position. She loved her motorcycle whether others understood her passion or not.

"I don't see you much, but when I do, you're always repairing that piece of junk. Is it really worth the hassle?"

"Yes." Dislike for machines, including motor vehicles, stood as a rare personal detail Stalker shared without encouragement. He deemed them noisy and accused them of promoting laziness. The fact that he suffered from motion sickness probably influenced his opinion.

"Really?" Stalker's eyes widened. "How? I mean, shit, you run faster than that thing. Why do you need it so much?"

Heard that before. Several reasons. People didn't think.
—Thoughts of Wrathchild, Hocmar 28, 2134, on the Nirnivian calendar

After an annoyed shake of the head, she enumerated on her fingers. "Doesn't get tired. Can carry passengers. Good for long distance. Holds big weapons too heavy for hands. Looks cool. Need more?"

"Nah, that's fine." Stalker tapped the bike. "Whatever, I think I'm bugging you. I'll get out of your hair."

Chapter 12

Tigal 33, 2133, on the Nirnivian calendar

With a tired smile on his face, Daniel Ricdeau poured a glass of his first-class uisge. Due to his lack of attention, he almost overfilled the glass. While stocking liquor in Valardir—let alone consuming it—broke regulation, he allowed himself that particular treat on stressful days. Lately, he had indulged more than usual. Between the mess caused by the security improvements and Doctor Death's apparent hack of their systems, morale had sunk to an all-time low. Witnessing everyone in such low spirits proved depressing. The fact that they operated in the now-infamous safe mode only exacerbated the issue.

On the other side of the desk, Tigh waited with his beverage already supplied. Contrarily to Daniel, his goblet contained druikinaka juice instead of alcohol. Once the serving was finished, both men clinked their glasses, then took a sip. Well, Daniel took a sip—Ron gulped half the glass.

"What a shitty week," the Koporal said, reaching for the juice bottle. For his response, Daniel nodded without a word. "Those goddamn techs are a freaking disgrace. They're beyond late on the motion detectors' fixes, and progress has more or less stopped because of the hack. If it yielded results, it'd be okay, but they still have no idea what happened." He snorted. "Ah, freak, worse than that, there ain't no signs of an attack, they say. Can't find anything. Ah well, that's just peachy, but something's wrong!

The records show the call. James isn't bullshitting us. Why would he?" After a grunt, Tigh sampled his juice again. "They have the nerve to quote their contract to me when they can't do their stupid job. Oh, we're not soldiers, you have to treat us with respect. Fine, let me tell you to respectfully kiss my wrinkled ass. If they weren't protected by their civilian contractor status, I'd whip them into shape. They have no pride for their country. They are not patriots!"

And there was the rub. Daniel suppressed a groan. No question about it, the delay caused by the incident wasn't what brought on Tigh's tirade. Rather, he fumed because that Jonathan fellow had defended his rights. Deep down, Jonathan impressed Daniel. He had dared to stand up to his Koporal, and he'd displayed no fear when debating the Commander himself. Several men and women who had faced death on the battlefield had failed the same test of courage. He wished to point this out to Ron but understood it would only worsen his mood.

"They're caught in a jam. I'm sure they're doing their best."

"Yeah? Too bad their best sucks."

"When it comes to Ostark, everyone's best sucks. Remember back in the war, when—" He dismissed his own comment with a wave. "Forget it. We've been dealing with this ordeal for long enough. Let's talk about something else." A pause followed as he pondered another topic of conversation. "Did you watch the game yesterday?"

"Yes, and our boys screwed up again. Let me tell you, if I was their coach, I'd—"

Daniel stifled a laugh. No matter the subject, his good friend found a reason for complaints. It could grow tedious on occasion, he admitted that much, but still, it was part of why he enjoyed Ron's company.

Chapter 13

Tigal 34, 2133, on the Nirnivian calendar

Though it demanded more effort than he'd hoped, Plague made quick progress with investigating the illicit transmissions abusing their communication array. True, he accomplished this feat by ignoring his other tasks perhaps a bit too much, but he still considered it an achievement. Now came the time to reveal his findings, and butterflies invaded his stomach. As he prepared for the video conference, he wondered whether the other founders would share his opinion on the matter. Somehow, he doubted it.

Soon, Plague finished the preparations and a video feed displaying Stalker and Diabo filled his screen. Despite his lacking sight, he guessed their posture. For certain, Stalker adopted the neutral expression he usually conveyed to conceal his feelings. A hard-to-read man in general, he liked to keep his thoughts to himself unless obliged to share them. As a result, Plague had no idea how he'd react to what he planned on proposing. Diabo, on the other hand, posed little mystery. The crimson beast almost definitively sat cross-armed and glowering at his camera, implying a bad mood. Not a surprise, by any stretch. He rarely displayed a joyful emotion. No question about it, he'd resist Plague's suggestion, but Plague had expected that much from the start. No point delaying.

After they exchanged standard greetings, Plague said, "So, yeah, it wasn't easy, but I think I pinpointed the source of the strange signal."

"Ya think, huh?" A scowl came from Diabo. "Don't sound too sure, do ya?"

"There's a margin of error, but I'd say I'm about ninety-eight percent sure. The transmission is from an apartment building in the city of Ishadel. That's Nirnivian territory all right. My guess"—coughs interrupted Plague's sentence, and he reached for his glass of water to soothe his irritated throat—"is that there's an Ostarkiran spy living there. Good news for NISDA is he didn't infiltrate Valardir—too far for that. Still, we should jump on every opportunity to take away any edge we can from Doctor Death. Thing is, we're not in a position to investigate the residents and find the spy. NISDA is better suited for that, so it seems to me we should give them the info and let them deal with it."

Stalker grunted. "They'll probably assume we're messing with them and ignore us. But I agree we can't do much here, so that's all right with me." The tension in Plague's chest lessened, and he almost exhaled in relief. Despite his misgivings, Stalker stood on his side.

Furious, Diabo shouted. "Are you two total idiots? Ain't no way that's a good idea!" Then a thundering crash echoed. Plague winced and deduced he slammed his fist on his desk, damaging the furniture. "NISDA's so dumb, even if they believe us, it'll take them months to act, and they'll mess it up anyway. You wanna get rid o' the spy? Let's do it now. We got plenty o' bombs. Building go boom at night, no more spy, just like that." A click echoed as he snapped his fingers.

After bending his neck and rubbing his chin, Plague said, "Effective, but we'd kill many innocent Nirnivians."

A derisive chuckle escaped the red monster's lips. "Got a conscience, huh? Gimme a break. We ain't gonna win as freedom fighters without some collateral damage, boys."

With a sigh, Plague shook his head. "I'm not talking about ethics, boss. I'm worried about practical matters." Again, a coughing fit assailed him. "Most of our resources come from rich Nirnivians who disagree with the uneasy peace but won't go against the Council because they have too much to lose. They give us money, food, weapons, clothes, the whole nine yards so we can fight Ostark, not Nirnivia. If we start murdering Nirnivian citizens, they might pull support and we'd be screwed." To accentuate his point, he mimicked slicing his neck with his fingers.

Unimpressed, Diabo snorted. "We killed Nirnivians before."

"Yeah, but not on purpose."

"Quit spinning your bullshit, won't ya, Plague?" He groaned. "That apartment building's a dump. Our benefactors ain't gonna bail 'cause we blew up a couple o' poor." A slight tremble affected his voice. "Bastards like them don't give a shit 'bout people who ain't in their circles. Ya wanna know why they help us out? 'Cause they want action and results, that's why, and we're gonna deliver. 'Sides, who cares if they split? We got other means. Plenty o' weapons to steal from Ostark. We can get food from Project Cyano. Ain't no problem."

Annoyed, Plague rubbed his brow and huffed. "Project Cyano is in its infancy. It's a start, we grew decent crops already, but it ain't enough. Not yet. And weapons, we're well stocked and are getting a good amount from our raids on Ostarkiran transport. But make no mistake"—he leaned forward—"losing our Nirnivian suppliers would be a major blow."

Diabo chuckled. "Ah, whatever, they ain't gonna care, I tell ya. Sure, they'll bitch fer a while, but they'll get over it. Trust me. Anyway, I'm the boss, ain't I?"

At that moment, Stalker harrumphed as if clearing his throat. "Yeah, you're technically the boss. But don't forget, Plague's the brain, and you agreed to listen to him when we put you in charge. Besides, we're two against one."

"You little shithead!" Already loud, Diabo's volume increased. Swallowing hard, Plague lowered his gaze. "This ain't no democracy! Ya wanna challenge me? Don't make me laugh."

It was Plague's turn to harrumph. "Boss—"

"I'm gonna snap you in two, you son of a bitch! You both gone soft on me, did ya? Ain't you remember why we started this freaking thing? To freaking kill all the Ostarkirans we can, that's why!"

"Diabo!"

"And now you gonna let that spy live? You guys are scum!"

Plague raised his voice to a shout and said, "Diabo! You're right, you're the boss. We'll obey your orders."

The tirade continued until Diabo processed Plague's latest words. "At least one o' you got some sense." As the crimson beast spoke, Plague noticed a slight movement from the blur representing Stalker and deduced he typed on his keyboard. "This ain't over, Stalker. We gonna talk 'bout your loyalty later."

Soon, Plague's suspicion ended up confirmed. A text message from Stalker popped up on his screen and his text-to-speech software read it for him. The master of camouflage wondered why he caved and wished for a follow-up conversation between the two of them. "So, Plague, I'm counting on ya to figure the science stuff. Ya know, size o' the bomb needed, that kind o' thing."

"Of course, boss, I'll look into it."

***

A minute after the video conference, Plague went ahead and called Stalker. Despite the fact that the master of camouflage had failed to reveal his reason for the secret conversation, Plague could guess his motive. Stalker's recent clash with Diabo offered a clear hint. At any rate, it seemed obvious that Stalker preferred keeping their leader in the dark about this transmission, and they prepared for such an eventuality. Plague switched the encryption keys, ensuring no one from BBR could eavesdrop. Thanks to the nature of their communication array, discovering the exchange would be difficult, let alone tracking its sources and destination.

The moment he appeared on the screen, Stalker skipped the greeting and said, "You sure gave up quickly, Plague."

A shrug came from Plague. "Yeah, well, it wasn't worth crossing Diabo over. He was so pissed, he might've gone ahead and snapped you in two. Diabo loves making idle threats, and that's probably all it was, but I figured we shouldn't push him. You know how he is, always angry at everything. But since we're giving him what he wants, he'll forget about it and calm down."

"Yes, um, actually, that's why I wanted to talk to you. Is it just me, or is Diabo getting more and more unhinged? He's never been a patient or reasonable man, but these days it's like he's gone mad."

"Hey, I'd say none of us are a model of sanity." The memories rushing back to Plague caused his jaw to tighten. "We're angry at Ostark too. I can't blame Diabo for his revenge fantasy."

"Okay, that's true. I'd like to make 'em pay, but he's taking it to a whole new level." He paused. "And he's forgetting the original arrangement. He's supposed to be a figurehead. You're the one really in charge of the operation." After a deep breath, Stalker continued. "I'm thinking you should consider making it official."

As expected, this was what he wished to discuss. Feigning shock, Plague laughed. "Excellent idea! People are dying to follow a blind leader with a decaying body." Sarcasm dripped from his words. "That's why we needed a figurehead in the first place, remember?"

"I mean, yeah, back then it felt necessary, but things change. You have a lot of respect in BBR, and we aren't desperate for recruits like we used to be." The blurred motion Plague witnessed and the resulting sound suggested Stalker slammed his fist into his left palm. "We could pull it off."

Huffing, Plague dismissed the notion with a wave. "Nah, the time isn't right. The majority of the troops are loyal to him. They believe in him. His power is too stable. We'd be crushed. Besides, you're overreacting. I admit Diabo's in a bad mood lately, but there's no reason for a coup yet. That's a drastic and desperate measure. No point risking BBR's existence over a small squabble." Plague stopped and then scowled. "And, I'm not convinced Diabo is wrong. The more we wait, the more intel the spy is leaking to Ostark. Whatever NISDA would do wouldn't be as quick as Diabo's way." The frown intensified. "I hate it. It's messy and beyond immoral. I mean, I ain't no saint, but exploding Nirnivian buildings is taking it quite far even for me. Maybe that's why I didn't consider it myself. I don't know what's best, so I'll go along with Diabo's plan. At least it'll keep BBR united for a while longer."

A groan came from Stalker, "Fair enough, but what about our patrons? I doubt they'll be as accepting of our methods as Diabo thinks they will."

Plague acquiesced. "Me too. Some will, but we'll lose major support. I'll call everyone I can first and let them know what's coming. If I'm persuasive, it might be okay. If not, well, we'll have some extra arguments to try and change Diabo's mind."

Chapter 14

Jonathan took a closer look at the small device he and his team were investigating. An impressed whistle parted from his lips. What a brilliant design. Straightforward, yet ingenious and effective. He ruefully admitted he'd never considered the possibility.

"This is definitively Ostarkiran," Jonathan mumbled as he pointed to the gismo. "I'd guess it's from Doctor Death himself. I've got to hand it to him, it's state-of-the-art."

"Yeah..." Brian smiled. "Well, we found the source of our troubles at any rate. We're pretty lucky overall."

"I'm ninety-nine percent sure, but let's make it a hundred before we relax." Jonathan adjusted his slipping glasses. "We can't be too careful." He glanced toward their fidgeting guide. "Got any idea who installed this here?"

"N-no!" the nervous man responded. "This is a freaking public restroom in a mall. We don't track people... I'm sorry, we can't help!"

Jonathan nodded in agreement. Some might deem the man's jumpiness suspicious, but not him. The poor fellow feared he'd be blamed for the incident. Jonathan doubted that would happen; nothing indicated guilt.

"Don't worry, I agree with you, but I wouldn't be doing my job if I didn't ask."

Jonathan manipulated the small gadget with his fingers. The cold metal brushed against his skin. Yes, he had most likely located the cause of their problems. All in all, they were fortunate. They'd discovered it faster than expected, and the damage ended up less severe than his most optimistic assumptions suggested. The "phones" in Valardir were wireless, except when plugged in. Wireless technologies had earned a reputation of being unsafe, but they secured their network using paranoid techniques. Picking up a conversation from outside proved impossible; no waves escaped Valardir. A spy could manage from inside, but their system suffered from greater weaknesses that a smart foe would exploit first.

Similarly, no one could call a Valardir phone from the outside, or so they'd believed. The Ostarkirans had somehow built an emitter accomplishing that feat through a simple yet unintuitive principle. The fact that they had overlooked this possibility sent a shiver down Jonathan's spine. What else had they missed? Thankfully, the trick posed minor risks. In appearance, the device lacked any means to extract information from Valardir's network. Their few remaining secrets were safe for now.

"Anyway, Jonathan, great job!" Brian gave Jonathan an encouraging slap on the shoulder. "You figured out the problem in two weeks, that's damn impressive."

"It's not over. There might be other emitters, and we have to study it more so we're sure it doesn't have any extra functionality. And the security issue needs a 'patch' so it can't work anymore. We also must confirm this isn't a decoy. Finding this thing was too easy."

Brian laughed. "I get your point, but easy? Without you, this would have taken months! You're a genius. Besides, yeah, there's more to do, but it's a major victory! You deserve a medal."

"Yeah? Well, I won't get one."

"I know."

***

Omoro 1, 2133, on the Nirnivian calendar

Now that the crisis had been resolved, Jonathan returned to the motion detector troubles. A dismantled sensor lay on his desk as he studied its insides and wondered if he'd ever discover the problem. This was outside his area of expertise. While he toiled, his door slipped open by itself. This had happened before, and back then, the sudden intrusion had surprised him. At the moment, however, he guessed the visitor's identity without looking. Once he spun his chair around, his eyes rested on the short, balding Koporal, confirming his hunch. Jonathan forced a smile.

"Mr. Tigh, to what do I owe the honor?"

Ron moistened his lips. "I heard you figured out the phone mystery. We have our differences, but I'm a big enough man to admit you did an excellent job. Congratulations, and thank you." Obvious sarcasm tainted his words, and the fake clapping accompanying them added to the insult. Jonathan remained calm and listened. "I'd give you a sterling review if not for the fact that the security improvements fell even more behind schedule." Tigh shook his head as he produced a disapproving clicking sound with his tongue. "High Command made it clear these are a priority, and I regret to say we're disappointed."

While he resisted a groan, Jonathan crossed his arms. "Figuring out how Doctor Death contacted James took precedence—the Commander told us that himself. Oh, and speaking of him, I warned him it was impossible to do both in a timely fashion. He wasn't happy, but he understood. It's not like we had a choice. Valardir was compromised."

A nod came from Tigh. "Ah, that's another thing." The senior brandished a lecturing finger. "You and your colleagues caused quite a ruckus over nothing. Please be more careful when assessing threats in the future."

Jonathan shrugged. "At the time, it was the logical conclusion."

A scowl appeared on Tigh's brow. "Yes, well, your mistake decreased morale and cost us money." He snapped his fingers. "That reminds me, when I last came here, you quoted your contract and said you're not soldiers and I can't treat you as such." The old man rubbed his chin. "I've been thinking—maybe that's part of the problem. If I could, you'd be more efficient. Sometimes having a fire lit under you is a great motivator. Your contracts are ending soon, and I'm a member of the committee drafting the new ones. I'll take that into consideration for my recommendations."

Jonathan waited a second before replying to keep his cool. "That's within your power, but right now, we're under the current contract, and what you've said could be interpreted as a threat, Mr. Tigh. I'll have to report it." He smirked. "It's my duty as a good employee."

Ron's mouth gaped in mock shock. "A threat? Oh no, Mr. Rivers, I was only stating facts aloud. But go ahead and follow your gut. I will."

On that note, the Koporal left. Jonathan watched him exit the room as he adjusted his glasses. No question the old man meant to taunt him, but he had learned his lesson since his previous tirade. He had remained polite, though the tone had proved insincere. Despite Jonathan's claims, he expected a formal complaint would be rejected in this case. Not that it mattered. Tigh could show off if he wished, but he lacked the power to rescind their contract. Sure, he had a role in the committee, but he couldn't decide on his own. Even if he swayed the other members, the final paper needed approval from the Commander. There was no way Daniel Ricdeau would go along with his revenge scheme. Besides, thanks to the video cameras, he possessed recordings of Tigh's two recent visits. Upon viewing them, any idiot would reach the conclusion the Koporal had acted not for the good of Nirnivia but out of a petty personal vendetta. Jonathan felt confident that this evidence would cause a scandal. A smirk formed on his face. Out of principle, he avoided starting fights, but he relished finishing them when provoked.

Chapter 15

Omoro 2, 2133, on the Nirnivian calendar

Crouched beside the furnace, Stalker finished wiring the device. Beads of sweat dripped from his brow. Infiltrating an apartment building posed little challenge and caused him little stress, as he had performed similar missions in more hostile territories. Explosives, however, played with his nerves. From the moment he had taken possession of the bomb, he'd imagined it detonating without warning, scorching him in the blast. At least it'd be over soon. He'd found the perfect location and installed the bomb. Now, all that remained was programming the timer, and he'd be set.

As he pressed the required buttons, footsteps echoed from the staircase. Stalker stifled a curse and darted behind a nearby column. Then he forced his body to remain immobile and, through his mutation, blended into the environment. That should work. A man arrived in the basement. He walked at a slow pace with a hunched posture while he hummed a tune. The song proved familiar, but Stalker failed to identify it. While a trivial matter compared to the rest of the situation, he assumed his brain would devote itself to the task for the whole day, against his will. He resisted a sigh. Gorumars' minds focused on such irrelevant nonsense.

Against his hope, the elder approached the furnace. Stalker's muscles tensed and his perspiration increased. Why should he tinker with a heater during a heat wave? If anything, the residents would demand air conditioning.

Soon the reason became clear: the old man aimed not for the contraption, but rather a nearby shelf. Once he arrived, he reached for a toolbox resting there and lifted it. Despite its obvious weight and his apparent delicateness, he showed no visible struggle. Perhaps he possessed greater strength than first impressions suggested.

At any rate, once he obtained the sought-after item, the senior began to leave. Stalker almost exhaled in relief, but he stopped himself when the man looked toward the bomb. "Uh... what's that thing?"

A tinge of regret assailed Stalker. Resigned, he shook his head and reached for his knife. He took no pleasure in what came next and even considered abandoning the mission. In the end, loyalty to BBR prevailed. He seized the old man from behind and covered his mouth with his hand, muffling any potential call for help. With his target immobilized, he brought the blade toward the man's throat and whispered, "I'm sorry."

It was a quick kill, no point prolonging the suffering. The deed accomplished, Stalker allowed himself a second or two to recover and then set up the timer. Though he gave himself a wide margin of error, he nonetheless escaped the building as fast as possible. Once he attained safety, he grabbed his radio and contacted Diabo.

"Yes, boss, it's done. No, no one saw me."

***

Conversation proved limited, not that Wrathchild expected otherwise. As usual, when awaiting the results of a large mission, Diabo's mood grew somber. Well, more somber than normal. Sometimes he paced around the cave serving as his office, and sometimes he sat at his makeshift desk. Like everything in their various hideouts, the piece of furniture ended up lightweight, cheap looking, and easily packable, all of which were important characteristics in their profession, where a sudden evacuation might become necessary, though as a consequence, their living arrangement lacked comfort. Some resented this fact, but not Wrathchild. She'd suffered far worse conditions during her youth.

As much as Diabo displayed impatience, Wrathchild endured a sense of dread. Stalker's mission had come as a surprise. The others had kept it a secret and decided not to mention it to her. When she'd asked Diabo why, he'd answered that they assumed she'd be against it. That was an understatement.

Didn't like it. Should've been used to it. We played dirty. Knew from start. Killed lots of people before BBR; still felt wrong. Blowing building filled with innocents—a bit much. NISDA be on ass... Not many upsides. Heh, no way change Diabo's mind. Didn't bother try. Only anger him.

—Thoughts of Wrathchild, Hocmar 28, 2134, on the Nirnivian calendar

At last, Diabo's radio beeped, and he reached for it as a wicked smile formed on his face. A shudder assailed Wrathchild. The implications seemed clear: Stalker had finished installing the bomb and was contacting the boss to inform him as instructed.

"Roger that, Stalker," Diabo said through his transmitter while his smirk became larger. "Good job. Don't stick 'round. Get your ass outta there quick."

The confirmation took the air out of Wrathchild's lungs. She gasped. As she imagined the explosion, two young visages popped into her head. A teenage boy and girl, gagged and suspended against a wall in a dark room. Whoever had tied them had removed their shirts, rendering Sebastian bare-chested. At least the assailant had had the bare minimal decency to leave Molly's bra on. Large scars ran down both of their abdomens. The memory lasted a mere instant, but Wrathchild's eyes watered. A mix of sadness, terror and pure rage overcame her. She huffed and forced herself to breathe in an effort to relax. Despite this, her legs weakened. She'd collapsed... and then a strong hand grabbed her shoulder.

Adrenaline surging through her veins, Wrathchild's instinct took over. Without thinking, she escaped the grip and spun. Her fingers wrapped around her sword's handle. Before she unsheathed it, she caught a glimpse of Diabo. The crimson beast adopted an expression filled with a concern he seldom showed.

"Hey, Wrath, something bothering ya?"

"Kinda... explosives bring bad memories." After a moment of hesitation, she added, "And blowing up Nirnivians sucks. Not our targets."

"Questioning my methods?"

Risks and foolish undertakings made up the majority of Wrathchild's life. She spent her whole existence on the verge of death, rushing from one insane situation to another. Still, even she wasn't crazy enough to oppose Diabo's approach. Those who did usually regretted it, though not for long.

"No, no!" Without quite realizing, she stepped backward. "Sucks, but no choice."

The red monster stared into her eyes as if gauging her sincerity. An unconvinced groan escaped his lips. "We strike when we can. There's an Ostarkiran spy in that freaking building. Ain't no way to identify 'em fo' sure. If we wait, they might leave. We attack now, get 'em all.

Nirnivians ain't our target, but they ain't our friends either." He brandished a warning finger toward her sternum. "Don't ya forget that. Give 'em a chance, and NISDA'll kill you dead like that." Diabo snapped his fingers. "Freaking assholes, we fight their goddamn war—shit, we win their war for 'em and that's how they thank us. Make no mistake, even if we brought 'em Doctor Death's head on a platter, they'd execute us in a second. 'Sides, nobody's innocent no more."

While she understood it'd serve no purpose, the following words escaped her lips against her will. "Freaking kids might live there. That's sad."

A shrug came from Diabo. "Nah, it's not." His brow wrinkled into a harsh scowl and his mouth contorted into a grimace. "Not anymore... there ain't no rules in war, not if you wanna win. We all damned ourselves a long time ago; a few more dead kids ain't gonna change that." On that note, Diabo turned away, but not before Wrathchild noticed pain and perhaps even sorrow creeping into his eyes. "Back then, Doctor Death didn't show mercy. That bastard gotta be stopped, and Rose ain't got what it takes for that. Anyway, those kids are better off dead than in a world where that son of a bitch wins."

So cruel... heh, always been; getting worse. Was kinda right. Rose too idealistic for war, but not in charge of NISDA. He took things other extreme. Had good reason hate Doctor, still... wondered why followed him. Why not leave shithole? Maybe joining been mistake? But, couldn't go... could escape, didn't want abandon him.

—Thoughts of Wrathchild, Hocmar 28, 2134, on the Nirnivian calendar

"Listen to me, Melissa." Startled by the mention of her birth name, Wrathchild lifted her gaze. "A freaking conscience is a luxury we can't afford. Keep it in check or you'll be dead meat. You know your life's more important than any snot-nosed Nirnivian kid's." After swallowing hard, she half-nodded. "Look, I got a soft spot for ya, so I'm gonna give you a one-shot deal. If this life ain't agreeing with you anymore, go ahead and leave. Go back to Rose and beg for mercy. Only one rule: don't you dare sell us out. If you betray me, I'll sneak up on ya when you sleep and I'll break your neck." Diabo's frown intensified as he mimicked the gesture. "Gimme your word you'll keep your mouth shut and you're free. Just ask yourself: if you do that, do you really think she'll forgive ya?"

A tempting offer, and yet despite her doubts, Wrathchild didn't hesitate, not even for a second. "Leave you? Never! With you till end."

Diabo gave her a light tap on the shoulder. Though meant as a friendly gesture, it packed considerable power, and her muscles screamed in agony. She expected the blow would cause a bruise. Mustering her courage, Wrathchild resisted showing any sign of pain. Not long afterward, she left for her "bedroom" and sat on her "bed": a simple sleeping bag. The cave lacked privacy, but she had somewhat more than most at her current location. After verifying no one was watching, she took a photo out of her pocket. The image depicted a younger Melissa standing beside Rose. Both smiled for the camera.

Not sure why kept picture. Nostalgia? Heh, understood couldn't go back. Liked looking at it. Was careful not be seen. Might've angered Diabo. Guess just nice remembering better times. Knew Diabo was right, wouldn't forgive. My place with him anyway.

—Thoughts of Wrathchild, Hocmar 28, 2134, on the Nirnivian calendar

She examined the snapshot a few minutes and then hid it again. Afterwards, Wrathchild prayed in silence. Religion wasn't very popular in BBR, as most considered it to be a remnant of their former lives best discarded. As such, it was safer if her prayers went unheard.

Chapter 16

When Mr. Cursak, the defense secretary, and I entered his office, the president sat at his desk and filled out paperwork. He hated such mundane tasks, but it was part of his duties. Normally, we wouldn't have bothered him, but we had bad news to report, and he'd be disappointed if we delayed delivering it.

—Thoughts of Evelyn Losier, Hocmar 28, 2134, on the Nirnivian calendar

Evelyn Losier and Roland Cursak entered the small utilitarian office. The Good Doctor kept it devoid of artifice. A large wooden desk stood as the single piece of furniture, though it lacked the habitual photos of wife and kids. Nothing ornamented the walls either. The president operated from several rooms in various secret facilities. He changed locations often to remain hidden from his enemies. Evelyn approved of the tactic, but she didn't understand why all his work areas were so bland. She realized he'd never cared for aesthetics and valued efficiency over style, but this seemed extreme.

Evelyn remembered how different his predecessor, Phillip Laforge, had been. The old fool had set up a bureau covered with artwork and expensive ornaments intended to flaunt Ostark's prosperity. Wherever space permitted it, he displayed pictures of himself accompanied by important politicians and celebrities, diplomas from his time at university, or other trinkets showcasing his standing. He planned to impress visitors with the excessive design and widely succeeded. Since the Good Doctor had declined to inherit Laforge's office, a minor politician no one cared about inhabited it.

The mechanical man sat at his desk with two stacks of documents before him. If Evelyn remembered correctly, the right one indicated papers requesting his attention, while those on the left he had taken care of earlier. The right pile towered above its neighbor, highlighting the enormous workload the cyborg needed to tackle. Despite the effort it demanded, he read through each sheet, making sure he understood the content, before signing it.

"Ms. Losier, Mr. Cursak, I welcome you." While he greeted them, he continued toiling without pausing. "To what do I owe the honor?"

Both of them glanced at each other before bowing their heads. Even in this situation, the Perz's bright brown eyes gave her shivers. Evelyn swallowed hard and then her lips parted as she prepared herself to make the announcement, but Cursak proved faster. His eyebrows lifted and pulled together as he stepped forward.

"This morning, we lost contact with three of our spies in the middle of a transmission, and we haven't been able to reach them since." He cleared his throat. "This does happen on occasions. BBR's communication array is impressive given their resources, but it's far from the most reliable piece of tech. Still, it's a cause for concern, and we investigated it as best we could." A tremor shook his voice. "We've intercepted a feed from a Nirnivian broadcast claiming BBR blew up the apartment building where they lived. The spies, Mr. Frasier, Mr. Lodal and Ms. Feror, are MIA and were most likely killed in the explosion—a very unfortunate turn of events."

"Indeed." The Good Doctor paused and dropped his pen. The smile displayed by his electronic eye's emoticon turned downward. "They shall be honored for their sacrifice."

Evelyn nodded. "They died as Ostarkiran heroes." She hesitated for a moment. "At least they almost completed their mission, so they obtained most of the information we wanted. BBR hurt Nirnivia more than us."

The mechanical man stared at her in a manner that froze her in place. Such a chilling glare... "Ms. Vice President, this is not about their mission. Loyal Ostarkiran soldiers died while performing their duties, and that is a tragedy regardless of the effect on our nation."

Mr. Cursak didn't say a word, but I could see he agreed just by looking at him. The thing is, I did too. I don't rejoice in the death of soldiers, but we were at war. Weren't such losses a necessity? Shouldn't our defense secretary be willing to sacrifice our men if it meant victory? If Cursak and the Good Doctor worried about their troops' well-being, shouldn't they have ended this war ASAP instead of dragging it on? The president had earned our trust time and time again, so I didn't doubt him, but I didn't understand his strategy either.

—Thoughts of Evelyn Losier, Hocmar 28, 2134, on the Nirnivian calendar

"I, um..." Embarrassed, Evelyn scratched the back of her head. "You're right, I'm sorry. I didn't mean it like that."

"I accept your apology." The Good Doctor resumed his paperwork. "My dear friends, I believe we have the regrettable task of contacting three unfortunate families. I wish to express my most sincere sympathies for their loss in person if it can be arranged."

"As you please, Mr. President." A sad but admiration-filled smile formed on Roland Cursak's face. "But, may I point out that you're a busy man, and your precious time might be better spent on more pressing matters?"

"You are correct, I am indeed busy. However, that is no reason to forget what is truly important. Besides, death could have been avoided. They ignored some cumbersome security measure during their communications. If only that had not been so, BBR would not have located them. I tried to warn them of the dangers, but alas, to no avail. That I didn't manage to convey how crucial it was is a failure on my part, and so it is only fair that I apologize to their families in person."

"Then it will be so. Of course, we'll have to arran—"

Once again, he reminded me of how much he cared for his people. This wasn't necessary, it'd be a superb publicity stunt, but I can't think of any other president who did the same. They would've mentioned the tragedy in a speech at best, or when answering some interviewer's questions, and let some senior officer handle the rest. He wasn't doing this just to look good, either. He was already more popular with the general population than any of his predecessors. I'll admit I didn't understand how his mind worked, and that sometimes led to conflicts, but I was convinced he was a great man.

—Thoughts of Evelyn Losier, Hocmar 28, 2134, on the Nirnivian calendar

Chapter 17

As he clutched his cue, James braced himself for defeat. Hunched over the table sporting a smirk, Brucie aimed for unconditional victory. Ever since he had learned that Janice had taught James how to play Rubarg, the bodyguard had expressed interest in a match between them. Well, that was the polite way to say it, but in truth, he'd taunted James with smack talk every chance he had. Somehow, they had never followed through until that day. The surprise cancellation of a meeting had left an unexpected gap in Rose's schedule. Of course, Kristina, the diligent assistant, had suggested that her employer should use this opportunity to progress with other tasks. The prophet had declined, explaining she needed a break, and so she had contacted her friends and they had headed for the rec room to put Brucie's skills to the test.

From the very first move, Brucie had gained the upper hand. James had expected to lose, but not in such a humiliating way. To be fair, he'd had his share of successes during the match, but the fact remained that Brucie crushed him.

I hate to admit it, but he was good. Maybe better than Janice... I didn't tell him that, though. His ego was big enough already.

—Thoughts of James Hunter, Hocmar 28, 2134, on the Nirnivian calendar

Still, Rose cheered James on and stayed on his side when it became clear she had backed the wrong horse. Even when the bodyguard prepared for what should be his final play, she smiled and patted James's shoulder. She assured him he had done great and that he'd win next time. Though he appreciated her kindness, James deemed her prediction beyond improbable.

And so, there he stood, on the brink of annihilation. Sneer widening, Brucie retracted his cue and... a strident beeping echoed through the room. At first, James gasped and his heart skipped a beat as he imagined the alarm came from Valardir's security systems. Soon, he noticed the TV produced the sound and relaxed with a few deep breaths. Shocked, Brucie dropped his stick and stared at the screen while Rose brought her hand to her chest and huffed. The MegaNews logo appeared on the monitor, and a voice said, "We interrupt the current program for an emergency news broadcast."

After presenting his longest finger at the woman reporter and shouting, "Shut up, won't ya?", Brucie refocused on his last ball. The expletive failed to deter the journalist, which was not surprising given it'd be impossible for her to hear, and she went on, "Good day, everyone. A tragedy occurred in the city of Ishadel when an apartment building exploded. Over fifty innocent people have died. MegaNews has received a tape from BBR, in which the terrorist organization claimed responsibility for the act."

"What?" The word came from Brucie. Shocked, the bodyguard's assured trust wavered and the struck orb rolled out of the planned path, missing its mark. Despite being pale by nature, Brucie's skin tone whitened to a ridiculous degree. His mouth gaped, pearls of sweat formed on his brow. He glared at the television and stepped toward it, trembling.

I had seen Brucie lose his composure before, but nothing like this.

—Thoughts of James Hunter, Hocmar 28, 2134, on the Nirnivian calendar

As for Rose, thanks to her darker complexion, she didn't reach Brucie's pallor, but she still looked as if she has been stricken by sudden sickness. Her palms covered her cheeks and her eyes watered.

"No... why?" she asked, though no one could answer. "BBR are sadistic terrorists, but they have no reason to attack Nirnivia. Why would they murder those poor people?" By then, the screen displayed ruins of the building along with firemen and medics responding to the scene. Rose averted her gaze, whimpering.

Concerned, James rushed to her. "Are you okay?" The alleged Melkar acquiesced without glancing at him. As for Brucie, he remained stiff as a statue.

When James returned to the television, the image changed. Now MegaNews played the videotape they had obtained. Diabo's large, muscular frame filled the view with its crimson shade. The cruel yellow eyes stared at the camera.

"...'cause an Ostarkiran spy lived there, and we got proof. Sorry fo' your loss, but we ain't got no other choice: NISDA are freaking cowards who won't do their job."

As I saw him, intense terror crept inside me. He was an abomination. Even on TV, I could sense his rage. If someone told me he really was the devil, I might've believed it. That he'd threatened to dissect me someday didn't help. I couldn't react. I was paralyzed by fear.

—Thoughts of James Hunter, Hocmar 28, 2134, on the Nirnivian calendar

Rose's face grew red and she gritted her teeth. "A spy?" She let out a disgusted groan. "A lousy spy? He killed fifty people over a spy the Ostarkirans probably don't care about?" She rested her hands on her hips. "What a lunatic! What if they weren't home?! He's not thinking. He just attacks again and again, innocent bystanders be damned. We have to stop him or he'll end up destroying both Ostark and Nirnivia!" She sighed and her defiant posture devolved into a resigned bow. "Who am I kidding? We can't even handle Doctor Death. Oh dear Ulgorack, please help us."

At that moment, James regained his senses and pointed at the monitor, unaware of Rose's monologue. "That's him! The red monster who said he'd dissect me!"

Brucie flinched, then turned toward James. An intense glower overtook his features. "Red monster?" The bodyguard approached James and poked him in the sternum with his index finger. Against all odds, the minuscule blow possessed enough strength to cause James to recoil. "Shit, man, he ain't no monster!"

"Brucie!" Rose said with her fingers joined in what reminded James of a praying position. "Please calm down."

"I guess he's an asshole. A terrorist? Sure! Got an ugly red body? Freaking yeah!" With his lips twisted in a grimace, Brucie grasped James by the collar and lifted him from the ground. A sob escaped James as his feet danced in the air. "But he's a person!"

By then, Rose stood behind her bodyguard and seized his shoulders in a pleading embrace. "Please stop, Brucie! Hunter doesn't know. He didn't mean anything by it."

Obeying his employer, Brucie let James go and left the rec room at a brisk pace. Terrified, James collapsed on the floor. Brucie hadn't hurt him, but the incident had weakened his legs and rendered him a nervous mess. While breathing rapidly, he scratched his head.

"Um, what was that about?"

Rose offered him a hand for him to stand up and he took it, yet stayed down for a second or two as he recuperated. "Diabo is Brucie's brother."

"What!?"

That didn't make any sense. Brucie was a normal guy, and Diabo was a monster. I remembered Daniel Ricdeau had mentioned there were mutants in this world. Actually, I'd met a few myself, and Rose might be one, though to say that was considered blasphemy. I'd figured Diabo simply had back luck. Turns out things weren't so simple.

—Thoughts of James Hunter, Hocmar 28, 2134, on the Nirnivian calendar

"I understand if you'd rather not see Brucie right now, but I have to go to him. I can't leave him alone like this."

"No, uh, I'll go with you."

***

When we exited the rec room, Brucie had already disappeared. Technically, he could've gone anywhere, but Rose guessed where he had gone.

—Thoughts of James Hunter, Hocmar 28, 2134, on the Nirnivian calendar

As Rose and James entered the gym, Brucie attacked the punching bag with a series of rapid blows. Several grunts and groans along with a dull thud accompanied each strike. If the bodyguard noticed the duo's arrival, he failed to show it. Instead, he remained tight-jawed and focused on his assault. After a moment of hesitation, Rose took a few steps toward him, though she chose to stay at a respectable distance.

"Are you all right, Brucie?" the winged woman asked, resting her palm upon her heart.

With a gulp and a scratch behind his head, James forced himself to look up. "Um, I'm sorry, Brucie, I didn't know." He recoiled and lifted his arm in a defensive gesture the instant he finished the sentence, expecting a furious glare. Instead, all traces of anger vanished from Brucie's features, replaced by sorrow. He waved James's apology away.

"Forget it, man, I ain't mad at ya." A resigned sigh came from Brucie. "You're right, Pierre's a monster—a freaking murderer. That's the problem, ya know. Truth hurts." Desperate, Brucie sat on the floor and wrapped his hands around his head. "Dude, it's just so unfair!" His voice trembled. "When he was Pierre Garland, he was a cool guy, ya know? Big bro, watching my back. We trained together. Sometimes we boxed. I never won, but I loved it. Shit, he was the reasonable one, keeping me outta trouble. And a babe magnet. Got my skills from him. Now he blows up apartment buildings."

In a deliberate manner, Rose joined her bodyguard on the floor. "Pierre used to be a good man." She patted Brucie's shoulder. "With any luck, he might realize his mistake and regain his senses."

A distorted chuckle escaped Brucie's lip. "Heh, ya mean well, but don't ya dare feed me that bullshit! I ain't so stupid, ya know? My bro's a criminal. He ain't coming back. At best, he'll get prison fo' life."

"I'm sorry, Brucie."

"It's okay, yer trying to help. Should be used to this crap now. It's been a while. Shit, if he'd never become that... thing."

"He became a mutant later on?"

I didn't mean to say that out loud—it just came out. I was worried I might've offended him, but he didn't seem to mind.

—Thoughts of James Hunter, Hocmar 28, 2134, on the Nirnivian calendar

"Kinda, ya see..." He sobbed. "Ah, dammit, I can't... won't ya explain it to him, Rose?"

A nod came from the prophet. "Not long after Doctor Death appeared in Ostark, they started capturing Nirnivians, both civilians and soldiers. We had no idea what they wanted with them, but they eventually stopped. To this day, Ostark's motives are a complete mystery. Most of those prisoners died, but we rescued a few." The alleged Melkar shivered. "One of the survivors was Pierre Garland, Brucie's brother. When we saved him, he had become the red monster you've met." Rose exhaled. "We don't know what the Doctor did exactly. Pierre refused to talk about it. The other prisoners were in a strange shape too. Each had different mutations."

"Pierre ain't ever been the same after. It's all his fault! All his goddamn fault that freaking—"

Brucie paused there. From the corner of my eye, I noticed Rose tense up. I had the feeling she was about to interrupt him. Maybe I was imagining things, but I doubt it. Now, I'm pretty sure I know what he was about to say. Back then, there was no way to figure it out.

—Thoughts of James Hunter, Hocmar 28, 2134, on the Nirnivian calendar

"—Doctor Death bastard! I hate that asshole. I only saw Pierre once after that. 'Twas terrible."

***

The apartment building failed to convey even a minimal sense of style. Suspicious stains, damaged walls, cobwebs, pests that had no business in a Gorumar's home—Brucie encountered each of these and beyond. Perhaps most disturbing, he passed at least six people slumped on the floor with a dazed expression. They didn't move and showed no sign of noticing Brucie when he walked past them. With a sickening sensation overtaking his stomach, he assumed them to be junkies high on snaprocks or other popular drugs. For a time, he'd risked following the same path, and witnessing the fate he had avoided left him quivering. Thank Ulgorack Pierre had helped steer him away from this future.

Soon, Brucie found his destination: a door marked by the number 404 scribbled in a barely legible manner. The door possessed the same dubious qualities as the rest of the living arrangements. Scratches covered its surfaces and the paint was long faded—that was, where it remained. In several spots, it had vanished, revealing the cheap wood underneath.

Brucie formed a fist with his right hand and lifted it, about to knock, but then hesitation grappled him and he swallowed hard. What awaited him on the other side? Had anything of his brother survived this ordeal? Of course, he'd learned of what had happened and had seen Pierre on TV, so Brucie was aware of the torture his sibling had endured and the resulting deformed appearance. When his mom and he had discovered Pierre's rescue and return to Nirnivia, they'd immediately attempted to locate him. The fact that he had chosen not to visit them gave them the impression he might not want to see them, but they had to try.

It had taken considerable effort. Pierre lacked a phone or any simple means of communication. Through intense research and begging those with the answer for information, they'd succeeded despite the low odds.

Now that Brucie stood in front of his goal, however, he wavered. How would Pierre react? Would he refuse to meet his own brother? After a few deep breaths, Brucie steeled himself and knocked. No response, yet the subtle sounds of someone attempting to conceal his presence reached his ears. With Pierre's large body, mastering stealth proved a challenge, it seemed.

Gritting his teeth, Brucie knocked again and said, "Yo, bro, open up, will ya? I know you're there!"

"Go away, Brucie." The voice sounded harsh and ragged, far from the deep, soothing tone Brucie remembered. Yet a trace of Pierre's former gentleness remained.

"Come on, bro, I haven't seen ya in months! Mom misses ya; she's worried, open up! I'll stay all night if I've got to!"

An annoyed grunt echoed from inside the room. Then heavy footsteps sent vibrations through the floor, and the door opened. Brucie's mouth gaped as the crimson mass his brother had become appeared in the door frame. At least he resisted the temptation to recoil. Yellow eyes peered upon Brucie from above due to Pierre's superior height. The uncommon color and coldness they displayed crushed Brucie's heart. Still, he forced a smile.

"Yo, bro, long time no see. How are ya holding up?"

"How do ya think, Brucie?" Pierre glared. "That Doctor Death freak screwed me up. I feel like crap."

Embarrassed, Brucie scratched the back of his head. "Yeah, dude, I'm sorry. Ya know I ain't good with emotional stuff. We were all messed up when ya were captured. We thought we'd never see ya again. Mom cried every freaking day. Not me, 'cause I'm a man and all, but shit, I missed ya. It's so good to get ya back." In a moment of nostalgia, Brucie almost punched Pierre's shoulder but decided it might be a bad idea. "Why didn't you call? Was a major pain finding ya."

Brucie positioned himself in a way that suggested he wished to enter the apartment, but Pierre blocked the entrance without flinching. "I didn't call 'cause your brother is dead, Brucie. I ain't the man I used to be. Get outta here and don't come back. Ya don't wanna be involved with a guy like me."

"Dude! That just ain't true! Look, you went through shit and it changed ya, but you'll always be my bro, ya know? We're family. Mom wants ya back, don't do this to her. Come home. She'll cook ya a feast! She'll be so happy. Whatever weird crap you're dealing with, we'll help you get through it, ya know? Hey, maybe later we'll hit a bar for old time's sake and—"

A terrible growl escaped from Pierre. Though not that loud, it possessed a menacing quality, and Brucie flinched without quite meaning to. "You think anyone in a bar wanna hang out with me now? I'm a monster, I ain't wanna be seen in public no more and they ain't wanna see me either. What's next, huh? A boxing match? Crazy bastard, I ain't just red, I got super strength and this skin is hard as steel. I'd kill you."

A shrug came from Brucie. "Okay, dude, forget 'bout the bar, but hey, there's tons o' mutants. You don't look so outta place. Anyway, come home with me, won't ya? For Mom's sake."

It seemed that, at that point, what little patience remained in Pierre vanished. In a quick motion, the older sibling struck Brucie. Not with a punch or even a slap. No, the giant only poked him in the sternum with his index finger. The resulting touch propelled Brucie onto his back.

"Get outta here, Brucie, I ain't your brother no more!" And then he slammed the door shut.

***

"He didn't wanna see me," Brucie said as a few tears rolled down his cheeks. "I thought 'twas a temporary thing, ya know... but a few weeks later, he formed BBR with two old pals also turned freaks by Doctor Death. Ah, man, the threats he made to that robot douche. Now he's Diabo and all like 'the end justifies the means' and shit. He was right, he ain't my bro no more."

After all that, I understood BBR's motivation better. Still had no idea what they wanted with me, though. What value could I bring to their cause? I'm only an average human: weak, dumb and totally useless. BBR already had amazing mutants in their ranks. I didn't have any skill comparable to Wrathchild or Diabo himself. What were they hoping to gain by experimenting on me? Whatever it might've been, I doubted their logic. At that point, I was too concerned with Brucie to care about those questions, but they often came to my mind afterward.

—Thoughts of James Hunter, Hocmar 28, 2134, on the Nirnivian calendar

The three of them stayed in the gym in silence. Nothing Rose or James could say would improve the bodyguard's mood, but at least they showed support through their presence. Four or five agonizing minutes passed, and then Brucie looked at his employer. "Rose, I'll be fine. We should go."

Concerned, Rose touched Brucie's shoulder. "Are you sure?" A nod came from Brucie. "Okay, then, I have plenty of work ahead of me." She sighed. "I must contact the families if possible and offer my condolences." The prophet shook her head. "I wonder if I'll manage. There are so many victims. Also, I should write a eulogy." She sobbed. "Won't this pointless war ever end?" They walked halfway toward the door before Rose stopped and faced her bodyguard. "Actually, Brucie, you should take the day off and rest. I can find a soldier who'll watch over me for a while." With that, she wished them a good afternoon and left.

Something bothered me about the way Rose acted. She talked like what had happened devastated her, but somehow that didn't quite ring true. I mean, I sensed her sadness—she clearly wasn't happy about it—and yet it almost seemed like she put up a front. As if she realized her reaction wasn't convincing, so she exaggerated it. No question she cared about the people, I knew her well enough to understand that. Still, it felt off.

—Thoughts of James Hunter, Hocmar 28, 2134, on the Nirnivian calendar

"I know what ya think, dude." Brucie slapped James's shoulder, though thankfully with moderate strength compared to such previous love taps. "You're cursing yourself 'cause you didn't take the chance fer another peek at her butt."

"What?"

A chuckle came from Brucie. "Just messing with ya. Nah, ya think her reaction is kinda fake. Don't blame her, dude, stuff like that's been happening through the war. Every freaking tragedy, she does one o' those mass eulogies. First couple o' times she cried for hours. Now she's used to it. We all are. For us, a building blowing up, that's routine, ya know? But she ain't gonna accept that, 'cause those people's lives are worth the same as those who died before. So, she forces herself to show the same level o' emotion, even if it ain't convincing."

I have to admit that was one of the saddest things I've ever heard.

—Thoughts of James Hunter, Hocmar 28, 2134, on the Nirnivian calendar

Brucie sighed. "But enough with the heavy stuff, ya know? We ain't finished our Rubarg match. How 'bout we play another game to settle the score?"

"Um, yeah, sure, why not?"

For the record, he won, but that shouldn't come as a surprise to anybody.

—Thoughts of James Hunter, Hocmar 28, 2134, on the Nirnivian calendar

Mutiny

Chapter 1

Tigal 30, 2133, on the Nirnivian calendar

Not long ago, learning the game called Kuhard seemed like an impossible task. It was so complex: I had never seen anything comparable back on Earth. Rose never gave up. I probably would have, but she enjoyed teaching me so much. Despite the challenge, I eventually managed to play for real, even if Rose sometimes had to point out that I'd made an illegal move.

—Thoughts of James Hunter, Hocmar 28, 2134, on the Nirnivian calendar

On the board, Rose dragged her berserker backward, decapitating James's last cook. Based on the current winning condition, she'd defeated him. Despite this, James's slight smile widened a little. The mere fact that he'd noticed implied improvement on his part. At first, he'd doubted he'd ever manage to grasp the rules, but now that seemed like a possible goal. Besides, being angered by a loss proved difficult in Rose's garden. Between the gentle fan producing wind that shuffled his hair and the artificial sunlight, the room provided a convincing representation of a beautiful day at the park.

"You win again! Third time in a row."

Rose offered an encouraging smile. "Don't feel bad, Hunter, that's to be expected. Nobody becomes a Kuhard master so quickly." She softly giggled. "I hope I don't come off as mean, but you're my favorite opponent!"

Enthralled by her obvious delight, James joined her in laughter. "Enjoying your winning streak, huh?"

"Well, yes. Don't blame me, Hunter, it's natural for one to celebrate her first three victories, isn't it?"

"What?" Due to surprise, that came out louder than intended. James frowned before adjusting his voice for the next sentence. "Um, you mean you've never won before?"

"No." A light blush reddened Rose's cheeks. "I love Kuhard, but I'm not particularly good at it. I mostly played against Daniel, my adoptive father. He won some regional championships, you know? And he was far too skilled for me."

"He never let you win even once?" an incredulous James asked.

A nostalgic glimmer shone in Rose's eyes. "No. In Kuhard, there is no mercy. It's tradition that you always give your best, no matter what." She gestured at the remaining pieces. "That's why I'm not giving you any chances either. I'm playing the same way I would if you were my dad."

"That's fine with me, but I'm not a kid! He, um, could've let you win at least once, just to make you happy. Parents do it all the time where I come from."

Rose shrugged, seemingly not understanding why James seemed so shocked by Daniel's behavior. "Dad did that too, but not with Kuhard. It's tradition," she repeated. "I didn't mind. Sure, I wanted to win, but in a way, seeing him try so hard motivated me to do better. Besides, he never went easy on Laurence either."

"Uh?" James's hand shielded his heart. "Who's that?"

"Oh..." With a swift motion, Rose covered her mouth. "Sorry, I forgot I never mentioned him. Laurence is my brother... well, adoptive brother technically."

"Ah, so Daniel and Madeleine also have a son?"

I admit I was surprised he had never come up in conversation. No one ever talked about him and I wondered why, but it wasn't my business.

—Thoughts of James Hunter, Hocmar 28, 2134, on the Nirnivian calendar

"Yes. He lives far away, which is why you haven't met him. And with me stuck in Valardir, I haven't seen Laurence for so long myself."

"You must miss him." In his mind, James added, "And the rest of the family too."

Rose's pupils darted to the left. "Yes..." She sighed. "Anyway, I played against a few other people, but I never beat anyone. Once I thought I would. You aren't my first student, Hunter." As the alleged prophet uttered those words, a touch of sadness flooded her voice. "That honor belongs to my deceased husband. When I met Miguel, he hadn't even heard of Kuhard. I taught him. When we began our first match, I figured he didn't stand a chance. It takes more than one game to become a great Kuhard player, and indeed, Miguel wasn't great just yet, but he already bested me. I made a stupid mistake at the last moment, but the fact that he had been able to exploit it was remarkable. Miguel loved Kuhard at least as much as me. We played often, and he became incredibly skilled. He won several championships and even surpassed Dad. I wasn't near his level, but I cherished every game." Rose adopted a sorrowful smile filled with such intensity that it sent a shiver down James's spine. "Hunter, I appreciate what you're doing. I know you don't like Kuhard, but you won't say so aloud for my sake. I haven't played in so long. Thank you."

"Um, you're welcome," James whispered while scratching his head. Then he added, "I don't hate it or anything. It's growing on me."

"Good!" The winged woman tilted her head sideways and beamed. "Enough to be up for another game?"

Turns out I was. I lost again, but I had fun anyway. Win or lose, what does it matter when you appreciate the other player's company?

—Thoughts of James Hunter, Hocmar 28, 2134, on the Nirnivian calendar

Chapter 2

Tigal 34, 2133, on the Nirnivian calendar

Out of nowhere, we reached the Nirnivian new year. Well, it was unexpected for me anyway since I had no idea when their holidays were—or what they were for that matter. Rose told me there'd be a party at the cafeteria to celebrate. I figured there wouldn't be much of a turnout given it's in a guarded military facility, but I ended up surprised. While it wasn't the biggest crowd ever, more people showed up than I would've imagined.

—Thoughts of James Hunter, Hocmar 28, 2134, on the Nirnivian calendar

When James entered the refectory, he almost failed to recognize the room. Dimmed lights greeted him, contrasting the normally well-lit area. A wide range of multicolored ribbons and balloons hung from the walls and ceiling, contributing to a festive atmosphere. Even the tables themselves offered an aura of luxury. Though they were simple wooden boards devoid of any impressive qualities, the staff had covered them with sublime white cloths that concealed their bareness. Intricate details woven into the fabric captured James's eyes. They illustrated complex scenes he assumed came from Nirnivian history. Every time he glanced at them, he noticed a new detail. Curious, he caressed one with his fingers as he advanced. The soft texture confirmed they must've cost a pretty penny. As if that wasn't enough, beautiful and unique centerpieces adorned each table. Some consisted of artful flower arrangements. Others depicted scenes, including several in which James recognized Rose. In all honesty, the decorators had achieved a triumph. Too bad the plain old chairs they always sat on for lunch diminished the effect.

In the upper left corner rested a large stereo playing music with an energizing rhythm. They had shuffled the tables around to clear the middle so that would-be dancers could take advantage of the situation, though James doubted he'd join them. Opposite, a buffet consisting of a multitude of meats, vegetables, bread, fruits and other delights awaited. Despite the distance, the enticing aroma reached James's nostrils, and he deduced the cooks had procured ingredients a few cuts above their standard fare. His stomach grumbled in anticipation.

As Rose, Brucie, and James waded through the room, he observed the crowd. Most seats remained empty, a fact he'd expected. The prophet led them to an elevated table near the middle. Clearly it was meant as a position of honor. Unused to such attention, James froze along the way. This couldn't be for him. Once Rose discerned his reticence, she turned around and touched his shoulder, leading him forward. James sat to the right of Rose while Brucie chose the left. Speaking of the bodyguard, he wore a sharp black suit and a tie, which reminded James of a businessman. That unsettled him a little. He had grown used to Brucie acting like a buffoon, and the serious attire contradicted his expectations. Rose, however, wore the same white dress she always did.

While they chatted about various subjects, people filled the chamber. Far more than James had presumed. Curious, he asked Rose why they chose to celebrate in Valardir of all places. She explained that she was the reason. Due to Doctor Death's abduction attempts, she couldn't leave the complex, so it made sense for her family to join her here. As for the others, they consisted of soldiers, politicians with clearance, and other high-society persons who saw passing this evening with the Melkar as a status symbol. A touch of disdain tinged her voice, as if the fact that they viewed her in such a manner bothered her.

A few minutes passed before James spotted Janice walking toward them. An expansive black dress wrapped the gigantic woman, and she carried an equally impressive purse. He didn't realize before, but he had never seen her carrying a handbag until that moment. Then again, it might not fit with the military attire.

Maybe it's sexist on my part, but it felt a little strange seeing someone so muscular in a dress. At least it did for a minute or two, before I got used to it. I had to admit it looked great on her.

—Thoughts of James Hunter, Hocmar 28, 2134, on the Nirnivian calendar

"Hey, James, what's up?" she asked while presenting her fist. After James offered the requested bump, she took the chair next to him, effectively squeezing him between the two Ricdeau sisters.

A chuckle echoed from Brucie. "Ya freaking clever bastard!" He winked. "Ya got the best seat in the place."

"Don't mind him." Janice sighed. "He's just jealous."

"Damn straight I am!" The bodyguard patted the free space at his side. "This baby's lonely without you, ya know?"

A wrinkled hand tapped Brucie's shoulder from behind. Startled, he jumped. Daniel Ricdeau stood there smiling. The group had been so focused on their discussion that no one had noticed him.

"Ah, don't worry about it, my boy. My old butt will be your baby's companion." As announced, he sat down beside Brucie. "And, just like that"—he snapped his fingers—"you have the best seat in the place!"

Madeleine now arrived, trailing her husband, and she joined him at the table. "Quite frankly, my dear, as fond as I am of your anatomy, I expect your posterior is not to Brucie's liking."

"I guess not, but it has a lot more experience than Janice's!"

The high priestess allowed herself a rare giggle. "I cannot deny that."

It was a pretty calm party, but I had fun. The food was amazing—the best meal I've had in Nirnivia for sure. And we laughed so much. Between Brucie, Daniel and Janice, there wasn't any lack of joking around. The only annoying thing was that once in a while, someone asked for Rose's blessings. I guess that gave me an idea of what it's like to be a celebrity who's constantly interrupted during meals.

—Thoughts of James Hunter, Hocmar 28, 2134, on the Nirnivian calendar

Midnight grew near and a camera crew prepared equipment so Rose could address the nation and usher in the new year. She went with the techs to prepare. Less than a minute after she'd left, Janice asked James, "So, buddy, any resolutions?"

"Um"—he scratched behind his ear—"not really, no. I haven't thought about it."

"I guess our new year doesn't mean much to you, uh?"

"You could say that." A light blush reddened James's cheeks. "I don't even understand how your calendar works. How about you? Got any resolutions?"

Janice pointed at her own torso with her thumb. "Me?" She smirked and joined her hands behind her head. "No way! When you're this awesome, who needs improve—"

Before she managed to finish her sentence, quick fingers seized the scarf around her neck and unraveled it. Shocked, Janice gasped. Both she and James turned toward the culprit: a chortling Brucie, who waved his prize. "Hey, I gotta blow my nose! This'll be perfect, ya know!"

"Oh, that's it..." The massive woman stood up and cracked her knuckles. "Your crotch's meeting madam fist." On that note, Brucie fled, with Janice in pursuit.

Shaking her head, Madeleine tried a sip of her drink. "It appears Mr. Garland will never grow up." She sighed. "I suppose some things never change." She paused and gazed at James. "Tell me, Mr. Hunter, how are you adapting to your new life?"

"Um, it's difficult, but I'm getting used to this place."

"We do not often have a chance to chat. I am relieved that you are feeling better." She reached out and touched his hand in a comforting manner. "My dear, you gave us quite a scare. Especially Rose. She feared you would not make it."

Though James opened his mouth to answer, Rose then began her speech, so he remained silent.

"Good evening, everyone, this is Rose Ricdeau: the Melkar. The last few years have been difficult, to the point where we lack enthusiasm for this celebration. However, I urge you to be optimistic and remember that this year might lead to the end of the war. Besides, we must not let our current situation make us forget what's truly important: our family, our friends, our hopes and dreams. If the greater picture has been dark lately, then we must find comfort in the little things. Now then, it's almost midnight." The public counted down in unison with the holy prophet. "Ten... nine... eight... seven... six... five... four... three... two... one... happy new year!" The whole room was filled with energy.

Not long after they finished, Brucie and Janice returned to the table, both laughing. Janice reclaimed her shawl. By the bodyguard's joyful demeanor, James assumed the threat of dick punching proved an idle one. Minutes later, Rose also arrived.

Everyone exchanged handshakes and hugs, us included. It was a bit strange. When Mr. Ricdeau hugged Janice, it looked awkward. Janice scowled, and I think she almost pushed him back. He wasn't exactly eager himself. It wasn't like that with Rose, and it confused me at first, but then I figured maybe it was because she was in the military too. In daily life, Mr. Ricdeau had to treat her the same as any officer under his command. That's an awkward situation in itself.

—Thoughts of James Hunter, Hocmar 28, 2134, on the Nirnivian calendar

Amid the celebration, Janice spotted someone in the distance and frowned. "That poor girl doesn't understand the meaning of fun."

By following her gaze, James laid eyes upon Kristina Dupree. The assistant sat at a discreet table alone and, as always, poked at her minicomp.

"I know. I invited her to join us, but she declined. She's quite shy. To be frank, I'm surprised she's here, but unfortunately not surprised she's on her own."

"That is so sad." Madeleine shook her head. "Does she not have any family she can spend this occasion with?"

The alleged prophet shrugged. "I'm not sure. Kristina doesn't talk much about her personal life. Her parents died a while back in a car accident, I can tell you that. I believe the other members of her family live in different cities." There was a pause, during which a resolved expression formed on Rose's face. "I'll go wish her a happy new year and use that as a pretext to stay with her for a while. You guys don't mind, do you?"

Madeleine smiled. "Of course not, my dear. In fact, it would be a pleasure to join you."

"Thank you, I appreciate it. The thing is, I doubt Kristina would be comfortable with so many relative strangers around. I'll be back later."

Daniel Ricdeau acquiesced. "Take as long as you want, princess." Blood rushed to Rose's visage, and she fired a quick glance at her father before leaving. Once she disappeared, Daniel said, "Oh, I forgot myself and embarrassed her. Again... ah well!" A wide smile formed on his lips. "Kristina might not understand the meaning of fun, but I do!" He got down on one knee and grasped his wife's fingers. If they weren't already married, James might've assumed he'd propose. "Would the loveliest lady in the room afford me her first dance of the year?"

Madeleine Ricdeau touched her cheek and giggled. "How can I refuse such a charming man?"

They both headed for the "dance floor." James watched them; both seniors showed a decent amount of spryness. After a short while, Janice leaned toward him and said, "Hey, should we join them?"

"Um, I don't know..." He hesitated and lowered his head. In response, Janice gave him a begging look.

"Please, just one 'friendly' dance. I don't have a boyfriend, so I never get the chance."

"I'd dance with ya!" an enthusiastic Brucie shouted as he stood up.

Janice chuckled and dismissed the proposal with a wave. "With your two left feet? Ah, sorry, but I like being able to walk." A rather mean riposte, but her good-humored demeanor implied jest. Brucie retorted with a playful extension of his tongue.

"You should dance with her, Hunter." Rose's voice came as an unexpected shock, and James's heart skipped a beat.

"Uh, what?"

"Oh, Kristina decided to go home already. Anyway, take her up on her offer. Janice is a great dancer." The alleged prophet cackled at her sister. "Do you remember that party five years ago?" Janice bit her lip and then averted her gaze. Though she mumbled a reply, James failed to hear what she said.

Again, Janice acted so cold with Rose. Actually, I don't think she said one thing to her that day other than that inaudible whisper. It's not like she treated everyone like that: Janice was friendly and talkative. I couldn't help wondering what was going on between them.

—Thoughts of James Hunter, Hocmar 28, 2134, on the Nirnivian calendar

"It's a bad idea. I'm like Brucie, I have two left feet."

"Hey, screw you, dude! Ya ain't know what you're talking 'bout!"

"It's not a competition. I just want to have fun." Janice lowered her volume. "It's not really about Brucie's dancing. It's because he has terrible breath. Stinks a mile away."

"Ah, come on!" The bodyguard threw his hands in the air. "Get off my back, won't ya? It ain't that bad; I'll check it right now." With his palm, he covered his mouth and nose and blew. A disgusted grimace twisted Brucie's features. "Never mind, ya lucky bastard."

"I win this round, don't I?" She returned her attention to James. "And I'm not letting you off the hook either."

Before he had a chance to refuse, she grasped his hand and pulled him toward her desired destination. Though James sent Rose a begging stare, the Melkar declined to intervene, and in the end, he relented. Butterflies assailed his stomach, and he shivered at the thought of making a spectacle of himself. Already, he imagined scenarios where he stumbled and fell, bringing hilarity for the crowd. Besides, while his disappearance separated them, he had a girlfriend back home and wondered what Nadia's take on these events would be. He reminded himself that Nadia danced with friends on occasion, so she should be okay with it. Then again, people could be tolerant of their own behavior while condemning it in others. Objections still filled his brain when they started dancing.

Rose hadn't exaggerated. Janice was amazing, and I think she held back for my sake. She could pull sick moves I'd never attempt in a million years. Um, I guess her mutation helped with that. I mean, perfect balance and all. Despite my fears, I avoided looking like an idiot for the most part by moving as little as possible. Nobody paid attention to me, and I admit it was fun. Well, nobody except two people: Rose, who clapped her hands to the rhythm, and Brucie, who gave us the finger for some reason. I ignored him, but Janice had plenty of fingers of her own for the both of us. Just when I felt glad Janice had made me do this, disaster struck.

—Thoughts of James Hunter, Hocmar 28, 2134, on the Nirnivian calendar

The upbeat tune they jammed to eventually stopped, and without warning, a far slower type of music began playing. James swallowed hard as those around him started reaching for their partners' waists. Sweat formed on his brow and he eyed Rose and Brucie. Janice caught the furtive glimpse and deduced the implication.

"Come on, give me another one and you're a free man, I promise."

"Um, I..." Embarrassed, he scratched the back of his head. "Uh..."

"Oh... don't worry, I'll lead."

Yeah, that sounds about right.

—Thoughts of James Hunter, Hocmar 28, 2134, on the Nirnivian calendar

"Let me show you." In a quick motion, she seized his hand. "This goes here." She then put it on her hip, and James winced. "It's all right, it's not like it's on my butt or anything."

"My girlfriend might think it's too close for comfort."

"Oh, don't be silly. We're just two friends dancing! Besides, she's in a whole other universe." She grinned. "And if she ever gives you lip about this, I can beat her up! I'm allowed, I'm a woman too!"

Okay, I knew she was joking, but I still worried about Nadia. If Janice punched her, she might break in half. Anyway, we began swaying around like the other couples, and that was my first slow dance. Nadia had often asked me to, but I'm not comfortable doing that kind of stuff in public and she's not as... motivating. Yeah, let's go with that. She's not as motivating as Janice, so she always ended up going with some of her friends instead. Soon, the song was over and, as promised, Janice led me away. I figured we'd return to Rose and Brucie, but no, she took me to an empty table.

—Thoughts of James Hunter, Hocmar 28, 2134, on the Nirnivian calendar

"All right, James, wait here for a sec. I'll be right back."

"What about...?" His head bobbed toward the prophet and the bodyguard.

"Ah, they'll manage without us for a few minutes." On that note, she disappeared into the crowd. When she reemerged, she carried her handbag and opened it. She plunged her fingers inside and fished out a small box wrapped in yellow paper and a red ribbon tied in a bow. "Here, I got this for you."

"Oh"—James flushed—"you shouldn't have... I don't have anything for you."

"Don't worry about that. It's not like I expected you to. Go ahead. Open it." She smiled.

Curious, James obeyed. The distinctive sound of ripped paper tickled his ears. Soon, he glimpsed the concealed package, but it proved to be a plain brown box devoid of unique features. No way to guess the contents, so he opened the carton. Inside rested a black rectangle most of whose surface consisted of a screen, though a few buttons could be spotted. A mere second passed and James recognized the thick tablet-like device they called a minicomp. He gasped in shock.

"Thank you, Janice. I appreciate the gesture, but uh..." He rubbed behind his head. "It's too much, I can't accept this."

A giggle came from Janice as she rejected his reticence with a wave. "Don't be ridiculous, it's an older model and only cost me a couple bucks. I know you're often alone and bored, so I figured it'd give you something to do." She scowled. "Too bad the techs are paranoid about this kind of stuff. They literally tore out some circuits so it can't access the GlobalNet for security reasons." She shrugged. "Ah well, that's life in Valardir for you. At least there are still plenty of games on there; better than nothing."

"Much better! Thank you again."

After that, we returned to Rose, Brucie, and the others and kept the party going until way past my normal bedtime. The next day, I woke up after noon, but it's not like it mattered anyway, right?

—Thoughts of James Hunter, Hocmar 28, 2134, on the Nirnivian calendar

Chapter 3

Osmoro 1, 2134, on the Nirnivian calendar

After he readjusted his glasses, Jonathan reread the document for the third time. The moment he had torn the envelope open, he'd predicted trouble. He had known the contents to be their new contract for the year. Despite being prepared for the worst, upon his first reading, he believed his eyes had tricked him and began a second pass. The text remained the same, confirming he hadn't fallen prey to his imagination. He'd expected something like this, and recent events only increased his suspicion, yet High Command had gone beyond his most pessimistic scenario. Unwilling to spread unfounded rumors, Jonathan had kept his apprehension from his colleagues. No point in discretion now. They had received the news, and they'd be furious. Not that he blamed them.

As if to validate Jonathan's assumption, his doorbell rang and he opened the door. His good friend, Brian, entered in a rush, followed by Giselle. "Hey, Jonathan"—Brian waved the papers he held—"have you seen this piece of crap?"

"That's harsh. Crap is disgusting, but it has its uses in nature."

Too angry for a genuine laugh, Brian forced a chuckle. "Yeah, fair enough. I can't believe Commander Ricdeau approved this. Not only do they have the guts to cut our salary, they're also increasing the work hours and slashing what little benefits we have."

Giselle nodded. She had lost a front tooth long ago. A large gap lay where it had once stood, and a whistling sound echoed as she spoke. "And they won't pay for overtime anymore, but they can force us to stay late." After a pause, she scowled. "Is that legal?"

Jonathan sighed. "Technically, no, but they'll claim it concerns national security, so it's an exception under the Deboros Act, and the Council will back them."

Incredulous, Giselle gasped. "So, there's nothing we can do?"

"We could sue and bring it before a judge, but the chances we'd win are almost zero because, well, NISDA has a point: if they need us to do overtime, it's probably related to national security."

Giselle crossed her arms. "You sound like you agree with them. Guess you don't care, your wife's bringing in the money."

An allusion to the fact that, as a lawyer, Madison earned more than him. Perhaps Giselle had meant to insult his masculinity. If so, she'd failed, and he decided he'd ignore the rebuke. "On the contrary—yes, we'll be okay financewise, but I barely see my son as it is and this won't help. Besides, we're in this together."

"What about their excuse?" Brian groaned. "They say Doctor Death's recent breach of our phone system made them go over budget. Smells like bullshit."

Again, Jonathan nodded. "It is. Look, they really are over budget and I saw this coming for a while. Thing is, the breach isn't the cause." He rubbed his chin. "Oh, it cost a bundle, no question, but they were in the red before. I suspect the security upgrades cost them more overall, but they won't admit that because we warned them and they didn't listen. And that's only the beginning. NISDA is broke and so is the whole country. The Council can't give them more. They're desperate, so they're using the breach as an excuse to mooch off us."

Enlightened, Brian snapped his fingers. "That's why you asked Commander Ricdeau if he was threatening us when he brought up our contracts."

"Yep, I wanted to test his reaction. He acted well, but he didn't fool me. Still"—he pointed at the papers—"this is ridiculous and way worse than I thought. Bastards."

Brian chuckled. "If they expected us to accept this quietly, they'll be disappointed. Everyone's in an uproar and starting to look for jobs. Seems like NISDA will lose a bunch of employees, and it serves them right."

"Fair enough, but there aren't many companies hiring." Jonathan shook his head. "They'll lose good people, but most will have to stay or become unemployed."

Giselle hunched over. "You sure make it sound like we have to shut up and take it."

"No, we can't give in. I have a plan, sort of..." Jonathan clenched his fist and fired an authoritative stare at his comrades. "Brian, Giselle, spread the word around: important meeting about the situation at my house tonight."

Surprised, Brian frowned. "Tonight? You're in a hurry."

"Everyone's riled up and we can't let them cool down before we act." A pensive Jonathan caressed his chin. "Don't use internal email or chat. Better if the higher-ups don't suspect anything for now."

Over the years, Jonathan had learned to appreciate history and the lessons it taught. Even back in high school, he'd often spent free periods reading ancient volumes his peers had deemed useless and boring. His strange hobby had earned him mockery then, but today, the same old books might provide a solution to their plight.

Chapter 4

Lies are messy business—Plague had learned that much as a teen, and yet sometimes they proved to be indispensable. No question, he had taken a gamble when he'd pretended to Stalker that Diabo's plan might be the superior option. In truth, he deemed his boss's idea ludicrous and expected a massive backlash from their Nirnivian supporters. Diabo believed in the attack with fervor, however, and Plague deduced that any attempt at dissuading him would fail. As for Stalker, he took an equally firm stance on the other side. Plague feared a fatal showdown. What was the point in preserving their patrons if BBR tore itself apart from within? So, he'd concocted a fine batch of bullshit and deescalated the situation, all while wondering at what price.

For better or worse, he'd learned the answer this morning, and he now related the information to both Diabo and Stalker via video conference. Still lacking proper sight, Plague imagined his colleagues' reactions. Poor Stalker—he pictured his head bowed down with a fist clenched in frustration below the camera's reach. As for Diabo, he likely adopted his usual posture: arms crossed and firing a furious stare that implied any reproach or rebuttal would come at a great price. The bad moods were warranted. Despite Plague's efforts, roughly fifty-seven percent of their so-called sponsors had pulled the plug on their deals. He'd predicted a massive backlash, but not this massive. This turn of events left BBR lacking precious resources. Matters would have been direr had Plague not cajoled their most important benefactors before the explosion. Alas, many of them had ended up unreachable, mitigating his success.

After he finished announcing the news, Plague waited for replies. A short silence followed his speech, but soon, Diabo's gruff voice reached his ears. "It ain't no problem. We get plenty stealing from Ostark, and if it ain't enough, there's always Nirnivia."

Then Stalker shouted, "Are you freaking in—" In his mind, Plague imagined the master of camouflage throwing his arms in the air, about to unleash a series of expletives, only to be stopped by the crimson beast's glacial glare. "We can't do that. We'd lose the rest of our support and we'd get NISDA on our ass."

"Dunno 'bout that. NISDA's already looking fer us."

"Yeah, but they're half-assing the job. They'll step it up if we give 'em a reason to!"

Plague cleared his throat. "I agree with Stalker. We shouldn't provoke NISDA any more than necessary. The thing is, we might not have a choice down the line. I can't think of any other sources except Nirnivia and Ostark, and we're pretty much exploiting every opportunity in Ostark already. There is a major problem beyond NISDA, though: stealing from Nirnivia will piss off more of our funders, and we'll be caught in a vicious cycle."

A derisive snort came from Diabo. "Both o' ya are such pussies. Those who stayed didn't care 'bout exploding an apartment building; they won't give a shit 'bout stealing some food and guns."

Stalker chuckled. "Hmm... that sounds familiar."

Gripped with a sudden sense of dread, Plague gritted his teeth. Indeed, the red monster had made a similar argument when defending the assault on the Ostarkiran spies. How wrong he had been then, and Plague doubted he'd appreciate the reminder. Against all odds, Diabo ignored the remark and remained quiet. Plague exhaled in relief. Perhaps he hadn't heard. "You have a point, Diabo, but there's still a major risk. Let's keep any looting from Nirnivia as a last resort. We can manage for a while. How about I do a detailed inventory to see what kind of shape we're in? I can make a good guess, but I'd rather eliminate any doubt. Once I know what we need, I'll contact our remaining supporters and ask them if they can increase their contributions. I'll even probe 'em to get a feel for how they'd react if we did go through with Nirnivia-based raids."

"Sounds like a pussy plan to me," Diabo groaned. "Ya guys always hiding behind numbers and science and shit. Ain't gonna win no war if you 'fraid of losers like NISDA."

Stalker sighed. "Come on, boss, we're not scared. No point making more enemies if we don't need to."

"Yeah, whatever, fine. Ain't no problem with me. Do your stuff, Plague. Just don't ya fo'get I'm in charge. If I decide we go ahead with this, ya two better listen even if you ain't done with your goddamn research."

Determined to keep the peace, Plague nodded. "Of course, boss."

"Good! Get to it, I'm outta here." A bit of static echoed, followed by silence. After a few seconds, Stalker yelled, "What the freak's wrong with him?"

"He's just Diabo being Diabo."

"No, he's an idiot being an idiot." He grunted. "Ya sure you don't wanna overthrow him?"

Plague laughed. "Let's not go down that road again. Diabo's not wrong. We might have to listen to him in the long run."

"Yeah, because of him. He put us in this spot."

"That's true, but it's too late to change it. Don't worry, Stalker, Diabo agreed with us." He shrugged. "Everything's fine."

"Sure, until he changes his mind. Then what?"

"Let me handle him. I'll figure a way to manage Diabo. We won't go through with his plan unless we have to."

Chapter 5

When Jonathan had invited his colleagues over to his house for a meeting, he'd expected most wouldn't show up. After all, he lacked any kind of authority to order them around. It seemed he had underestimated the anger inspired by the new contract, since almost everyone came. Of course, some had chosen not to, but the turnout proved so great he soon ran out of space. Undeterred, he formulated a plan. As a bunch of technicians, they possessed knowledge allowing them to set up a private live feed on the GlobalNet. Those who arrived late could return home and watch it from there. Sure, the footage would be low-quality, but they'd hear his proposition.

His idea had seemed simple when he'd thought about it in his office, but being confronted by the massive crowd left Jonathan uncertain. When he replayed his speech in his head, it sounded ridiculous. Did it have any chance of working? Would anyone here be crazy enough to listen? Would he himself be willing to follow through?

At any rate, he thanked the nonexistent gods that Madison wasn't home. Oh, she'd approve the cause, no doubt, but she'd be annoyed by having her basement filled with strangers without any warning. He'd hosted gatherings down here before, but those had consisted of at most ten people playing cards. This was a whole new level. Everyone stood shoulder to shoulder; no space remained for movement. A mass of feet covered the floor to the point where he failed to discern the carpet lying underneath. A few guests even sat on the coffee table. He'd ask them to relocate, but to where? Takeout food and canned beverages littered every area not occupied by a Gorumar. No seating options were available except the furniture not intended for this purpose.

As the gathering's size implied, a roaring mess of voices ran through the air. Complete chaos made it impossible for Jonathan to understand distinct conversations. Despite their talking, several of his colleagues stared at Jonathan, wondering what he wished to discuss. Even those who focused elsewhere often fired curious glances at him.

As Jonathan recited the words he'd prepared in his mind, a hand touched his shoulder. He turned and saw Brian next to him, smiling. Quite frankly, that his friend had managed to navigate this pandemonium impressed him. "Oh, man, Madison's gonna kill you. What a mess!"

Jonathan dismissed his concern with a shrug. "Nah, she won't. She'll understand why I did it... after a while. Besides, I'll clean up before she comes back."

A chuckle came from Brian. "That'd be smart, but I'm not sure it can be done!"

"I guess I'll find out. I'll let you know how it turned out."

"Yeah, please do." He gave an inquisitive look. "When is this thing starting, anyway?"

"When I've calmed down my jitters, but that's not going to happen, so how about right now?" Jonathan listened to the cacophony and his lips twisted in a grimace. "If I can get through." He harrumphed to no effect, then clapped his hands and yelled, "Everyone, please!"

Still, people failed to react. Undeterred, he kept repeating his plea until a couple hushed. One by one, the horde fell quiet. It took a while, but sooner than he anticipated, they stopped talking and stared at him with inquisitive eyes. After a hard swallow, Jonathan opened his mouth, only to pause. Sweat covered him, and he shivered. With a final sigh, he forced himself to proceed.

"Hello, everyone. I've asked you to come here tonight because of our new contract. As you're aware, the terms are rough and—"

Prey to a sudden rage, a female screamed, "That's the understatement of the decade!" Scanning the crowd, Jonathan recognized Giselle. The woman shook the offending papers. "This piece of shit should be illegal."

Several similar remarks erupted in unison. Jonathan attempted to regain control by lifting his hands in the air and begging them to stop. However, before long, he realized his endeavor was futile. They needed to release their pent-up anger, and so he waited. The uproar lasted for five or six minutes, but it then died down.

"Got that out of your systems? Good." He cleared his throat. "Giselle is right, but we can't depend on the law. If we sue, it'll take years, and we'll probably lose. Not because we're wrong, but because fighting NISDA in court is fighting them on their ground. Don't forget, the courts are part of the same system as the government and NISDA. They support each other."

An objection rose through the assembly. Jonathan couldn't identify the man in question, but that didn't matter. "That's not true! There are cases where judges ruled against the Council itself!"

"Sure, it happens, but it's rare, and those battles were difficult. Listen, we can go that way, and maybe we'll win, but I doubt it. We have a better chance if we fight NISDA on our terms instead."

"And what's that supposed to mean?"

"This." The crucial moment had arrived. Slight trembles assailed Jonathan, and he hoped no one noticed as he reached for his tome. He lifted the battered green volume above his head, showcasing it. "This is a history book from before the old war. It holds the answer. Long ago, back when survival wasn't as critical, companies still took advantage of their workers. Working conditions were terrible and unsafe. The hours were brutal. People accepted it for a while because they were afraid of losing their jobs. They had children that depended on them, like us. And so, they shut their mouths until the companies were so greedy they pushed too hard." There was a dramatic pause.

"The people realized they were weak on their own, so they organized groups they eventually named unions." Jonathan formed a fist and struck his other hand. "Together, they fought oppression. They refused to work and manifested in the street, which they called striking. They risked everything, and there were cases where it ended badly. More often than not, though, they won because their employers needed them, so they negotiated. The unions didn't stop, however. They stuck around and kept protecting workers' rights. Until the old war happened. After that, society was devastated. Workers' rights weren't the concern they used to be. Everyone had to struggle to survive. There was no nine-to-five anymore. There couldn't be. It took so long to rebuild that the concept was forgotten, except by history buffs. There's nothing special about those who invented unions. We can do the same and force NISDA to revise their terms."

The crowd remained mute. Incredulous glares fixated on Jonathan, perhaps debating his sanity. After a while, Giselle spoke. "But... what if NISDA fires us?"

Jonathan shook his head. "They can't. There aren't enough qualified people searching for a job to replace everyone. There's no way they'd manage for long if they got rid of us, so they won't. As a group, NISDA wants to survive, just like you or me."

Another random voice emerged from the crowd. "But how about salaries? NISDA won't pay us for nothing. We need money!"

Again, Jonathan acquiesced. "Yes, but this is for the future. A few years under this contract and we'll have lost way more money than whatever the strike will cost us."

"That's easy for you to say. We're not all married to rich lawyers!"

"Okay, I deserve that." A scowl formed on Jonathan's brow as he contemplated the argument. "You're absolutely right. I don't have to make the same sacrifice. But remember, the people who invented unions were facing the same dilemma. They chose to fight anyway, and they won! How did they survive? Mostly through donations from concerned parties. We can find the same support if we try hard enough. Depending on charity is scary, I get that. Look, I'm only giving you our best shot of fighting this bullshit. I understand if you don't want this. You can choose your low-ball pay and crappy conditions, or you can stand up for a better tomorrow." He stopped and scanned the troupe with a penetrating gaze. "It's up to you."

The crowd turned somber. As he studied them, Jonathan discovered nothing but hesitation. People chewed their nails, fidgeted their fingers, bit their lips. Terrified murmurs spread, and the few words Jonathan caught matched their speakers' demeanor. Ah well, it was a long shot.

Defeated, yet not discouraged, he almost proposed they adjourn and sleep on it when a single cry resonated:

"Strike! Strike! Strike!" A surprised Jonathan located the source: Giselle.

Soon, Brian joined the rallying chant, and the solo morphed into a duo. Then more voices rose, until the whole mob shouted in unison. Well, almost. A couple of reticent visages remained, such as Octavio, who lowered his head and rubbed the back of his neck. That was all right. They could afford a few dissidents. The question was, how many would remain once he had finished?

"Your enthusiasm warms my heart, and it helps renew my fate in Gorumars. But before you decide, I have to warn you…" He gave a resigned sigh. "There are laws written against forming unions. They're from long ago, from when Nirnivia was on the verge of death. These laws haven't been used for centuries. Some councillors might not even be aware they exist. They're antiquated and obsolete, but they are there."

"So, we could go to prison?"

Jonathan frowned. "No, that's unlikely. For the most part, the laws impose stiff fines. There's potential jail time for those in charge, but even then, it's for extreme cases." A bit of queasiness assailed him, but he recuperated in a second. "Since this is my idea, I propose I be the leader so I'm the one who'll take the biggest risk. We'll put it to a vote so you can chime in, but it seems only fair."

"That's noble of you," Giselle said, "but between no salaries and fines, how are we supposed to feed our families?"

For this, Jonathan lacked a good answer, and he went with honesty. "I don't know. We'll figure it out." Again, the mob fell silent. His teammates glanced at each other, and alarmed whispers spread. Still, the "strike" chant resounded again, weak at first but growing stronger every second.

Though the number of dissenters grew, the majority stayed committed to the cause.

"Looks like we've made our decision." Jonathan beamed. "I'm proud of you. It takes courage to stand up for your rights. I know some disagree with my views, and that's fine. We're talking about a big risk, and if you'd rather not take it, I suggest you leave now and return to work."

"That's exactly what I will do, and I urge everyone to follow my example," a high-pitched nasal voice yelled.

Dazed by the interruption, Jonathan turned toward the turncoat. He failed to locate him or her at first, but then he noted Austin Green attempting to progress through the mob. People moved out of his way as he walked. A few grimaced at him or brandished vulgar gestures, but thank God nobody attacked him. His appearance helped assure his safety. Poor Austin waddled forward, armed with a cane and hunched over. His back couldn't straighten properly since the car accident that had left him with a ravaged spine.

"Is this a one-man show, Jonathan, or will you let me speak?"

"Is it in my habit to stop people from expressing their opinions?"

Austin scratched the patch of curly red hair surrounding his bald head. "No. You're a good man, Jonathan, but you glossed over a few crucial things."

Boos and taunts emerged from the crowd. Jonathan urged everyone to calm down and let Austin express himself, but his effort failed. Some shouted that Austin was a greedy asshole scared for his money.

"No, I have savings. I'd be fine. This is about Nirnivia's well-being." Several coughs intersected his musing. "If we go on strike, we're putting NISDA in a tough spot. This may be the uneasy peace, but for all intents and purposes, Nirnivia's at war with Ostark. NISDA losing their techs for weeks, maybe months, will make them vulnerable to cyberattacks. It will be chaos, and Ostark will capitalize on it." A sarcastic grin appeared on Austin's visage. "You forgot to mention that fact during your pitch."

Jonathan chuckled. "Oh, I didn't forget. I was about to bring it up when you interrupted me."

"Hard to believe, but you're such a straight arrow, I trust you."

"Listen, you are one hundred percent correct, and it's a major concern, but it's also why we stand a chance. NISDA needs us, and if we strike, they'll have to resolve it quickly. They'll fold so fast it won't matter."

"Hmm..." A reluctant Austin lifted his neck and his pupils darted upward. "That sounds logical, I admit." Despite his compromised balance, Austin leaned forward and almost tumbled. "But it's a huge gamble, and I can't condone it. I'm sorry. I agree with you, our new contract is unfair, but this is beyond us."

Jonathan nodded. "That's understandable, and I share your apprehension. Those who feel the same should think about the moral aspect of our strike. I can't blame anyone who decides against it." After this admission, the crowd hushed and people hesitated. In the end, several left, but the majority stayed. Jonathan swallowed hard. It seemed they would do this.

***

Somehow, Jonathan succeeded. Against all odds, he sold his colleagues on the concept of forming a union. Not that it had been easy—their discussion lasted until well past midnight. It remained to be seen how long they'd stay united. The contract infuriated them, and while rage is an excellent motivator, it cools down. Still, for the moment, they planned on starting their strike. Some decided otherwise and would keep working, but the majority went along with the plan. Based on his history books, they had a term for people who refused to strike: scabs. They tended to be viewed as traitors and often became the victim of threats and violence due to their lack of solidarity. So far, no one showed signs of ill will toward the likes of Austin Green, and Jonathan hoped that wouldn't change. He'd worry about those concerns later. For now, however, he had more practical matters to take care of.

As expected, the enormous meeting had caused a terrible mess in his basement. Greasy cardboard that had once contained food and empty beverage cans littered the area. Not everyone had had the courtesy to wipe their feet before entering, so traces of mud stained the floor. A disgusting jerk had even left his mucus-filled tissues on the sofa. At least Jonathan hoped it was mucus, for the alternative seemed worse and far more disturbing. Despite the late hour, Brian joined him in the cleaning operation, and Jonathan appreciated the gesture. He'd rather have the job done before Madison arrived.

While the task at hand proved intense, things progressed well. Jonathan grabbed the last carton and dropped it in the garbage bag. During the motion, he spotted an object on the floor, and he approached. There were broken shards of a vase along with a poor flower and a puddle of water. Someone must've bumped into it. After a sigh, Jonathan picked up the sharp pieces, careful not to cut himself.

"That's not a precious gift from Madison's mother, right?" an anxious Brian asked.

Jonathan dismissed the notion with a wave. "Nah, it's just some cheap decoration. The valuable stuff is upstairs."

"Oh, good."

"Yeah, I guess."

With a frown spreading on his face, Brian walked toward Jonathan and rested his hand on his shoulder. "Are you okay? You've been silent ever since everyone left."

"I'm fine, I..." He shook his head, and his pupils darted up. "I dunno, I..." Jonathan grimaced. "I'm scared I might regret what I've done tonight."

"What?" A laugh escaped Brian's lips. "Austin got to you?"

"No, I'm fine with the strike. It's the union that bothers me."

"Uh?" Puzzled, Brian scratched his head. "Why?"

"It's like..." Jonathan paused and reached for a microfiber cloth in his pocket. "How can I explain?" Then he removed his glasses and scrubbed them. "Which provides better services, the government or a company?"

Confused, Brian shrugged. "I don't know, they both suck if you ask me."

Impressed, Jonathan pointed at his friend and made an approving clicking sound with his tongue. "Great answer! People debate this a lot, and they take their position to heart, but the truth is, both sides are terrible. Sure, one can be superior in various situations, but that doesn't make it good. It just means it's less bad. They suck in different ways, but they still both suck, and both end up screwing us over, though the details vary." He paused and rubbed his chin. "That's because, despite their differences, at their core, the government and business are the same thing: a group of people, and those are trouble." He scowled. "Don't get me wrong, Gorumars can accomplish amazing feats by banding together. But that goes in both directions and can result in a far bigger mess than anyone can produce alone. Our union is also a group of people, so it might get messy real fast."

Annoyed, Brian tilted his head and lifted his nose. "Yeah, okay, I guess you're right technically, but if everyone fretted about that, nothing would ever be accomplished."

"And that's why I got this ball rolling. But I can't help but worry about it."

"Hey, you're the history buff. Did anything happen in the past that shows unions can be a bad idea?"

"Hmm... good point." As he pondered for a second, Jonathan stroked his chin. "Kind of... there are cases where unions were blamed for bankrupting companies by being greedy." He fondled his eye. "That's possible, but between you and me, I suspect that was propaganda from business owners. I can't say it never happened—freak, it probably did at least once—but I doubt it was frequent. No, the biggest concern for me is stories where the unions acted in their own interest even if it harmed the employees they swore to protect. I can believe that." Jonathan cleared his throat. "With a group, no matter its goal, eventually that goal tends to shift to ensuring the group's survival and enriching those in charge. Even charities are involved in scandals. Think of how often they're accused of using the money to line their pockets."

"Look, Jonathan, you're thinking too much." Brian snickered. "I can't imagine our scrappy union becoming powerful enough to cause major problems."

"I agree, but it's not just about us. If we succeed, then we'll resurrect the concept of unions. Others will copy us. We're making history, and that's scary. I feel I wouldn't be taking my responsibilities seriously if I didn't consider the implications of my actions."

With a laugh, Brian patted the green volume Jonathan had laid on a nearby coffee table. "Hey, at least this whole ordeal might put you in those books you love so much."

"Yep! For better or worse..."

Chapter 6

Osmoro 3, 2134, on the Nirnivian calendar

The raid went down in a familiar manner. Allison beset the Ostarkiran soldiers with terrible visions, thus incapacitating them. After that, the BBR troops finished them off with ease. Despite Wrathchild's absence during this particular attack, the conflict ended in minutes. Driving your enemies mad by assailing them with nightmares proved an effective strategy, though Diabo had never doubted it would be.

Covered in his victims' blood, Diabo strode with pride toward the military transport truck. He wondered what treasures the vehicle contained. They found all kinds of nice things in these, from high-tech weapons to research materials. Some of his men were already inspecting the cargo. He approached and nodded to one who stood close by.

"Hey, so anything interesting in this baby?"

The goon tilted his flat hand from left to right gesturing his indifference. "Seems like the usual, boss."

Diabo shrugged. "Good enough. Gonna check it out myself." On that note, he took another step... and a loud boom resounded as a ball of fire engulfed him. The incredible force from the explosion propelled his impressive mass several meters backward. After his short flight, Diabo collapsed on the soil with a crash. Flames scorched his skin as he screamed in agony. He had never endured such torture, not even when Doctor Death had experimented on him.

The ludicrously large syringes plunged into his body, electroshock treatments, and cruel vivisections—none approached the same level. With a gasp, he attempted rolling to extinguish the blaze, but a strident pain stopped him. Broken bones, or so he assumed. A glimpse at his leg where a bone stuck out of his flesh confirmed his suspicion as his surviving troops rushed toward him.

***

Was worried. Ran too fast. Almost hit people. Couldn't believe was injured. Never needed medical care before.
—Thoughts of Wrathchild, Hocmar 28, 2134, on the Nirnivian calendar

Her mad race left her out of breath, but at last Melissa reached what they called their infirmary. The place stood in such disarray and lacked resources to the point that it hardly deserved the name. Still, given their living conditions, it was the best they'd managed to achieve.

Once she arrived, Wrathchild looked around and eventually found him. Diabo lay on a makeshift bed—well, what remained of him, anyway. Hideous scars covered his face. The explosion had reduced his left eye to a puddle of goo and broken his single yellow horn. A cyan blanket concealed the rest of his body, but Wrathchild noticed his visible arm lacked a hand.

Various medical equipment surrounded Diabo. In particular, she discerned a IV tube piped a clear liquid into her boss's veins and a beeping ECG monitor. The latter displayed a jagged line, indicating at least some sort of heartbeat, though, to her untrained eye, it appeared erratic. Wrathchild spotted the doctor dressed in red-stained white scrubs and approached her.

Wrathchild bobbed her head toward Diabo. "How is he?" she asked, almost yelling out of nervousness.

Surprised, the medic turned and stared wide-eyed at Melissa. It took a second before she recovered. "I've never seen him in such bad shape. No one else would've survived that explosion. Even for him, it's a miracle he's alive!" The woman noted Wrathchild's gaping mouth and perspiration-soaked brow, so she added, "It's okay, he'll be fine. Remember who we're talking about here. His body isn't only ultra-strong, it heals rapidly."

"But..." A hard swallow came from Melissa as she pointed at the missing limb. "Lost hand, eye... ain't gonna be happy."

"I won't bet on it, but based on previous experience, they'll likely just grow back."

There was a gasp as Wrathchild brought her fingers to her lips. "Can do that?"

The physician acquiesced. "He lost a thumb once and it grew back two days later." She patted Wrathchild's shoulder in a comforting manner. "Our boss is far from gone, but it will take a few weeks before he's one hundred percent."

"Can talk?"

"I'm sorry"—she shook her head—"but right now, he's in an artificially induced coma. He'd be in unbearable pain otherwise. I'll let you know as soon as he can speak with you."

"Thanks." Wrathchild rubbed her chin as she contemplated the situation. "Can't lead. Stalker's second-in-command. His chance to shine." In her mind, Wrathchild added that, in truth, this meant Plague would be the leader. Stalker would serve as a decoy to hide the fact that BBR's fate depended on a sick blind man with an unreliable life expectancy. Most lacked this knowledge, which was why she kept this detail silent.

Felt many things for Diabo. Fear; knew what capable of. Hate; 'cause what made me. Pity; was devoid of joy; only lived for revenge. More than all, love. Worried might not survive. Was foolish. Little bomb wouldn't kill him. Still, couldn't help it.

—Thoughts of Wrathchild, Hocmar 28, 2134, on the Nirnivian calendar

Chapter 7

What served as Rose's office used to be rather luxurious, but that had been long before she'd arrived in Valardir. Years of service had ravaged the once-lavish décor. Scratches covered her desk and other furniture, such as the small table upon which a vase rested. A resistant coffee stain sullied the very chair she sat on, though that did little to diminish the comfort. As for the carpet, tears and wear revealed its age. Why, if you stuck your face close enough, for some reason, a lingering unidentifiable odor would reach your nostrils.

On the opposite side of her bureau, Constance Prim laid a folder on the wooden surface. She proceeded to open it and spread the relevant contents so they'd be in plain view. Despite her long blond hair and obvious feminine shape, she reminded Rose of her father. The fact that they both were Zarg contributed to this, but it had more to do with her body language. For instance, the moment Constance finished positioning her documents, she joined her fingers in a pyramid. The pose implied power, strength, and self-confidence. Traits well suited to leaders.

In a corner, Brucie stood fully erect and immobile. His role as bodyguard required a strange mix of elusiveness and presence. On one hand, you wanted people to sense the menace you'd represent if they dared cause trouble. On the other, it was best not to take their focus away from their current tasks. Brucie played the part to perfection, his vigorous physique showcasing his capabilities, yet blending in with the office. Looking at him now, Rose almost forgot he was the same man who made juvenile jokes during her daily life. To Constance, no doubt, he appeared serious and joyless, and Rose stifled a giggle at that thought.

"I must admit, I'm not sure how to address you. Would you prefer Councillor or Your Holiness?" Constance asked, a slight blush coloring her cheeks.

"Let's keep religion out of this: you're speaking with the politician today. Please call me Councillor or Ms. Ricdeau, whichever makes you more comfortable."

"Right, Councillor it is, then." She forced a smile. "I've been meeting with councillors a lot lately, so the term is familiar. I must say, reaching you was a challenge." Cross-legged, Constance started a slight kicking motion with her left foot while she rearranged her papers. "I work for NISDA, but I only had access to level one. The procedures for getting to level five are daunting."

The overall demeanor Constance adopted suggested to Rose that she'd rather forsake this small talk and dive straight into the issue. In all honesty, that would've suited her fine. What was the point of chitchat if it was so contrived? Regardless, she attempted a sincere laugh and obtained a similar degree of success.

"Well, you don't get the most secure complex in Nirnivia by letting people walk around as they please."

"Quite true!" Constance agreed with a nod. "NISDA is Nirnivia's only defense against Ostark and BBR, so Valardir's security is paramount to its survival." Rose leaned forward in anticipation, though she figured what came next. "Councillor, as you're aware, NISDA faces several challenges. The economy, in general, is poor and our budget has been slashed repeatedly."

"Actually, the Council has increased it every year since the war started."

"Yes, but I'm talking about before that. Our current budget is a fraction of what it was ten years ago, and the uneasy peace is draining our resources. It's simply not enough. The recent Doctor Death breach didn't help either." She harrumphed. "When drafting the technical support teams' contract, we had no choice but to decrease their salaries and make other adjustments." Constance scratched behind her ear. "I won't lie. The cuts are extreme. We expected a backlash, and it's justified, but we're acting out of desperation. Believe me, those in charge are not happy about this, least of all your father. The problem is, the techs are taking this worse than we hoped." Constance gave an incredulous exhale as she shook her head in dismay. "They've informed us that they created a union!" She put emphasis on the last word as if it were the vilest scheme ever conceived.

By the delivery, Rose imagined that the revelation had been intended to shock her, but she didn't react. Constance had contacted some of her colleagues earlier and she'd heard the news from them. If her lack of surprise disappointed Constance, she decided to hide it.

In a calm tone, Rose said, "Yes, I'm aware. I've used the opportunity to brush up on unions. They sound like a way for oppressed people to fight back and better their conditions. Seems like an appropriate response based on what you told me about how NISDA is imposing on the techs."

"But..." Constance leaned forward, wide-eyed. "Your Holiness—" The woman cringed at her mistake as her arm began a short upward motion. Rose expected she would've face-palmed had she failed to resist the temptation. "I mean, Councillor Ricdeau, unions are against the law! Beyond that, they threatened to go on strike. There are no questions about it, they are violating the Deboros Act."

Rose wrinkled her forehead. "The Deboros Act is a relic from a time when promoting individual rights over society might've caused our extinction." The frown intensified. "The fact that it hasn't been repealed by now is a travesty. I can't condone using that law, and should the Council consider the possibility, I'll vote against it."

"I understand your point of view, Councillor, but those times you are talking about aren't gone. For all intents and purpose, the uneasy peace is a sham. We're at war, and this strike will weaken NISDA, our only line of defense against Ostark. Do you really think Doctor Death won't exploit this opportunity?" The moment Constance uttered the cyborg's name, Rose grew paler and started shivering. Embarrassed, Constance scratched her head. "I apologize. But it's the truth. People could die over this."

"I can't deny you are right. This ordeal causes major trouble."

A relieved Constance acquiesced. "And it's not just NISDA. Others might follow the techs' lead and throw our whole political system into disarray. It's in the Council's— nay, Nirnivia's best interest to resolve this quickly."

"Ms. Prim, I can't speak for the other councillors, but I expect most will be on your side due to the situation. As for myself, well, I wish to solve the issue ASAP, but I don't have all the facts yet, so I can't guarantee where I'll stand should the Council have a major vote about this." She sighed. "Even if I end up favorable to your views, there are lines I won't cross. These aren't bad people. They're hard workers taking care of their families."

"No one at NISDA would say otherwise." Constance clenched her fist. "But our backs are against the wall. We gave our techs the best offer possible under the circumstances. Their demands are reasonable, but the sad reality is that complying would destroy NISDA."

Skeptical, Rose crossed her arms. "Prove it to me and I'll certainly be willing to defend NISDA's action."

"With pleasure, Councillor." Constance adjusted her glasses. "First, look at this chart." In a swift movement, she reached for a paper displaying a blue curve on a graph and tapped her pen on the highest peak. "This shows NISDA's expenses for the last few weeks. Notice the sharp increase here. That's when D—when Ostark contacted the human."

Rose's jaw tightened. "He has a name: James Hunter."

After a nervous chuckle, Constance corrected her mistake. "Mr. Hunter, then. At any rate, this graphic makes it plain to see the incident strained NISDA's budget. We need to recoup the loss."

"The data is accurate and convincing, but there's a problem." With a groan, Rose opened a drawer and pulled out her own sheet. "I prepared myself for this meeting and glanced over NISDA's financial report."

"Then you know I'm not lying."

"I never accused you of doing so, but you are using incomplete data in an effort to hide an embarrassing detail." Constance's lips parted to counter, but Rose stopped her by lifting her finger. "I have the same chart here, but it goes back months further. Look at the curve. There's this massive spike weeks and weeks before the hack, and it's much steeper than the one you showed me. What's the cause? The security improvements NISDA demanded. Without these, the breach would be a far less serious matter in terms of finance." Rose glared. "I don't appreciate being manipulated, Ms. Prim..."

"Oh, um... uh, that's um..." She tugged at her collar. "I didn't mean to deceive you or anything suspicious." Sweat covered Constance's brow. "I was trying to keep the discussion focused on pertinent matters."

"Please spare me the half-baked excuse. Such a massive cost is pertinent to a discussion about the budget."

"Yes. Yes, it is." Constance swallowed hard. "I'm sorry. There's immense pressure on me right now by my superiors. I don't enjoy using those kinds of tricks, I swear. Much like NISDA, I'm desperate. But it doesn't change the fact that NISDA is on the verge of bankruptcy and the techs are, in part, responsible. They are the experts. They should have warned us the security measures were financially unsound."

Another moan came from Rose as she fished out a different document. "Here's a report written by Jonathan Rivers, the leader of this new union if I remember correctly. Mr. Rivers is thorough. It describes in painful detail why the improvements were a bad idea, and NISDA ignored him." She leaned forward. "Ms. Prim, I understand NISDA is in a tough spot, and I want to ensure its survival. Our country's future depends on it. The problem is, how is it fair that those who pay for this mistake are the ones who tried so hard to prevent it?"

"If you care so much about punishing those responsible, you should look at your father." Terrified by the sentence that slipped out of her mouth, Constance covered her lips. "Oh... oh my God... I'm so sorry."

"You have no reason to be. Dad is part of the problem, and I will talk to him about it to find a better solution." Rose offered a comforting smile. "Don't worry, I won't mention what you said. Still, I'd like you to answer. How is it fair?"

Defeated, Constance crumpled on her seat. "It's not... but it's the only way."

"Please forgive me for not taking your word for it." Rose stroked her eye. "I'll study the question myself and reach my own conclusion. If you're right, I'll do everything in my power to persuade the techs to come back to work under the present contract."

"That's... fair, Councillor. Speaking of which, should you decide the current terms are appropriate, well..." She scowled. "I... I don't want to do this. I've been ordered to."

"Go ahead. I wouldn't want your supervisor to be disappointed in your performance."

Two quick nods came from Constance, and then she gulped. "Councillor, you won't like this, but please keep an open mind. My superiors feel that, due to your unique role as a prophet, you might be in a good position for... persuasion."

Indeed, Rose disliked where the conversation headed, but she concealed her disgust. Constance lacked sincerity when she expressed concern for the staff. Clearly the woman put NISDA's interests over them. However, her reluctant body language indicated she disapproved of this particular idea.

"I believe I understand your meaning. As the Melkar, people do listen to me. Using my religious authority to manipulate the other councillors would be unethical. Besides, my colleagues are professional, so my status won't influence their judgment as it might an average citizen's." Rose wondered if maybe her words appeared condescending toward the general population. Too late to rephrase it. She could only hope it didn't sound as bad as she imagined.

Taken aback, Constance raised both her palms before her. "No, no, I didn't mean the councillors, but rather the techs. Your Holiness—I believe this title is appropriate, since I am now addressing the Melkar—if you denounced the strike in a sermon, they would likely stop."

Rose closed her eyes and hunched her head. She stayed like that for a moment as a flow of emotion overwhelmed her. From rage to sadness, she was struggling to stay calm. A minute passed and then she opened her mouth, though not her eyes.

"You might disagree, Ms. Prim, but what you are asking is despicable. As the Melkar, I am a prophet and a guide. I suggest spiritual paths and help understand religious concepts. It's not my place to order people around, especially not for matters unrelated to faith."

"Your Holiness, I realize this is unconventional, but no one is talking about ordering them. You suggest paths—well, you could suggest that stopping the strike would be best for everyone." Constance faltered for a second and then proceeded. "You are the Voice of God, you know more about these matters than I ever will, but I feel you are wrong. To me, it seems this is connected to religion. If people die because of their actions, won't our employees edge closer to nothingness? You might save their souls by convincing them to end this."

Rose winced. "It's not that simple. Many variables guide the gods' verdict. Even the Melkar can't predict toward which destination a decision will lead, as intentions matter and I can't know their intents."

"Oh... still, on occasion, controversial methods are necessary for the greater good. Life is painted in shades of gray, and sacrifices can be inevitable."

"The greater good." There was a pain-filled laughter. "Numerous tragedies happened in the name of the greater good. I'd rather not cause one more." Rose rubbed her forehead as if prey to a migraine. "This is a complex matter. I will take your suggestion into consideration." In truth, she had no intention of doing so, but she wished to conclude this meeting.

"Thank you for your time." Constance got to her feet and shook Rose's hand. The deed done, she then spun around and headed for the door. Rose prepared herself to exhale in relief the moment she exited the office. The preparation proved futile as Constance stopped midway and turned. "Your Holiness... if I may, I have a personal request. As a NISDA operator, I neglected my spiritual obligations. I have sinned; I've wandered toward nothingness. Will you please confess me?"

Stunned by the change of subject, Rose blinked twice. The woman was requesting a rite in which people implored the gods' mercy so they would forgive their transgressions. While not a magic eraser that removed your evil deeds, most priests believed it could bring a sincere repentant toward the correct path. Those who performed that ceremony were known as confessors, and Rose wasn't among their rank. Despite this, her followers often begged her for confessions.

Unconvinced, Rose studied Constance's demeanor. Whether a genuine request or an attempt to befriend her by showing an interest in religion, Constance displayed no signs of lying. Frankly, Rose didn't like the representative very much. And yet, honest or not, it didn't matter—Constance had a right to the sacrament.

Some alleged that a confession by the Melkar didn't count; some assumed it increased the ritual's significance. Rose had no idea which was accurate. In fact, many debated whether the rite possessed any value to begin with. For this reason, she always provided a fair warning.

"I'm not a confessor. I will confess you if you wish, but I would advise you also seek a real confessor afterward."

"I understand. Please do." The response failed to surprise Rose. Everyone demanded the service despite her lack of credentials. It wasn't one of her normal duties, but people tended to view the Melkar as more than she was. And since she wasn't even a prophet, they put far too much faith in her.

Rose rested her hand on Constance's brow and recited a special prayer. She never grew comfortable in her role and doubted that'd ever change, but at least she had memorized every line by now.

Chapter 8

I was supposed to have lunch with Rose, but at twenty minutes past noon, she still hadn't showed up. I guess her meeting lasted longer than expected. The thing is, I got bored, so I figured I'd go to her office. When I arrived there, a man leaned against the wall, his arms crossed. I had no idea who he was, but I had a bad feeling.

—Thoughts of James Hunter, Hocmar 28, 2134, on the Nirnivian calendar

Five minutes had passed since James had arrived. From his corner, he stared at the stranger once in a while, averting his gaze between each glance so he wouldn't be noticed. Something about him seemed off. Between the long black hair arranged in a ponytail and the trench coat he wore, he gave off a non-military vibe that contrasted with Valardir's atmosphere. Not that James fit the décor himself.

Always the shy one, James decided he'd keep his distance and made himself small. Despite his low profile and silence, however, the man eventually turned toward him, smiled, and said, "Hey! You must be James Hunter."

"Um..." After a gulp, James scratched the back of his head. "Yeah... how do you know my name?"

The man shrugged as he pointed at James. "Simple deduction: who else would be waiting for Her 'Holiness' dressed like that?" Something about the emphasis on the word *Holiness* suggested sarcasm, but James couldn't be certain. At any rate, the man approached at a brisk pace and, once in range, presented his hand. "I'm Jonathan Rivers, the jackass who took away your phone."

"Oh"—as requested, James grasped his palm and shook it—"that's fine, I wasn't using it much anyway."

"Wow, I've met visitors before, but you're my first human." He chuckled. "It's crazy, if I hadn't recognized you, I wouldn't have realized you're not a Goru—"

The door slid open, interrupting his sentence. Rose stepped out, wearing her familiar white dress. Behind her trailed Brucie, who greeted James with a wink. Of more interest, an unknown blond woman in a deep blue business suit accompanied the prophet. She possessed a professional aura similar to Kristina Dupree's, though somehow, James sensed she lacked the assistant's extreme diligence. When she spotted Jonathan, the mysterious woman's mouth contorted in a disgusted grimace.

"Well, well, well, if it isn't Mr. Jonathan Rivers."

"Constance Prim! I'd say it's a pleasure, but I'm honest by nature."

Constance groaned out loud. "I thought you and your colleagues stopped working. Why are you here?"

"Oh, there are rumors you've been bribing councillors left and right and that her 'Holiness' was next, so I came to check if there was any truth to it." He shrugged. "I'm allowed. They haven't revoked my clearance. I assume it's coming, though." Then he faced Rose and proceeded in a mock whisper. "Did you take it? I studied sacred texts in my days and, religiously speaking, it's frowned upon."

Rose adopted a scowl and opened her mouth, but before she answered, a blushing Constance stepped toward Jonathan. "I have been meeting with councillors to discuss the situation you've brought on us. There are no bribes involved. That a traitor dares to make such an accusation is ludi—"

As Constance spoke, Rose peeked at Brucie and bobbed her head in the direction of the bickering duo. As instructed, the bodyguard plunged between the two and separated them. Potential blows averted, the alleged Melkar said, "That's enough. Mr. Rivers, Constance is telling the truth, and I'm appalled by your behavior. Ms. Prim, he's not a traitor. None of the techs are. I won't tolerate slander from either of you."

Both apologized for their conduct. Jonathan in particular lowered his head in what appeared to be genuine guilt and regret. Soon after, Constance left, though she did warn Rose not to listen to a word Jonathan said. Once she disappeared, Rose exhaled and prepared her widest smile. "I'm actually glad to see you. I've been trying to contact you so we can discuss the strike."

Surprised, Jonathan blinked twice and tapped his sternum with his index finger. "Meet with me? Why?"

"Isn't it obvious? Like it or not, I'll play a part in resolving this issue, and I wish to hear from both sides so that I have a fair perspective."

"Oh, I didn't expect that." Jonathan gave an impressed nod. "None of the other councillors contacted me. Thank you. We can meet if you want, but you're a busy woman and I'd rather not waste your time." He sighed. "It's very simple. For years, the other techs and I have slaved away for NISDA. The hours are terrible, the pay below average and the benefits almost nonexistent, but we did it because, despite what Constance Prim thinks, we love Nirnivia and take our duties seriously. As thanks, NISDA is cutting our salaries by forty percent, making the hours worse without compensation, and removing what little benefits we had."

He shook his head. "Listen, I get it—times are tough, budgets are tight—but enough is enough. At this point, NISDA is straight out taking advantage of us. I can give you a copy of our contract as proof."

"I already have one, and I agree. It's a bad offer, and that's putting it mildly." The prophet bit her lip. "On the other hand, NISDA is in dire financial trouble and I doubt the Council can help. Our own budget is... stretched." There was a slight pause. "NISDA can't crumble, Mr. Rivers, especially not with the uneasy peace. I hope you realize that."

Jonathan acquiesced. "Trust me, I don't want NISDA to fail. Look, it's true, NISDA isn't swimming in money, but there are ways to reduce expenses without cutting our salaries by almost half!" He formed a fist. "How about scaling back the security improvements? They'd save a bundle right there—not enough, but it's an easy step. High Command isn't getting any pay cuts and they are in part responsible for this mess. Hey, I understand why they're paid more than me. I'm fine with that, but you could slash their salaries by three-quarters and they'd still be a whole lot richer than us techs." He punched his open palm. "We're willing to make some sacrifices for NISDA's sake, but everyone has to pitch in."

As if prey to a headache, Rose rubbed her brow. "You have a point, but so does Constance: your strike is putting Nirnivia at risk. Please, reconsider. I'm not suggesting you give up, but there are other solutions. How about we draft an interim contract and negotiate from there? No need to interrupt work, and you'd keep getting your paychecks. Of course, I can't make this decision alone, but I'm confident I can convince the Council and NISDA to cooperate."

Reluctant, Jonathan winced. "Tempting, and I appreciate the offer"—he shook his head—"but I can't recommend it to my colleagues. They put me in charge of this union and gave me their trust. Frankly, I don't believe this would be in their best interest. NISDA would write in a clause that would punish any future strikes with drastic measures to cover their rear and we'd be surrendering our leverage. If it was only me, I'd be willing to risk it, but I can't in good conscience tell everyone else to take such a foolish gamble."

"And if innocent people get hurt because of your actions? You're okay with that?"

"No, but I'm not okay with being exploited either. It's easy to say the needs of society trump the needs of individuals. Freak, maybe they do in many cases—I don't know." He grunted. "The thing is, those individuals make up society, and if you keep stabbing them in the back for the"—he added finger quotes—"good of the whole, sooner or later every upstanding citizen has a knife stuck into their spines."

After a short silence, Jonathan exhaled and bent his head down. "I have a son, and he might suffer because of my choice. That terrifies me, but I'm more scared of having him grow up in a world where governments and corporations abuse him and he isn't allowed to defend himself. That's a big reason why I'm resurrecting unions."

"For the record, I'm not against the return of unions." Rose winced. "Though I am concerned about what will happen next."

Jonathan chuckled. "You are? Don't be, I can tell you what will happen." Shocked, Rose recoiled a touch, tilted her head and fired a questioning gaze. "No, no, I'm not a prophet. I leave that stuff to you. But it doesn't take a genius to figure it out. You'll act sympathetic, maybe even try to help us out. At the same time, you'll express worry about Nirnivia's safety. Then, if it's not resolved fast enough for your taste, you'll play the Melkar card. You'll address us in a sermon and warn us we're taking a step toward nothingness because we're putting Nirnivia in danger or some bullcrap. And it'll work because people blindly follow the so-called Voice of God. The strike will be crushed and you'll still look good in the eyes of the public. You'll have a clean conscience despite manipulating us because, hey, you supported us. You're a defender of the common folk! We pushed things too far—that wasn't your fault. But deep down, you'll know that it's all for appearance. You never cared about us, it's only politics."

That was new for me. He didn't trust Rose at all. Most revered her. The only exception had been Ron Tigh. Jonathan was a reasonable man who believed what he said. And Tigh— um, he was just an asshole to everybody. The "dear old" Koporal hadn't been polite, but he hadn't accused her of abusing her power either. To be frank, I didn't understand why Jonathan made that speech. To me, it seemed he alienated a potential ally he desperately needed. Yet I admired his courage. I wouldn't have the nerve to do something that reckless.

—Thoughts of James Hunter, Hocmar 28, 2134, on the Nirnivian calendar

"What?" Rose gasped. "No, I'd never... I'd never use my position like that. It'd be morally bankrupt. Abusing religious beliefs to bend my followers to my will when I'm supposed to guide them selflessly would be..." She wrinkled her nose. "I can't think of a word vile enough."

The tech shrugged. "And yet you do it every day."

Triggered by Jonathan's antagonism, Brucie's muscles tightened. Though the bodyguard remained otherwise calm, a sickness overcame James's stomach and he twitched in apprehension. As for Rose, her lips parted, but then she lowered her gaze and rubbed her chin.

"In a sense, I suppose, but not on purpose and certainly not for selfish gains. Someone with my reputation will influence others whether she intends to or not. And I swear I do care. Yes, I'm conflicted, like everyone involved, including you. That said, there's no question NISDA is giving you a raw deal, and I'll do my best to find a compromise that satisfies both parties. I can't promise success, but if I fail, it won't be for lack of trying."

"Really? Hmm... that'd only be fair. You put us in this tough spot, after all."

Taken aback, Rose's eyes opened wide. "What?"

Having had enough, Brucie approached Jonathan and towered above the skeletal tech. Jonathan stood his ground, though he sheltered his body with his arms. James doubted that would protect him much. The bodyguard pointed a menacing finger toward his target's sternum. "That's enough, dude. Ain't taking your crap no more. She's a great gal, the holy Melkar, and she busts her ass every freaking day fo' people like you. And you go and make up some bullshit accusation? Ya damn better apologize or I'll beat the shit outta ya!"

That went south quick. Worried, I fired Rose a glance, and she nodded as a response. Jonathan pissed me off too, but he didn't deserve a beating. Besides, I'm pretty sure Brucie would have gotten in trouble if he'd executed his threat.

—Thoughts of James Hunter, Hocmar 28, 2134, on the Nirnivian calendar

"Stop it, Brucie!" The alleged prophet dashed forward and jumped between the two men as a buffer. Brucie gritted his teeth. For a moment, James feared he'd shove Rose aside, claiming she put herself at risk. "Mr. Rivers is allowed to voice his opinion if he wishes, and as a public figure, I'll take his criticisms into consideration." She exhaled. "Besides, you're here to protect me from physical threats, and he poses no danger."

The bodyguard scowled, then crossed his arms. "Ain't so sure 'bout that. The guy hates your guts, so ya never know."

Jonathan harrumphed and waggled an explaining finger. "Hate is a strong word. I disagree with some of her political views and that's it. I have no intention of harming anyone."

"Yeah?" Brucie sneered. "Well, I don't trust ya. Don't fo'get I'm watching. One wrong move and—" With his index finger, he mimicked slicing his own throat.

Rose caught his wrist during the motion and snatched it away. "Enough, Brucie, you got your message across. Please forgive him, Mr. Rivers. He's very protective of me, which is desired from a bodyguard, but sometimes he gets overzealous." A pouting Brucie retreated at the rebuff, and Rose focused on Jonathan. "If you don't mind, I'd like to hear how you concluded this mess is my fault."

"Now, you're not the only one responsible, but you played a big part. Remember when you were elected to the Council?" A revolted quiver came from Jonathan. "Which goes against the Felicia Act, by the way. The first things you did were to push for social reform and convince the Council to enact a bunch of expensive welfare programs."

"What's wrong with that? We helped countless poor families. There's a good chance you enjoyed those benefits as well."

"Nothing's wrong with it, but the keyword is *expensive.* You were so desperate to look like a savior that you gave everything for nothing. Suddenly, Nirnivia had to pay for programs it couldn't afford and you wouldn't raise the taxes—that'd be bad for your reputation."

In denial, Rose shook her head several times in succession. "No, it wasn't about my image. I didn't want to impose an extra financial burden on the population."

"Whatever the reason, your brilliant solution was to cut NISDA's funding, and not just by a little." Jonathan mimicked a slicing knife with his hand. "You gutted them. The Council played along because, hey, their prophet said it was okay and the people who elected her loved it. Even the Commander didn't complain since you're his precious daughter." After a brief pause, Jonathan continued at a lower volume and in a somber tone. "Then, a few years later, the war started. NISDA was a mess, and far behind the Ostarkiran army. To be fair, I admit they would've been outclassed no matter what, but you made it so much worse. The Council reversed course then, but it was too late. NISDA never recovered."

"I..." Rose rested her hands on her hips, leaning forward—no doubt preparing a rebuttal, only to give up and slump. "That's true, I made a terrible mistake, but I had no reason to think Ostark would attack." She whimpered. "How could I know?"

"You couldn't, but you should've realized there was a possibility it would happen. It doesn't take a genius to figure out there might someday be tension with the country filled with people we were once at war with. Ms. Ricdeau, I believe your heart was in the right place back then, but you also have to use your head. Let me give you an example. One of your most expensive programs was the universal health care. I admit, it was a godsend for me when my son was sick, but it cost so much. Based on our intel, Doctor Death implemented a similar program in Ostark once he took power. The difference is, he studied the possibilities, looked at his assets and created a system that Ostark could afford and that gave the citizens the most bang for their buck. You just gave us the whole kitchen sink, consequences be damned."

Rose sobbed and a few tears rolled down her cheeks. Sudden anger grasped James as he witnessed his friend so dejected. A small part of him hoped Brucie would shut Jonathan up. Not cause physical harm, but frighten him like he had before. However, the bodyguard had learned his lesson and forced himself to stay quiet. Still, the bulging vein in his forehead confirmed that his restraint tested his patience.

"Are you crying?" Jonathan sighed and adopted a compassionate tone. "Don't. It's in the past and everyone makes mistakes. I'm not asking you to sit in a corner and blame yourself—that's useless. What I'm hoping is that you'll do your best to fix it. Please, don't use your religious authority to screw us over. That's all I have to say."

"Uh, hey, wait up!" On that note, James started walking toward Jonathan. The tech stopped as demanded and turned. "Um, you're wrong about her. She's a nice person, and she's trying to help you."

Jonathan smiled. "I hope so, buddy." And then he left.

In an obvious rage, Brucie clenched his fist. "What a total asshat!"

Rose sniffed and dried her eyes. "Don't be so harsh. He had some good arguments. For instance, I never should've joined the Council. That's one of my biggest regrets."

Yes, Jonathan mentioned a Council and how Rose was part of it. I had no idea what that was about, but it seemed like she had political power. That worried me a little because of Doctor Death's warning. There might be more truth there than I thought.

—Thoughts of James Hunter, Hocmar 28, 2134, on the Nirnivian calendar

"Um..." James began, but then hushed.

"Oh right, you don't know about the Council."

"That's fine, it's not important."

"No, it is. I'll explain during lunch."

Chapter 9

As promised, Rose explained about the Council during lunch. She wasn't thrilled about it, though, to the point where she barely ate. Sure, she bought food, but she mostly played with it in an anxious manner. No question she'd rather avoid this conversation, and I wondered why. Did the memories bring her pain like those of her marriage, or was there a more sinister reason? I couldn't help but remember how Doctor Death had warned me that she had dark secrets. Had he told me the truth? Was her role in the Council one of them? I chased those thoughts away, ashamed of considering this. Is the human mind so feeble and untrusting that it takes so little to doubt a friend?

—Thoughts of James Hunter, Hocmar 28, 2134, on the Nirnivian calendar

"About the Council..." As she uttered those words, Rose ran her fork through her mishusq puree, leaving an orange trail through her meal. "Jonathan didn't lie. I'm a member. It's surprising you didn't hear before."

"Um, wait... you're going too fast." James scratched his ear. "What's the Council supposed to be?"

"It's the Council of Hurdan, dude," the nonchalant bodyguard said, hands linked behind his head. Though his demeanor suggested a self-evident statement, James's confusion increased. "Those guys are in freaking charge o' the country, ya know."

Rose nodded. "That's the short explanation. Nirnivia is divided into twelve regions. Every five years, they each elect a representative who'll join the Council, Nirnivia's highest political body. The councillors vote on laws and make important decisions that shape our future. Sorry, Hunter, I should have told you. I didn't mean to hide it. The thing is, you panicked when you learned about me being the Melkar. I figured maybe I should wait before revealing my involvement as I didn't want you to be uncomfortable again. Then, over time, I grew scared you might be angry that I hid this detail from you, so I didn't dare mention it."

"Um, that's fine. Don't worry."

After what had happened earlier, I understood why she'd be hesitant to reveal she was a politician too. Yet I wondered if there was more to it. Besides, something about a prophet who's also part of the government didn't feel appropriate, and wouldn't the two conflict with each other? Back home, mixing religion and politics tended to cause trouble.

—Thoughts of James Hunter, Hocmar 28, 2134, on the Nirnivian calendar

"The truth is"—her voice trembled—"Jonathan was right. I shouldn't be on the Council. What he forgot to mention is that I never intended to participate in the election."

***

It all began back when Rose turned twenty-one. During a routine evening, she watched TV in her house. Perhaps displaying a touch of harmless narcissism, the program she chose starred herself. On the screen, she performed an interview concerning the current election. Since people preferred their councillors to be experienced, the youngest member ever was thirty-six, and that proved an anomaly. Still, experts predicted the record might soon be shattered given Rose had reached the age where she could pose her candidacy.

"Your Holiness"—the reporter offered a respectful nod—"several Nirnivians claim you should be a candidate."

"That's an understatement." The Rose on the display giggled. "It seems I can't go anywhere without someone making that suggestion." The present Rose smiled as she heard her own statement. Today, she'd received fifty-two letters debating, pleading, and sometimes begging her to run. She remembered earlier after a sermon while she talked with disciples, a young girl had approached. The poor child muttered that her mommy said if the Melkar was part of the Council, Nirnivia would prosper. Too innocent to understand the meaning, she asked for Rose's participation to ensure her mother's happiness. Such a cute kid; she hardly managed to pronounce the sentences. Unable to bear the burden of refusing, Rose replied she would think about it. Of course, she had no intention to since she'd decided against it before anyone had raised the possibility.

After a short pause, the journalist continued. "So, you aren't considering that particular option?"

"No, my duties as the Melkar are too important." She shrugged. "I cannot let politics distract me. Besides, the Felicia Act forbids members of the clergy from pursuing a political career. Priests are forbidden from candidacy, so I shouldn't be allowed either. I am touched by my followers' faith in me, but I'm not above the law."

"Since you won't be part of the race, is there any candidate you'd like to support?"

"I'd rather keep my political preferences private. I will say this: I am certain our future councillor will do the region of Ulkar proud."

"We sure hope so." A frown appeared on the reporter's brow. "If you don't mind indulging me in a hypothetical scenario—if we somehow did elect a madman, so to speak, would you use your status to oppose him?"

A pensive Rose rubbed her chin. "I doubt that would be necessary. The Council is made up of several members. A corrupt councillor cannot do anything without the support of others. That's the big reason why we implemented such a system." She paused for a second. "I am hopeful these measures are sufficient."

"And if the system fails us despite our checks and balances?"

Rose saw herself on the screen cross her arms and tap her elbow with her index finger. The reporter attempted a trick question. It appeared harmless, but she'd learned those of his profession created controversies from nothing. A yes implied she craved political power regardless of her statements to the contrary and might draw criticism. A no suggested she'd abandon her people.

"It's hard to predict one's reaction when facing a crisis. Sometimes we do things we never imagined." She exhaled. "I feel I shouldn't publicly take a side on political issues, yet what kind of spiritual leader would let a tyrant ravage Nirnivia unchecked? Your question is too hypothetical to answer accurately. However, whatever I decided to do in such a situation, I would only act after careful deliberation."

The reporter wrapped the interview on that last comment. Exhausted, Rose shut down her TV and went to bed. A few weeks later, they counted the votes. Something incredible had occurred; something impossible. Ninety-two percent of the voters hadn't chosen any of the candidates. Instead, they'd written "Rose Ricdeau" on the ballots. Of course, since she wasn't an official contender, this ended up being an insignificant gesture. Then again, the number of valid votes proved too low to be considered legally binding. Not long after the unexpected results were announced, Madeleine, Rose's adoptive mother, visited her. The strange news left her agitated and rendered her skin paler than usual.

"My dear," Madeleine said as her fingers reached for Rose's shoulder, "have you heard about the election?" Rose acquiesced and opened her mouth to reply, but her mother kept on talking without giving her a chance. "The general populace refuses to understand! Now they will redo the entire election. What a waste of resources. I trust your decision remains firm?"

A reassuring smile formed on Rose's lips. "Of course, Mom."

"Good. As the Melkar, you cannot become a politician, and I do not mean because of the Felicia Act you are so fond of." Madeleine frowned as she waggled a lecturing index finger. "The Melkar cannot risk being corrupted by politics. To wield such tremendous power is not your place."

She rambled on and on, and Rose grew tired of that particular speech. Her mother had protested the idea of her joining the Council from the start. The thing was, Rose agreed, but Madeleine had forgotten that fact. The head priestess explained her position again and again, uselessly defending her point. Her dad, however, wasn't opposed to the notion. He stated that Rose could accomplish amazing feats as a councillor but then added that she knew best. Despite this claim, Rose had a distinct impression he believed she should do it. It brought her no joy to disappoint him, but principles were important.

"I know, Mom. I agree. The people obviously don't."

Madeleine crossed her arms. "We will have to change their mind."

A sigh came from Rose. "We tried before."

"Then let us try harder."

The next day, Rose heeded her mother's advice and addressed the issue during her sermon. She hoped to stop this foolishness right there.

"I would like to mention what happened yesterday. It is clear that my beloved followers want me to be a councillor. Your devotion touches me, and I am honored by your trust. However, the Melkar is a spiritual leader, not a political one. If I were part of the Council, it would negatively affect my duties, and that's unacceptable. Please, in the next election, vote for a legitimate candidate. I will decline even if the process is repeated a million times. All you are doing is wasting money needed for greater causes."

She performed such lectures on several occasions but achieved no success. The subsequent attempt occurred a few weeks later, and ninety-six percent of the ballots bore the name Rose Ricdeau: a four percent increase. This outcome depressed her. Friends and family attempted contacting her, but she disappeared as she sought a solution. Unable to find one, she turned to her mirror. Others alleged she spoke with Ulgorack himself; she assumed she deliberated with her own subconscious. Whoever or whatever she talked to, sometimes it helped her a lot.

"How can I convince them that I cannot be a councillor?" she inquired as she gazed into her own eyes. The reflection stared back with an unsettling intensity. A familiar discomfort crept inside Rose. It happened often when she consulted her mirror. The image resembled herself, of course, but there was something... different. Rose couldn't put her finger on what it was.

With a blank expression, her other self answered, "Perhaps you cannot."

She let out an exasperated moan. "Are you saying they're right? That I should be a councillor?"

"No, I am not. Decisions such as these are complex. They have unforeseen consequences, be it for good or ill. The best path is hidden to me."

As useful as it could be, her reflection failed her. Rose asked a few more queries, but she received the same ambiguous unhelpful responses. Since "Ulgorack" declined to rescue her, she relied on the people she trusted most instead. First, she met her father. Though aware he deemed she should be a councillor, she figured he might offer interesting insights.

"So, princess, you're in a bit of a pickle," he said with his fingers linked in a pyramid. A common pose for him, he employed it both as a display of authority and as an aid when contemplating a difficult problem. Daniel often called her princess when they were alone, a remnant from her childhood. A clichéd pet name for his daughter, she conceded, but Rose always enjoyed it. It made her feel special. Except when he uttered it in public; then it embarrassed her. "You want to convince people to stop throwing away the election. Well, you explained the situation several times—that didn't work. I think... you're going to hate this, dear, but I think you'll have to show some tough love. You should give another speech and make it clear that you're angry—throw a fit." The instant he finished his sentence, Daniel presented his palms in front of his body in a request for restraint. "Not too much, of course; don't overdo it. They'll stand down rather than anger the Melkar."

A groan came from Rose. "You're right, I don't like it. But it might be the only way." She shook her head. "Why are they so stubborn?"

"Well, princess, it's natural." He patted her back. "The Old War devastated our country. Our population is small. There are many mutants and a large chunk of our former territory is uninhabitable. The situation has improved, but it's still tough all over. If the Melkar were a member of the Council, she could use her new political influence to fix it and make Nirnivia great again." The elder widened his arms as if making a grand declaration. "With her wisdom and her connection with Ulgorack, there's nothing she couldn't accomplish. Now, don't take this the wrong way, princess, but I can certainly see their point."

"But the Melkar is a spiritual guide—"

"Not a politician," her father finished with a chuckle. "You sound like your mother. I agree, under normal circumstances, the Melkar shouldn't be on the Council, but these times are hardly normal, are they?" In a moment of hesitation, Daniel averted his gaze. "Princess, God doesn't speak to me, and unlike Madeleine, I'm not a priest. But have you considered the possibility that this whole mess is Ulgorack telling you that you should be a councillor? I mean, ninety-two percent of the people writing Rose Ricdeau on their ballots, that's shocking. I could see some wiseass trying it, but ninety-two percent? It's ridiculous."

Rose had to admit he displayed some level of logic. Ulgorack employed mysterious methods, so he might send her a convoluted message in this manner, but she doubted it. In need of more guidance, she turned to her mother next.

"So, he suspects Ulgorack wishes for you to become a politician." Madeleine's lips contorted in a grimace. "As much as I abhor the idea, I cannot deny the possibility. My child, you are able to understand God's will with greater accuracy than this humble priestess." She tilted her head. "Have you conversed with Ulgorack?"

"Several times." In her mind, Rose added that particular technique might've succeeded had she been an actual prophet. No point speaking those words out loud; she'd accepted years ago that others considered her the Voice of God no matter her beliefs. Her mom was not an exception. "All I got were evasive answers."

"It is written that communication with Ulgorack can be challenging." After a moment of hesitation, she proceeded with a cautionary tone. "Do not forget the possibility that Ulgorack is testing you."

Rose's eyes widened. "Testing me?"

"Yes." Madeleine nodded. "Maybe Ulgorack is tempting you with power to determine if you are indeed pure-hearted. Do not rush blindly, my child." She gave a comforting smile before continuing. "Rose, my dear, though you doubt yourself, you are the holy prophet. This is difficult, but I am certain that you will make the correct decision and I will support you no matter what that may be."

While her mother's confidence touched Rose, it provided little relief. Confusion still clutched her, causing several sleepless nights. Since she had asked the rest of her family, Rose figured she might as well visit her sister next.

Janice went straight to the point. "You want my opinion, sis?" The older sibling folded her arms. "Don't do it."

"So you think the Melkar has no place in politics?"

"No, that's not it." She giggled as she rolled her irises. "I'm no religious expert—I'll leave that to you and Mom." Janice grasped Rose's hand with surprising tenderness considering her size. "I'm just thinking about you. Rose, I know you. If you do this, you'll worry and worry about every small decision. Acting as a councillor is a full-time job; same for being the Melkar. Doing both, that's too much; you'll end up burning out. It's important you take care of yourself too."

Moved by her concerns, Rose beamed. They had shared a close relationship since childhood. Without her, Rose would be lost.

"Always protecting me, aren't you?"

Janice and Rose joined in an embrace.

"Hey, everyone's so hung up on the big issues; someone has to remember my little sister's well-being."

"Thanks!" With that, both of them enjoyed a pleasant laugh.

Rose conferred with other acquaintances she respected, and she even tried the mirror again, to no avail. Despite the numerous suggestions, the path forward remained unsure.

***

At the lunch table, Rose dropped her fork and stared at her plate. Despite the obscuring angle, James caught a glimpse of her watering eyes. "And so, Hunter, after the third election ended up with the same result, I decided to become a candidate after all. What foolishness—I let my idealism get to me." She scoffed. "What can I say except I was young and stupid? Though I wasn't deluded to the point of assuming I actually fulfilled God's will, I figured maybe Dad was right when he suggested I could do amazing things. Too bad I was wrong. I mean well, but I'm not a politician. I don't fit in. When you think about it, it's similar to the reason why I accepted my role as Melkar.

Apparently, I learn slowly, so I'm doomed to repeat the same mistakes again and again."

That story sounded completely insane. Almost everyone writing Rose Ricdeau in on the election ballots? How improbable was that? Yet no matter if my brain screamed it wasn't logical, my heart knew she told me the truth. Also, no doubt she despised her role as a politician. The disgusted expression she had whenever she pronounced the word councillor made that clear.

—Thoughts of James Hunter, Hocmar 28, 2134, on the Nirnivian calendar

After a long silence, James said, "There's one thing I don't understand." He winced as hesitation overcame him. "Uh, you obviously hate being a councillor, so... why not quit?"

The prophet sighed and shook her head. "Well, I considered it, but the people still want me on the Council. I could quit, but I'm afraid of the public's reaction. I fear some might believe Ulgorack is forsaking them. And with the war, I'd rather avoid a commotion."

James scratched the back of his skull. "Um, yeah, I understand."

"And now I keep getting trapped in situations like this strike." A few tears ran down her cheeks. "I'm at a complete loss."

With an uncomfortable harrumph, Brucie presented a thumbs-up. "Do your best, like always!" The tone proved cheerful and encouraging, yet James sensed the effort required from Brucie to manage it. "And when shit happens, don't forget we're here fo' ya."

"Yeah, you bet we are!"

Rose forced a smile. "Thanks, guys, I appreciate your support."

Chapter 10

Osmoro 7, 2134, on the Nirnivian calendar

At around six in the morning, Anya arrived at the lab. Once she parked her car, she exited the vehicle and walked toward the door. Clouds covered the sun, and due to the early hour, the air proved cold compared to Ostark's usual temperature, causing her to shiver. Once she reached the door, she rummaged through her bag in search of her key card. After a few seconds, she located it and opened the door by sliding it in the scanner.

Lately, Anya had been working on the test trials for the synthetic skins she and her sister, Tania, had developed with the Good Doctor. So far, the results had ended up positive. The transplants had gone well, with either no side effects or, at worst, minor ones. Anya remembered how Tania had grumbled about extra tests being useless in this case, and it seemed she was right. Still, she considered her sibling's impulsiveness dangerous and preferred proceeding with caution.

As Anya entered the laboratory, she removed her coat and hung it in the closet before proceeding to the main area. There, she saw her sister sitting at her desk already. Tania hammered on her keyboard at an impressive speed. How she managed to stare at that screen unblinking, Anya would never understand.

After a minute or two, Tania stopped typing and ran a finger through her pink hair. Then she stretched before reaching for her coffee and taking a sip. No doubt she needed it. Based on previous experience, Anya assumed she had stayed there the whole night. The president had tasked her with synthesizing a chemical compound. As always, when faced with a new scientific endeavor, Tania attacked the challenge filled with glee. In this state, sleepless nights spent on research were common.

"Hey, Tania," Anya said, "working hard this early, huh?"

Her twin giggled. "Oh yeah, it's so interesting! That stuff he wants me to replicate is out of this world. Never seen anything like it." Tania then rubbed her chin. "I can see it's plant-based, but I guess that doesn't help, since the Good Doctor already told me that. Don't ask what kind of plant it is, but you can bet your butt it's not from Ostark or even Nirnivia."

"How mysterious... it seems you have your work cut out for you."

A large smile formed on Tania's lips. "That's fine, it's how I like it!" Then her smile turned upside down. "So far, I've sent two test samples to the Good Doctor, but they failed his tests. But that's okay—I'll make sure to bring my A game for the next batch!" Filled with enthusiasm again, she closed her fists and shook them around as she giggled.

"Great!" Anya paused. "Hey, wanna hear about how the skin trials are going?"

Tania shrugged. "Nah, that's boring stuff."

Though Anya had expected as much, her sibling's demeanor made her laugh. While not a polite response by any stretch, she understood Tania meant nothing by it. When enthralled by a task, she forgot basic Gorumar manners and grew socially awkward. Ah well, how could Anya be mad at someone so passionate about their job?

Chapter 11

The rain poured down, soaking their clothes and causing discomfort. Adding to their misery, the drops proved cold and chilled Jonathan and his colleagues to the bone. They had picketed for two days, brandishing signs denouncing NISDA's unfair treatment. So far, they'd received little support from the general population. Rare passersby offered encouraging words, but most insulted them and fired accusations of laziness.

Despite the deluge and the adversity, his companions' spirits remained high. Of course, some regretted their decision, but they were a minority, and nobody had abandoned the cause so far. Most sang protest songs and chanted catchy slogans unaffected by the setbacks.

"Shitty weather for a strike, huh?" Brian said as he approached Jonathan.

"Yeah, but that's okay." He gave a concerned frown. "It's not the weather I'm worried about." Other than meeting with councillors, NISDA hadn't attempted to dissuade them yet. Jonathan realized that wouldn't last. Soon, their employer or the Council would make a move, and that would be much worse than the cold shower.

Brian grimaced and then leaned toward Jonathan's ear. "You're talking about Her Holiness, huh?" he asked in a whisper, hoping not to be overheard by the crowd. No one appreciated negative sentiments expressed against their alleged prophet. Jonathan nodded in silence. Indeed, she could become a serious problem. The beloved icon possessed the capacity to end their efforts with a short speech.

The fact that she had chosen not to up until now didn't surprise him. That was part of her attempt at playing both sides of the field as he had deduced before. Still, he'd acted too harshly with her. He had meant to show he'd figured out her manipulative tricks and wouldn't be deceived. He'd succeeded, but he might have been too forceful. She had the potential to be either a powerful ally or a powerful enemy. After what had happened, Jonathan feared it was way too late to befriend her. The notion disgusted him, but he should have kissed her ass like every other fool. Jonathan took a deep breath, relaxed and focused on the positives. Things had proceeded as planned. He decided to take comfort in that rather than agonizing about the future.

Chapter 12

Osmoro 9, 2134, on the Nirnivian calendar

No way around it, Rose would be late. The Council of Hurdan held an emergency meeting in the parliament. Given her self-imposed imprisonment in Valardir, joining in person would be impossible. Instead, her office possessed an advanced teleconferencing system that allowed her to attend such gatherings while remaining safely within the complex. There was only one problem: thanks to the very strike they meant to discuss, she'd lost her tech. Since NISDA lacked manpower, they had failed to provide a replacement.

Rose had never set up the communication equipment before, and it didn't go well. A visual survey of the various machines exposed a plethora of buttons, flashing lights, and dials. As for what they represented, she had no idea. Intimidated, she nonetheless studied the controls in the hope the labels would provide important hints concerning how to proceed. Her optimism ended up dashed, and her confusion only grew. Out of desperation, she attempted pushing a promising switch, but her effort resulted in a strident beep indicating she must've done something wrong. Panicked, she played with the panel until she managed to shut down the annoying sound.

A mocking laughter accompanied the scene. The source, a delighted Brucie, leaned against the wall with his hands behind his head. Annoyed, Rose looked at him and said, "Oh, real funny."

"Hey, ain't my fault gals suck with technology, ya know."

Rose scoffed. "You chauvinistic bastard! How about you give it a try and see how easy it is?"

"Yeah, sure!" The bodyguard cracked his knuckles. "Lemme show ya how the great Brucie Garland—"

Then Rose thought better of it and she presented her palm to stop him in his tracks. "Never mind! If you break it, it won't be fixed until the strike is over."

Brucie fired off an expletive-filled reply, but she ignored him. With a groan, she then reached for the manual, and her heart sank at its girth. It was about a thousand pages long. After a gulp, she started reading, though comprehension eluded her. Soon, the complex material overwhelmed Rose, and she stopped to massage her temples. She relaxed for a minute before plunging back into the volume. How long she struggled to catch a glimpse of meaning she couldn't say, but eventually, the door slid open. Rose turned her head for a quick glance and spotted a blond-haired silhouette. She assumed Kristina had arrived and kept focusing on her task. A second later, the assistant rested the coffee Rose had requested on the desk. While she hated that drink, she needed an energy boost.

"Wait," Kristina said with a gasp, "you're not set up yet?"

"I tried!" Rose gave a shake of the head, followed by a sigh, as she gestured toward the equipment. "This thing is impossible to figure out. What a nightmare. I won't be able to make it."

"Here, let me try." On that note, Kristina rolled up her sleeves and began fiddling with the controls at a rapid pace. If she doubted how to proceed, she revealed no sign of it. In fact, she displayed an assurance Rose envied.

An impressed whistle escaped Brucie's mouth. "She got ya beat, ain't she?"

"I'd say... wow! You're amazing. Is there anything you can't do?"

"It's nothing. I've watched the tech so often it's burned in my memory." Kristina shrugged.

"Don't sell yourself short! I've watched too, and I can't come close to get it working."

No answer came from the assistant, but her cheeks reddened at the compliment. Rather than embarrass the blond woman further, Rose spun toward Brucie. "You owe my gender an apology."

A smirk forming on his lips, Brucie offered an exaggerated bow. "Yep. Sorry 'bout that." He paused. "Ya know I was just messing with ya, right?"

"Yeah, yeah, no worries." The moment Rose finished this sentence, her screen turned on. Kristina had succeeded, Ulgorack be praised. Still, she was so late.

***

The monitor revealed a familiar sight: the chamber where the councillors assembled. Each of them sat in a chair around the ring-shaped wooden table. Except for Rose, of course. Instead of her person, her "seat" consisted of a display and a camera allowing interactions with the others. At the center of the table sat a hollow space that was useless in appearance, though it served a purpose. From the ceiling, three screens arranged in a triangle could descend when prompted. The unorthodox format allowed everyone to see whatever they showed.

Now that she had metaphorically arrived, Rose sensed the weight of her peers' stares, none heavier than that of Doug Thomson. A heavyset head-shaven man dressed in a gray suit, the honorable moderator stayed as calm as ever, yet a subtle scowl greeted her tardiness. Rose blushed. "I'm sorry," she apologized. "It took me extra time to figure the equipment out."

"No worries, Councillor Ricdeau, we expected this." He adjusted his small glasses. "You're here sooner than we hoped, in fact. You haven't missed anything. We waited for you."

Rose let out a relieved exhale. "Thank you, I appreciate it. And also thank you to my dear assistant, Kristina. Without her, I'm afraid you'd still be waiting."

Thomson had sounded genuine. Perhaps she'd imagined the scowl she'd perceived. Either that or something else had caused his expression. That suited Rose fine. She'd rather not be humiliated before a veteran like Doug, especially not one she respected so much.

Elected as a councillor three elections in a row, Thomson remained seventeen years later, though in a different role. The dark-skinned Perz now filled the infamous position of moderator, the thirteenth person on the Council. While he lacked the ability to vote on issues, he possessed considerable power. He served as the guide for the deliberations, ensuring polite exchanges during fierce debates. Should a councillor step over a line, Thomson could enforce punishment, such as fines and expulsion from a session. This alone granted moderators sway over the discussion, allowing them to influence the outcome if they desired. In addition, when a vote resulted in a draw, Doug received a special opportunity to break the tie. While she admired him for his dedication and integrity, Thomson intimidated Rose. Not that he meant to; he acted kindly toward her. Rather, it was because he had earned his reputation through his achievements while she had won her campaign because of her wings. His presence reminded her of this truth.

Doug Thomson leaned forward. "So, Councillor Ricdeau, you don't expect any more technical difficulties?"

"I think I'm good." She gave a quick glance at Kristina along with a nod. "And if I'm wrong, I have someone who can manage."

"Excellent!" The moderator nodded. "Everyone should be aware of our agenda; the strike is our priority."

Not wasting a second, Henry Smith pressed a button illumining a green LED set before him. This indicated his wish to speak. An emaciated man with hair colored black in a botched attempt to conceal his age, he was serving his first term. Some speculated it'd be his last. He had failed to impress the public, though, to his credit, he hadn't caused any scandal either.

"Those techs are being selfish. They are putting the nation in jeopardy for their own interests. Because of the Deboros Act, we can impose daily fines. I suggest we do so with the maximal amount."

Rose sprang to offer a rebuttal, but someone beat her to the punch—Councillor Erika Master, a sixty-eight-year-old woman who had aged gracefully. Few wrinkles tainted her visage, and her green eyes remained filled with energy and passion.

"If they were considered part of the military instead of contractors, NISDA would have more options. This strike would be crushed." She crossed her arms. "I warned you about this." Just like Erika—a smart person, but stubborn—she always lectured them about how if they'd listened to her earlier, everything would be better. Rose deemed the rants counterintuitive and purposeless. Thomson apparently agreed, since he interrupted the session by banging his small gavel. Upon hearing the resulting thump, Erika hushed as requested.

"Enough, Councillor Master! Maybe we made a mistake, but saying 'I told you so' doesn't help resolve the issue."

Erika accepted the criticism with a bow and apologized. Though Rose questioned her sincerity, at least she stopped her futile scolding. Also, the silence caused by Doug's ire allowed Rose to signal her intention to address them.

"I understand why Councillor Smith suggests fines should be imposed. However, I believe this course of action would be unfair." She exhaled. "The techs aren't doing this out of malice. They received a raw deal from NISDA, and so they are forcing negotiations. We are talking about people defending their rights and the well-being of their families, not traitors, as some accusations flying around propose. Fines are overkill. Without a salary, they're already facing a financial strain, so there's no need for extra pressure. If we do this, children will suffer, and I for one refuse to take this path."

"Councillor Ricdeau, you make a touching argument, but I should remind everyone that we are at war with Ostark. The military faces serious difficulties due to the strike." Henry clenched his fist. "Doctor Death will probably mount an attack."

Rose dismissed the rebuttal by shaking her head. "I disagree." The whole room gasped. "Look, there's no point pretending you don't know what I'm talking about. We are overpowered by Ostark. If he wanted, he could invade us without the strike. Yes, he'll use this to his advantage, but he won't attack." Her colleagues stared at the screen displaying her image. "He wants me, not Nirnivia's destruction. He would have captured me from the beginning if he were willing to annihilate our country, but he'd rather avoid war. That's the reason for this uneasy peace."

The crowd remained quiet, flabbergasted by her candor, and then Thomson cleared his throat. "With all due respect, Councillor Ricdeau, Doctor Death is a madman. I doubt anyone can tell what he's after or how he'll react."

Rose twitched at the rebuff. She couldn't help it. One would assume she'd be used to it all by now, but no. "Madman? Yes, you're correct." She shivered. "But you are also aware he told us that I alone am his target. He's a monster and a manipulator, but not a liar."

A soft smile formed on Doug's face. "Sometimes it almost sounds like you're defending him." If the message implied accusation, the tone conveyed deep concern for her well-being.

"I'm not. He's dangerous." She trembled. "I'm terrified of him. I don't want to think about what would happen if he captured me. But I'm convinced he won't attack us directly."

As a reply, Doug shrugged. "Even so, other Ostarkiran politicians might disagree and oust him from power. We aren't safe, Councillor Ricdeau, and you shouldn't pretend otherwise. In particular, you are not. Doctor Death will use this strike to get to you, and we cannot allow that. Nirnivia needs the Melkar."

Swallowing hard, Rose bent her head until her gaze met the floor. Her eyes watered, and she hoped they wouldn't notice. She answered with difficulty, her beautiful voice strained by intense emotions. "Again, you overestimate my value."

She regretted uttering those words, but it was too late. Long ago, when Doctor Death had replaced President Laforge, Rose had proposed surrendering herself. She was a single person, and she would sacrifice her life without hesitation to save thousands. The Council had rejected the option and pleaded that Nirnivia depended on the Melkar. The Voice of God served as a symbol of hope, and they would never abandon her. They also mentioned that nothing guaranteed Doctor Death would stop the war after her incarceration. Perhaps she was naïve, but she believed he would indeed end the fighting, or at least attempt to. Of course, if she had become his prisoner, her fate would have been sealed. What he would do to her wasn't clear, but she imagined an unpleasant and possibly lethal scenario. Still, part of her wished it had happened for the people's safety. But she'd be lying if she claimed that was the only reason.

Back then, she'd argued that Nirnivia had survived without the Voice of God for thousands of years, and they'd manage again. For better or worse, they refused to listen. She prayed her colleagues didn't see her tears. She preferred to avoid looking weak in front of them. Each of them understood the ordeal this conversation imposed on her, but breaking down like that made her feel beyond inadequate.

"No, Councillor Ricdeau, you are underestimating your worth. Even if you weren't the Melkar or a councillor, even if you were a homeless beggar with no family or friends, I still wouldn't sacrifice you. Nirnivia does not give in to threats." The rest of the councillors applauded in approval. Though a convincing display, in her heart, Rose doubted its sincerity. They sent soldiers on suicide missions without objection. Why not her if not because they deemed her a prophet?

Before Rose had the chance to imagine an answer to her own question, an indignant high-pitched voice tore through the air.

"We digress and digress, but it does nothing to solve the issue at hand." No need for visual confirmation; Rose identified the source as Priscilla Destro. Dressed in white as usual, she punctuated her speech with grandiose gestures, suggesting a sense of self-importance. That habit, along with how she wrinkled her nose no matter the circumstances, gave the impression she snubbed everyone. "Whether the strikers are acting out of malice is debatable, but either way, they are betraying not only NISDA but Nirnivia in its entirety. Fines aren't drastic enough! They deserve imprisonment for their crimes."

"The Deboros Act won't allow that," a hunched-over councillor named Gerald Mahoni said. As he talked, he twitched his fingers and kept his gaze fixed on the table. Most judged him to be a nervous wreck due to his fidgeting, but none denied his intelligence. "But there are possibilities."

Gerald possessed an eidetic memory. Like a sponge soaks up water, he absorbed knowledge from texts and conversations. Later, he recalled the details with impressive precision. He loved quoting obscure laws. Often, the Council depended on his peculiar skills, both to handle pressing matters and to solve petty squabbles over what had and hadn't happened in previous sessions.

"Those who wrote the Deboros Act put vague language in there." He licked his lips. "On the surface, while striking and forming unions are prohibited, the punishments are fines and not jail. This is because they feared the public would consider going that far to be an unacceptable violation of their rights, even in the face of extinction. Still, our predecessors snuck in loopholes in case they needed them later. Most of the techs are out of reach legally, but if we play our cards right, we could indict their leader, Jonathan Rivers."

The notion disgusted Rose, and she meant to condemn it, but Jade Carlson beat her to the punch. A sharp bang echoed through the chamber as she slapped the table, causing Rose to jump on her seat in shock.

"That's preposterous!"

Surprised, Doug Thomson fired her a warning glance, but the glare she shot back implied such fury he decided not to intervene. Rose swallowed hard. Councillor Carlson was a fierce woman indeed. "I'm used to despicable musings from you, Priscilla."

That proved enough to vanquish the moderator's hesitation. "Councillor Carlson, please refrain from personal attacks or I will—"

The old lady ignored him and continued. "But I didn't expect it from you, Councillor Mahoni."

Unlike many politicians, Jade retained a strong moral compass. She fought with devotion for what she considered ethical, critics be damned. And if the voters disagreed with her view, they could vote her out of there and she wouldn't complain. That was their right, and their civic duty. While there had been cases where she had reconsidered her position, these were rare. Rose herself had endured several debates with Carlson. She'd lost a few metaphorical feathers in the process and ended up standing down during most of them. Few dared to contradict the alleged Melkar with such tenacity, and Rose respected her for her convictions, though she didn't always agree with them. Thank Ulgorack, at the moment, they stood on the same side.

Poor Gerald started biting his nails. With a tinge of shame, Rose peeped at her own fingertips. That was a bad habit she'd once indulged in, but after years of effort, she had broken it. Not that the temptation didn't show itself on occasion.

"Uh, I'm only mentioning facts pertinent to the discussion. I didn't mean to imply I condone that course of action."

"I hope not." Jade sneered. "Councillor Ricdeau is right. The techs aren't traitors, and I won't let anyone here treat them as such. Rose is wrong for the rest of it, though. In fact, everyone so far has been wrong. Imposing full fines on the strikers would be cruel. Imposing none would be foolish. I'm sure they don't want to bring harm to Nirnivia, but they are nonetheless." Jade rubbed her chin with her index finger. "I suggest we fine them fifty percent of the maximum amount. That shows mercy and understanding to their cause, but also encourages them to settle this quickly."

Better than what Henry Smith had recommended, but Rose believed the penalties were too steep. A shiver ran down her spine at the thought of facing off against Jade, but she took a deep breath.

"Fifty is too high. They'd be crushed financially." A beginning of an idea formed in her mind. She frowned. "How is it fair that only the techs are being pressured? There are two parties here, NISDA and the techs, and they'll have to work together to resolve this. There must be incentives for both parties."

Jade offered a benevolent smile that implied a lack of experience on the part of her younger colleague. The act might've offended Rose, had it not been an accurate estimation of her capabilities as a councillor.

"I hope you're not thinking of fining NISDA. There's no legal grounds to do so, and it would make it that much harder for them to reconsider the current contract."

"No, that's not it."

Doug Thomson then joined in the fray. "And I'm not enacting Tabarar, in case you're wondering."

Frustration crept inside Rose, and she wished to shout that they should listen to her instead of assuming she'd propose such ludicrous notions. Of course she wouldn't ask him for a Tabarar vote. He'd refuse in less than a second, and she'd be laughed out of the room. In theory, the Commander controlled NISDA, and the Council had little to say about how the organization operated. However, should a dire situation occur—for instance, a Commander breaking the law—they could invoke Tabarar and take direct control of NISDA. Only the moderator could start those proceedings, and then it required a unanimous vote in the Council to pass. It was deemed a drastic measure for drastic events, and any moderator employing Tabarar for unjustified reasons would destroy their career.

"That's not where I'm going either. Tabarar isn't appropriate here, at least not yet, but we can try to persuade NISDA to collaborate with us and the techs. Potential fines on the strikers achieve this. We won't impose fines, but we'll inform NISDA that if they make a genuine effort to solve the problem, we will."

A short silence fell over them as they considered the argument. Soon, Jade nodded. "Hmm, that's interesting, but zero percent is too low. If we go with fifty, we put some pressure on the strikers, and we can increase that amount if NISDA plays ball."

"Maybe zero is too low, but fifty is too high! We can't do that to them!"

Erika shrugged. "How about we split the difference? Vote on thirty and finish this up before dinner?" Nothing was ever so simple. The debate raged on for hours. When it was over, Rose had succeeded in decreasing that number to twenty.

Chapter 13

Osmoro 10, 2134, on the Nirnivian calendar

The strike began on a somber note for the techs, but spirits grew higher on that particular morning. First, the sun showed itself and Jonathan admitted he enjoyed the break from the rain. No doubt his colleagues shared his point of view. Second, since the start, they had feared the prospect of drastic fines, and the Council settled that question. Yes, the Council had imposed penalties, yet they proved less severe than anticipated. The politicians had agreed on twenty percent of the maximum amount. While an important financial burden, it could have been far worse. Some claimed the low charges implied that the Council favored their cause. To Jonathan, that sounded like an exaggeration, but he assumed some councillors sympathized with their plight, even though they needed the matter resolved as fast as possible.

"Hey, Jonathan!" Brian said as he walked toward him, smiling and brandishing a sign. "Good weather, good news. Things are looking up!"

Jonathan nodded. "Yeah, but it's not over yet! Don't let your guard down."

"Looks like we owe this to your old pal the Melkar. She fought to lower the fines. Freak, they say she tried to remove them entirely."

Jonathan had heard similar claims and studied the available evidence, yet he was skeptical. Council assembly took place in private, and what happened inside remained secret, unless they decided to share information. This secrecy drew criticism from civil rights activists. Before the old war, most governments had broadcast political meetings live, so the voters saw their elected officials at work and judged whether they deserved their trust. Many, including Jonathan, deemed this an essential practice for a democracy. Sure, perhaps this wasn't feasible during Nirnivia's early years, but now they could reintroduce the notion. The Council, however, claimed nobody wished to see the sausage being made and that such a system undermined national security. Classic bullshit, a mix of truth and lies to suit their interests.

At any rate, Rose refused to comment on how the discussion had gone and her role in it. When confronted by the rumors, she'd declined to answer. While Jonathan desired transparency from elected officials, in this case, he agreed with her approach. Thanks to her alleged calling as a prophet, any expression of opinion tended to cause major shifts in the conversation. However this strike ended up settled, it shouldn't be due to religious beliefs.

Despite Rose's silence, the anecdotes had gained credence when someone had leaked recordings from the Council's session. There wasn't much to it, just a few sentences of Rose pleading for her peers not to levy charges. The voice on the tape appeared genuine, but no expert had managed to confirm its authenticity. It might be fake, or it could have been edited to alter the intended meaning. Either way, this outcome had resulted in a surge of approval for the strikers. Passersby now greeted them, and motorists honked in solidarity. Crazy. They'd increased their support before that by releasing the tape showing Koporal Tigh implying threats to Jonathan. The boorish demeanor displayed by Ron brought questions about NISDA's motives for the salary cuts and helped garner sympathy. Still, the Melkar's assumed endorsement rendered that video a mere footnote in comparison.

Jonathan scowled. "That's gossip. Don't assume she's on our side yet."

"Nah, just saying she might not be the complete monster you paint her to be."

"Maybe not, but I'm not convinced." He waggled a lecturing finger. "Don't forget, I predicted she'd pretend to support us at first, only to play the religious card to stop us later on. So far, she's following my prediction to a T."

With a laugh, Brian shook his head. "Always so pessimistic. Don't let the others hear you talk like that."

"I don't intend to."

Chapter 14

Osmoro 15, 2134, on the Nirnivian calendar

Our information network made it clear: the Nirnivians faced a crisis. As such, a promising opportunity presented itself. Without delay, we organized an emergency cabinet meeting to discuss the situation. I felt the president's impatience: he considered the assembly useless and itched to return to his precious Alcharia virus cure. I have no idea why that disease fascinated him that much.

—Thoughts of Evelyn Losier, Hocmar 28, 2134, on the Nirnivian calendar

"Don't you understand that this is our chance?" General Harold Torn shouted while brandishing a ferocious index finger. His mood had soured after the president had shot down his proposal for a full-scale invasion. "Nirnivia is in turmoil, and with this strike, it will only get worse. This uneasy peace is our worst mistake ever. If we had kept fighting, it would all be over. Now we can rectify our error and finish it."

Before the mechanical man uttered a word, Evelyn predicted his reply. He had made his position on the issue clear. Based on Torn's puffed-up chest, she expected he'd deduced the same. The posture might suggest strength in appearance, but it screamed of false bravado. The general had already lost, and he was aware of that fact.

"Indeed, it would be over due to Nirnivia's utter destruction. That is not our objective." He paused as he pointed his biological iris at Harold while the electronic counterpart displayed a sad face. "Or at least it should not be. For the moment, our goal is the capture of Rose Ricdeau. I do not believe changing our current strategy would be a wise decision."

Evelyn frowned. Torn creeped her out, and she understood why the president preferred avoiding another full-scale war. Still, the situation offered them an advantage, and she doubted inaction would prove a good choice. After a brief hesitation and a deep breath for courage, she said, "But isn't this our chance to finally reach her?"

The cyborg shook his head. "While there is wisdom in your judgment, I am afraid it is not so simple. Breaking into Valardir by force would require a major assault on Nirnivia. Many would perish, far too great a number to consider it a viable means to our end." While the monotone voice his body imposed failed to convey emotion, Evelyn sensed the fear the potential conflict inflicted upon him.

"Then maybe we can be sneakier? Have a few soldiers infiltrate Valardir and escape with Rose? It'd be impossible normally, but with the current confusion, we could pull it off."

The president rubbed his chin right below the speaker serving as a mouth. "We will certainly keep our eyes open for possibilities; however, I would not get your hopes up if I were you. Daniel Ricdeau will expect us to take advantage of their weakness. He also knows what we want. It is true that the Nirnivian military will be disadvantaged in the coming days and possibly weeks, but he realizes too well that this puts Rose in danger. I assume he will compensate, to the point where reaching her will even be harder. Of course, Lady Luck might favor us again. Regardless, I have full confidence that our friend James will deliver Rose sooner or later."

Why did he bother with the human? What could he do? Once he'd made up his mind, I could never change it, so I didn't argue. He had his secret plan, and he stuck to it. I thought it was a misstep, but I trusted him, so in the end, I let it go.

    —Thoughts of Evelyn Losier, Hocmar 28, 2134, on the Nirnivian calendar

Mr. Cursak, the defense secretary, cleared his throat. "We can still take advantage of our good fortune. This should make it easier for our spies to extract classified information, and I think we'll find clever ways to further demoralize the Nirnivians."

"I suppose." Evelyn nodded. A quick survey of the room revealed numerous disappointed expressions. Almost everyone shared her opinion that they should exploit Nirnivia's hardships. Still, the Good Doctor commanded such respect that none dared to debate his views.

The mechanical man also acquiesced. "Yes, I assure you we will use this occurrence to our advantage. I rule out an extermination, but we may attack a few special targets. However, the victims will be those posing a genuine threat, and not innocent civilians." He scanned the chamber with his piercing gaze. "Do not mistake my compassion for a lack of resolve." He clenched his fist. "Before this strike is over, Nirnivian blood will flow."

Chapter 15

That morning, Kristina arrived armed with paperwork. "What's this?" Rose asked when the assistant rested the form on her desk.

"It's for the Melkar funds for the needy. You have to fill it out."

"Sure, no problem. Thanks for bringing it to me." On that note, Rose grasped her pen and started writing the appropriate text in the correct spaces. About halfway through, her phone rang. She almost picked it up, but Kristina got to it faster. As the assistant lifted the receiver, she bobbed her head at the document, indicating she meant to allow Rose to finish her current task.

"Hello, Councillor Ricdeau's office." The exchange went on, and Rose paid little attention. A minute or so later, Kristina blocked the microphone with her hand and leaned toward her. "It's Constance Prim. She's calling about the Council's decision concerning the fines."

For a moment, Rose failed to remember the name. She scanned through her memory, rubbing her chin. At last, Constance's image popped into her brain. The delegate from NISDA who had visited her once regarding the strike. Now that she thought of it, she heard Constance had contacted various councillors in an attempt to change their minds.

"I'll take it, thanks." She seized the phone. "Hello, Ms. Prim, this is Rose Ricdeau."

"Councillor, it's a pleasure to talk to you again." If the words suggested that sentiment, the overeager tone conveyed the opposite. "I'm calling because NISDA is concerned about the Council's recent decision to fine the strikers only twenty percent of the maximum amount. While we understand the rationale behind your choice, we must stress that the situation is critical and must be resolved quickly. We fear that due to the lack of pressure, our employees won't be motivated to cooperate."

Rose suppressed a groan and rolled her eyes. "But they aren't the only ones who have to cooperate. NISDA shares part of the responsibility. You gave the techs a raw deal, and I worry that if we charged them full penalties, they'd have to give up before having a chance to negotiate properly. Work with them to find a reasonable compromise. From that point, if they refuse the new offer, we'll see about raising the fines."

There was a short silence. Rose imagined Constance's mouth contorting in a grimace. "Councillor, I appreciate your reasoning, but there's a major problem. Yes, I admit the current contract is far from ideal, but it's the best we can do. It's impossible for us to make a better offer."

Rose sighed, and then a sad smile formed on her face. "In that case, prove it and we'll act." The two of them exchanged a couple more pleasantries and then they hung up. Prey to a sudden headache, Rose moaned and massaged her temples. She glanced at Kristina.

"Constance gave up, but she's not happy about it. What's your opinion? Are we being fair?"

The assistant shrugged. "You don't need my approval."

Rose giggled. "No, but I value your input."

Kristina frowned. "I'd say the Council is being more than fair." She twitched. "But, based on what I know of NISDA's finances, I tend to believe Constance. It'd take a miracle to offer the techs a decent contract."

"Yes, I'm afraid you're right. Hmm, I suppose the Melkar might convince Ulgorack to grant us one if she prays hard enough." In her mind, Rose added, "Too bad I'm not her."

Chapter 16

Osmoro 21, 2134, on the Nirnivian calendar

Ever since the strike had begun, life had become even more boring for me. I wasn't seeing Rose, Brucie or really anyone anymore. Sometimes I went to the recreation room, hoping I'd bump into someone. It was always empty, though. Nobody had time to relax, it seemed. Given I was so sick of my quarters, I stayed there anyway and flipped through the channels on TV, but lately, the shows weren't that entertaining.

—Thoughts of James Hunter Hocmar 28, 2134, on the Nirnivian calendar

Annoyed, James realized that damn thing played on every station. On the screen, a scarred cyborg addressed the crowd. The same one James had witnessed not long after his arrival. The so-called Doctor Death spewed prerecorded propaganda on a loop. When James had first seen the mechanical man, his appearance had caused a major shock. However, the surprise had since vanished, and the repeating message proved grating.

"People of Nirnivia, you know who I am, and I realize you all hate me, but please listen to this—" With a groan, James pushed the arrow-shaped button on the remote. Following a flash of static accompanied by a screeching sound, the channel changed. The action provided little relief: the new station offered the same image.

"Your leaders—in particular, Ms. Rose Ricdeau—are lying to—" No matter how often he switched, he obtained the same result. A ball of frustration formed in his throat, expanding with each futile attempt.

"They are using your beliefs for their own selfish ends. Ms. Ricdeau is not the Melkar. She—"

The persistent announcement had started yesterday, and since then, the Doctor's ugly mug had dominated TV. James sighed and almost shut down the tube when a sultry female voice said, "Not exactly prime programming, huh?"

The words startled James, who had grown accustomed to solitude, but he recovered once he recognized Janice's voice. He turned around, and the sight of the gigantic woman confirmed his conclusion. Janice approached him, shoulders slumped and carrying cables twisted in a ring. As she got closer, he noticed the weak smile on her face and the bags under her eyes.

"Oh, hey, Janice. You surprised me."

She giggled, but the simple act required a visible effort. "Sorry. I saw you and I thought I'd say hi. I don't have much time. And I must look terrible."

"Oh, um, not at all"—a hesitant James scratched his ear—"well, maybe a bit tired."

"That's fitting. I'm exhausted!" Janice moaned as she dropped on the couch. She leaned back in her seat, eyes closed. For a moment, she remained silent, and James wondered if perhaps she had fallen asleep, but then she began massaging her temples. "Oh, James, they've made me a makeshift technician. So many things to learn. Everything's freaking crazy. You better get used to your new show. Don't ask me how the bastard did it, but Valardir's TV system is messed up, and we won't have a chance to fix it. Low priority. Oh, and you can't access the GlobalNet, so you wouldn't know, but check this shit out." With a smirk, Janice grabbed the minicomp attached to her belt. It rested in sleep mode, so bringing it back up to full power required a second. "They hacked NISDA's public globalsite."

She browsed through the site's pages, and James caught a glimpse of the propaganda replacing its former content. In all honesty, this was his first visit, and so he lacked knowledge of the original text. Yet somehow, he doubted it had spelled out Ostark's virtues while denouncing Daniel Ricdeau as a war criminal. Quite a few degrading images showcased Nirnivian leaders as villains—in particular, the picture of Rose dressed in a military uniform. A determined glare adorned the red-headed prophet's visage as she held several chains. On the other end of those restraints, her most devout followers trailed her like obedient dogs.

James grimaced at the unpleasant sight. "Doctor Death's spreading across all media."

"Yep, a freaking star is born," the soldier agreed in a sarcastic tone.

A shrug came from James. "Well, at least it's nothing serious." He gestured toward the minicomp. "I mean, who'd believe that junk?"

As he finished his sentence, the corner of Janice's lips twitched. "Yeah, but that's not the problem." She scowled. "Nobody's going to die because of this crap, and there's no major security risk. Everything the Ostarkirans accessed so far is public. But it's not about that. It's about reminding us how weak and helpless we are. Back during the war, we only survived because of Doctor Death's mercy. And now he's still toying with us, and we can't stop him. Worse, thanks to the strike, it won't be fixed for ages. That makes NISDA and the government look like a bunch of clowns. How are people supposed to trust in our capabilities to defend them when we can't handle a freaking globalsite? That can't be good for the population's morale, let alone us soldiers. Everyone's discouraged, and it's getting worse." She groaned. "Believe me, a depressed country is much more vulnerable."

I hadn't thought about that, but I guess that was the Doctor's plan all along. I doubt he converted anyone with his smear campaign, but it could sap Nirnivia's spirit and that'd certainly be a victory for him.

—Thoughts of James Hunter, Hocmar 28, 2134, on the Nirnivian calendar

Humbled, James lowered his gaze and stared at the floor. "Guess not."

At that instant, a man's head popped inside the chamber. Though unfamiliar at first, upon further inspection, James recognized Dylan, a Jonilan soldier Janice had introduced him to a while back. They had played Rubarg together.

"Sorry to interrupt, but they need you in the com room ASAP."

After a frustrated exhale, Janice acquiesced. "All right, I'll be right there." She hopped to her feet and then smiled at James. "It's been nice talking with you, James, but I've got to go now."

"Hey, James"—Dylan waved at him—"we're pretty busy, but once this damn strike is over, what do you say the three of us and Patricia have another Rubarg tournament?"

"Sure thing!"

With that, they both left, leaving James alone. A sigh escaped his mouth as he wondered what to do. In the end, he sat down by himself without finding a decent answer to that particular question.

And so she was gone, leaving me alone except for Nadia's picture. With that in mind, I slid it out of my wallet, stared into her blue eyes and forced a smile. As much as I loved her, it had been nice having company that could actually talk back.

—Thoughts of James Hunter, Hocmar 28, 2134, on the Nirnivian calendar

Chapter 17

With Diabo out of commission, Stalker found himself in charge of BBR. In theory, the role should've gone to Plague, but the decrepit mutant refused to lead due to his health. That put Stalker in an awkward position. A master of stealth, his strength lay in hiding in the shadows and keeping a low profile. As the boss, however, he had to be heard and seen by everyone. Being the center of attention made him feel exposed and vulnerable. Despite his recent disapproval of Diabo's methods, he wished him a prompt recovery. And it'd be best for BBR too. The explosion had done more than break the crimson beast's body. It had terrified his followers. Now people feared to participate in similar raids in case they suffered the same fate. Also, they'd believed Diabo to be invincible, and witnessing him reduced to a bedridden wreck had shattered their confidence. Many questioned BBR's chance of success. The odds had always been against them, of course, but that fact had grown clearer than ever thanks to Diabo's near demise.

In order to help diminish their men's qualms, Stalker had decided they needed to discover how Ostark had managed to cause the explosion at such a perfect moment. A simple bomb on a timer wouldn't manage the feat. Besides, a basic technique like that implied a suicide mission, and Doctor Death preferred not to waste his soldiers' lives. Stalker doubted Diabo served as a valued enough target to incite the cyborg to break this rule. Perhaps, then, someone had detonated the explosives manually. That seemed doubtful, though. BBR had killed every Ostarkiran, and any observer capable of accomplishing the task would've been incapacitated by Allison.

Plague had agreed that they must discover the truth, and he'd started working on a solution. Unfortunately, he faced an imposing problem: Due to a lack of evidence and clues, his lone option appeared to be crafting guesses out of thin air. That rendered his odds poor, but then their luck changed. A few days before, BBR had raided another transport. They'd won without trouble, and as they'd searched the contents, they'd discovered common explosives armed with a detonator unlike any other. The goons had defused the bomb and brought it back for study. After several tests, Plague had obtained results, and now he disclosed his findings to Stalker through video conference.

On the screen, Plague played with a small gadget. While Stalker discerned a shape manipulated by the zombie's hand, it lacked definition thanks to the grainy and skipping transmission. The occasional static burst covering their voices also made the conversation hard to understand, but they managed.

"This little baby," Plague said in his harsh tone as he gestured toward the apparatus, "was designed to destroy us."

Stalker gave an unimpressed shrug as he rolled his eyes. "Duh, who else is attacking their trucks?" As soon as he uttered the words, Stalker regretted his callousness. On occasion, his sarcastic bent showed itself.

If his behavior offended Plague, Plague's body language concealed it well. Stalker noticed no physical reaction. Instead, Plague went on, "No, not BBR. I mean us—the three founders."

Stalker recoiled in his seat a bit and frowned. "Huh? But Diabo and me aren't on every attack, and you're never part of it. How did the bastards know one of us would be there?"

"My guess is they didn't. This detonator, I noticed, reacts to me when I'm close enough."

After a second, Stalker understood the implications and snapped his fingers. "The truck exploded when Diabo got close."

Plague imitated a gun with his index finger and thumb, indicating Stalker had hit the mark. "Exactly! We tested it. It responds to DNA samples from me, you and Diabo, but no one else."

"Not even Wrathchild and Allison?"

Plague shook his head. "Nope—which isn't really surprising. Sure, they have special powers, but for different reasons than us. Wrath was born a mutant, Allison is a visitor, but we received gene therapy. Our DNA shares traits that aren't found in nature. This detonator detects those traits and"—he separated his arm from his body in a motion mimicking an explosion—"boom!"

Stalker gritted his teeth. "How is that possible? How can that thing detect our DNA without touching us?"

Ashamed, Plague lowered his gazed until it met the floor. "I'm sorry. We've studied the device, but... I don't understand how it works. It's just impossible. If I wasn't a man of science, I'd say it's magic. No doubt in my mind, Doctor Death invented that thing himself."

Stalker nodded. "Yeah... that son o' a bitch has a knack for doing the impossible. Whatever, the important part is, the Doctor's getting tired of us. Ostark hasn't been able to counter Allison yet, so they won't attack too directly. But offing any of the founders would crush BBR. Me and Diabo are on those assault teams all the freaking time, so this was meant to get rid o' us. Luckily for us, they made a mistake:

the charge wasn't 'nough to finish that douche Diabo. If it had been me..." He exhaled. "They ain't gonna mess up like this again. We've been hiding behind Allison and figured they couldn't do anything 'bout it. It became routine, and they used that to trick us. We'll have to be more careful."

"Yes." The decaying mutant acquiesced. "These bombs are easy to avoid. You and Diabo just have to stay far from the trucks. But I have a feeling the Ostarkirans have more in store for us."

"Yeah, no question there." Next, Stalker opened his mouth but hesitated for a second. "There's only one good thing about this. Since the boss is out of the loop, we can delay those stupid attacks on Nirnivia." He groaned. "But we can't always count on Diabo getting messed up to save our asses. We still have to get him to calm the freak down."

Plague dismissed the notion with a wave. "Don't worry about him. He's a firebrand all right, but he's manageable. Just remember: direct confrontation doesn't help with Diabo. That only gets him more pissed off. Diabo has a one-track mind, and he's impulsive, so trying to convince him on the spot backfires. The trick is to wait until he cools down and then it's easier to deal with him. Psychology, my friend, that's the key. Together, we'll manipulate him while making him believe he's in charge." He cackled. "Diabo is not too sharp a guy. He'll fall for it."

Unimpressed, Stalker crossed his arms. "And what if you're wrong about that?"

"I'm planning for that case too." Plague sighed. "But I'd rather not go there. Either way, short-term, we better make this work and we will. Trust me."

Chapter 18

Osmoro 31, 2134, on the Nirnivian calendar

In his office, Daniel Ricdeau reached for his coffeepot, eyes barely opened. Mid-motion, he yawned. His job demanded long overtime in the best circumstances, and the strike exacerbated that fact. Last night, he'd slept for three hours, which would be all right if it hadn't been the case since the techs had formed their union. Even at this precise moment, he remained in Valardir after hours to discuss the issue and discover a solution. His trusted Koporal sat on the other side of the desk, studying the notes from the latest negotiation session with a frown visible on his brow. More than once during his reading, Tigh scratched his head in confusion. As he watched his colleague, Daniel poured coffee into his white mug.

Many disliked Ron, hated him even. They deemed the Koporal harsh, abrasive, and unpleasant in general. Quite often, an officer or a councillor asked Daniel how he endured the man's antics. The truth was that it demanded little effort. Yes, Ron had a bad temper, so Daniel understood his lack of popularity. After all, they hadn't gotten along at first. Years of shared missions meant they'd had to grow used to each other, and eventually, acceptance had become friendship. Besides, while the Koporal's tantrums could be intimidating and annoying, when taken with the proper grain of salt, they provided considerable entertainment.

With that thought, Daniel brought the cup to his lips. He almost swallowed a sip when Ron glared at him. "For the love of God, Dan, what are you doing?"

Head tilted, a perplexed Daniel said, "Drinking coffee?"

"No, you're not: you poured yourself cream!"

A glance downward and indeed Daniel noticed the white liquid inside his mug. Baffled, he closed his eyes and laughed. The mistake might've embarrassed a younger version of himself, but at his age, he had suffered far worse. "Oh, my... I need some sleep, don't I?"

A grunt accompanied by a nod came from Ron. "Yeah, me too. I slept two hours last night." Tigh offered Daniel a sad smile. "And it'll be the freaking same tonight."

"I'm afraid you're right. We have to stay on guard: Doctor Death's planning something." Daniel paused. "You know, Rose caused a controversy at the Council. She said he won't do anything because while he wants to capture her, he'd rather not harm Nirnivia. She's delusional. Our old friend has something big coming our way." He shuddered. "I can sense it."

After a chuckle, Ron shook his head in a derisive manner. "Your daughter's holy connections gave her a wrong tip, huh?"

A glowering Daniel crossed his arms. "That's blasphemy." While he maintained a reasonable volume, menace infused his tone.

Unconcerned, Ron dismissed the accusation with a wave of his hand. "Oh please, cut that crap. You recognize a joke when you hear one."

"Sure, Ron," Daniel replied with a grin. If he'd tried that with any other subordinate, the poor fellow would have been horrified, but it took a lot more to shake up his Koporal. Many assumed Ron had learned Daniel's temperament by now and recognized when he kidded around. Though it was a reasonable assumption, the reality was that Tigh possessed nerves of steel. Despite his abundant complaints, when facing a dangerous mission, few things scared him.

As if something popped into his mind, Ron snapped his fingers. "Speaking of Rose, how are your two lovely daughters doing?"

"When it comes to Janice, I don't know!" Daniel shrugged. "I haven't been in touch. Busy and tired, I guess. I can tell you she's got her work cut out for her. She must regret joining the military." He jested... more or less.

The Koporal chuckled. "I wouldn't blame her."

"As for Rose, I talked to her yesterday. She's trying to figure out a solution, like everyone. Thanks to the Council's suggestions, we've been able to optimize NISDA's budget, but it won't be enough. Rose will donate money from the Melkar's fund for the needy to help out, but there are limits to what she can do on that front without hurting those who depend on her charity, and she won't go that far. I'm not convinced we can give the techs an offer they'll accept."

"This whole goddamn mess is my fault." Ron slumped back in his chair and bent his neck downward. "I pissed off that Jonathan guy, and he's screwing with me. Not only that, but that video hurt us. I've been an idiot."

"Yes, but you're putting too much of the blame on your shoulders." Daniel leaned forward. "The contract is what pushed them over the edge."

Tigh rolled his eyes. "Yeah, but I still screwed up. Once this is over, I swear I'll be more courteous."

Daniel snorted. "For two minutes."

"Yeah, you're right, I'm an asshole. I can't change that. But I wish I could think of a way out."

As he spotted an opportunity, Daniel rubbed his chin. "I'm glad you said that. There might be something you can do. Rose asked me if I'd be willing to take a salary cut myself to reduce NISDA's financial strain. I figured I'm a rich old man. I'll survive without a year of salary. So, I'm donating it all to the cause."

"What?" Ron squinted. "That's extreme, Dan."

"Yes, and even then, it won't be enough, but Rose hopes the gesture will convince other high-ranking officers to contribute." A grinning Daniel joined his fingers in a pyramid shape. "Since you feel responsible, maybe you'll join me?"

"Son of a gun!" Tigh grimaced. "Your daughter ain't messing around, is she?" He groaned. "Ah, what the freak? I've got plenty of savings. I'll give my salary for a year too."

"You don't have to go that far."

"Yeah, well, I doubt you'll get much charity from the others, so we both better give everything we can."

Daniel lifted his shoulders, only to lower them a second later. "Hmm, you never know. They might surprise us. Freak, you just did!"

Chapter 19

Yushidor 4, 2134, on the Nirnivian calendar

On several occasions now, Jonathan Rivers and a few other strikers had met with NISDA's representatives and discussed the techs' demands, NISDA's financial situation and potential compromises. Though those meetings could grow tense, they'd made undeniable progress. NISDA had revealed information that helped explain their position. Jonathan had already known they suffered money-wise, but the budget proved direr than expected. Still, through constant efforts and concessions, they discovered paths forward.

In fact, not long ago, NISDA had proposed an offer everyone hoped would mean a return to work for the techs. First, they'd reinstated overtime compensation, though at a reduced rate. More importantly, while a pay cut remained inevitable, it had been slashed by seventy percent. Most believed this to be the best possible deal under the current circumstances, and Jonathan counted among their number. His understanding had bolstered morale for the negotiators and promoted a sense of imminent success. Too bad it didn't turn out that way.

Jonathan had tried. For hours, he'd explained in detail the conundrum NISDA found themselves in, the new contract's virtues, and the hoops they'd jumped through to achieve it. Regardless of his efforts, his colleagues voted to reject the offer. While they accepted the condition related to overtime, they refused any reduction in salaries. From their point of view, they deserved the standard small cost-of-living raise, especially considering Nirnivia's high inflation. That they'd agreed to forgo that perk already served as a concession. No question, Jonathan sympathized with their position, but he realized they demanded the unattainable.

When he arrived at the gathering, a sense of optimism encompassed the room. As he sat at the table, those on the other side grinned and nodded at him, confident he brought good news. Then he announced what had happened, and the mood changed. Several of the negotiators remained immobile, slack-jawed and unable to react due to their shock. Quite a few glared at Jonathan, filled with hostility. Constance Prim's face turned red, and she clenched her fist in frustration.

"You are aware," a balding man adjusting his glasses said, "our last offer is extremely generous, all things considered. Mr. Rivers, we showed you the numbers. Several high-ranking officers donated a large part of their salary for you and your colleagues' sake. The Commander and the Koporal went as far as giving away the whole thing! Why, Her Holiness is even financing you through her charity. Surely you'll agree, we are trying our best."

Jonathan acquiesced. "Yes, I do."

"Then why?"

"It's not me." After a disappointed exhale, he threw his hands in the air. "I would've taken your offer, but my colleagues voted against it. They chose me as the leader of the union, and as such, I made an implicit promise I'd fight for them till the end. Since they decided to continue, it's my responsibility to keep that promise."

After a sharp groan, Constance Prim leaned forward, squinting so hard her eyes almost popped out of her head.

"Don't think we'll take this lying down. The Council has been lenient so far, but you've crossed a line. I doubt they'll show mercy from here on."

Jonathan gave a sigh followed by a quick nod. "Yes, I expect that much."

Chapter 20

Yushidor 5, 2134, on the Nirnivian calendar

Rose only rested her eyes, or at least that was the idea. The next Council assembly started in a few minutes. Dependable, Kristina had set up the teleconferencing equipment in advance, so she enjoyed a brief respite. She closed her eyes for a second and drifted into a light slumber. Perhaps not the best moment, but how she needed that nap. However, a familiar voice woke her up.

"Rose, I'm sorry, but you have a meeting soon, remember?" the blond assistant said as she gently poked Rose.

"Uh? Oh, thanks." Rose yawned stretched her arms. Kristina then offered a cup emitting a dreadful stink. Rose recognized the odor, and her mouth contorted in disgust. "Coffee? I hate coffee."

"I know, but if you don't drink up, you might fall asleep in front of all the councillors. You don't want that, do you?"

"I guess not."

Resigned, Rose took a sip. The sour taste made her gag as always, but Kristina had a point. Because of the strike, her political tasks had increased in number, and she was working too much for her own good. In fact, the ordeal was causing her to neglect her Melkar's duties. She had failed to address the population in a while. Her mother had chastised her about it, and Rose had promised she'd deliver a short lecture later that day. There was only one small problem.

"Um, Kristina, I'm supposed to do a sermon after, but..."

A smile formed on the assistant's lips. "You don't have anything ready."

"You got it." Rose squirmed. "I normally write my own material, and I realize that's not why I hired you."

Giggling, Kristina dismissed Rose's apology with a wave. "Don't worry, I'll prepare something. It's okay, don't feel bad about it."

"Thank you so much, you're a lifesaver." Not mere words, but rather an absolute truth. The blond woman often appeared distant and gloomy, but she proved reliable and dedicated no matter the circumstances. Without her, Rose had no idea how she'd manage.

***

The councillors' low spirit echoed Rose's mood to perfection. Throughout the whole session, people displayed a lack of energy and interest. The political meetings always presented their fair share of conflict, but today proved beyond ridiculous. Patience disappeared around the table and they snapped at each other. The poor moderator, Doug Thomson, had imposed three fines already, to little effect.

"Well, it's finally time to talk about what we're all waiting for." Doug Thomson's voice sounded tired and rough, as if he suffered from a sore throat. Despite his apparent discomfort, he chose not to reach for his glass of water but instead his folder, from which he pulled a sheet of paper. Then he fished out his glasses, placed them on his nose and started reading. "A few days ago, NISDA made a new contract offer to their techs. The Council helped in drafting it, and NISDA went above and beyond to prepare the best deal they could, but the strikers refused. As you can imagine, NISDA is furious and they are requesting we raise the fines to the maximum amount." Doug scanned the room. "Are there any objections?"

The weight of the chamber fell on Rose. She endured everyone's glare. "Um, I understand where NISDA is coming from, and I agree that the strikers are unreasonable, but one hundred percent..." Several disappointed moans echoed. In the distance, Rose spotted Jade Carlson roll her eyes. And did John Travers facepalm? "Look, I'm not against it fully. It's just that there has to be another way."

The instant she finished her sentence, Erika Master leaned forward and smirked. "Maybe if someone they respected and idolized tried convincing them, they'd listen."

Furious, Doug Thomson banged his gavel, interrupting Erika. "That's inappropriate, Councillor Master. Speaking of fines, you've just earned your second one today. I hope it was worth it. Please continue, Councillor Ricdeau."

She sighed. "I don't have any idea, and I can tell you have already decided. There's no way for me to stop you by myself." She paused as she winced. "So, I guess I have no objection, but due to my moral dilemma I will abstain from voting." And that was how the vote ended up being 11–0, a rare event indeed.

***

Less than a minute after the Council meeting ended, a notification for a voice chat request popped up on Rose's screen. A glance at the white window revealed Doug Thomson's picture. Surprised, Rose frowned. Why did the esteemed moderator need to contact her when they'd literally just parted ways? At least she hadn't removed her microphone, so taking the call should be simple. A press of the accept button would suffice. Yet a bit of apprehension assailed Rose, and she hesitated. Her bad luck with computers might strike again. Thank God Kristina took pity and accomplished the action in her stead while stifling a giggle, or Thomson might've hung up. Rose thanked the assistant under her breath as an image of Doug filled the monitor. He appeared to be in an excellent mood. He offered a pleasant smile as light reflected from his large bald head. Despite his calm demeanor, Rose sensed a tension in his jaw muscles.

"Councillor Ricdeau, thank you for taking my call."

"My pleasure. How are you and your husband doing, Mr. Thomson?"

"Oh, we're both doing great!" The smile widened, and a slight blush appeared on his dark cheeks. "In fact, we're celebrating our twentieth anniversary this weekend."

An impressed whistle came from Rose. "Wow, congratulations!"

"Thank you." Doug licked his lips. "Councillor Ricdeau, I have a delicate matter I wish to discuss." He shook his head. "Now, I don't approve of Councillor Master's behavior, but I understand why she did it. The strikers are putting us in a tough spot. NISDA is beyond disorganized at this point, and the situation must be resolved quickly. I'm afraid of what will happen if it isn't. As the Melkar, people listen to your opinion. If you address the techs, you might change their minds, and you know that would be the right course of action for them."

Rose sighed. "Actually, you're not the first one who suggested that to me. Manipulating people through their religious convictions would be unethical. The strikers have to make their decision for themselves, not because their prophet put the fear of God in them."

"Ethical concerns are important, and I respect your integrity." Thomson raised his hands as if shielding himself. "But, as leaders, sometimes we have to compromise our morals for the good of society. I believe this is such an occasion."

"Maybe so, but... I'm sorry, Moderator Thomson, the Melkar has to have higher standards than that."

A quick nod and then Doug bent his head downward. "Don't be sorry. You know these matters better than me. I trust your judgment."

Chapter 21

Yushidor 6, 2134, on the Nirnivian calendar

I got hungry in the afternoon, so I figured I'd grab a snack at the cafeteria. When I exited my room, I saw Brucie standing guard at Rose's door. That was strange. It happened often in the evening, but during the day, he was almost always with her.

—Thoughts of James Hunter, Hocmar 28, 2134, on the Nirnivian calendar

"Hey, James, my man," Brucie said as James entered the corridor. With a half-smile, the bodyguard presented his palm, and James high-fived him. "What's goin' on, bro?"

"Um, not much. Just grabbing something to eat." He had a moment of hesitation as he feared hurting Brucie's feelings with his next remark. In the end, he decided that seemed improbable. "Um, you guys having a lovers' spat?"

Slapping his thigh, Brucie erupted in a chortle. James relaxed as his jest had gone well. "Nah, dude, nothing like that. She wants her privacy. Ya know, doing stuff, didn't say what." Brucie scowled as he paused. "Ya wanna hear what I think? She's talking to her mirror."

"Uh, what?" Startled by the revelation, James stepped back. Yet, once he considered it, he recalled hearing Brucie mention that fact before, though he failed to remember when.

"Yeah, it's like, Ulgorack talks to her through her reflection and shit. I tell ya, it's freaking crazy."

"Really?"

Brucie nodded. "Sure, dude, the first Melkar did strange crap too. They say she had this weird-ass empty book. She wrote questions in there and then she wrote the answers." The bodyguard's hand started moving as if he scribbled a note with a pencil. "But she ain't the one who wrote 'em; Ulgorack did it through her. Freaky stuff. I guess the mirror is Rose's way of doing the same thing, ya know?"

Damn, I couldn't believe my ears. That was so easy to fake, it was absurd. I could've explained to him for hours how ridiculous he was, but I didn't want to piss him off, so I shut up.

—Thoughts of James Hunter, Hocmar 28, 2134, on the Nirnivian calendar

Then Brucie snapped his fingers as something popped into his mind. "Hey, yeah, that's right, check this out." With a giggle, he reached for a minicomp attached to his belt. After switching it on, he grabbed the stylus and poked at the device several times in succession. That conjured up images of Kristina in James's brain. "Some guy filmed her way back when. Ya know, before she lived here. A paparazzi asshole."

The bodyguard waved for James to approach and showed him the screen. It displayed Rose staring at a mirror, her lips parted with surprising energy, as if she engaged in a passionate debate. The whole time, her arms moved in dramatic gestures. At one point, she turned around, began massaging her temples and took a few steps back before returning to the reflecting glass. That was when James averted his gaze.

It felt wrong looking at her. Kind of like peeking at her undressing. Um, I mean, she was fully dressed, I swear, but... I

was still intruding on a private moment she didn't want to share.

—Thoughts of James Hunter, Hocmar 28, 2134, on the Nirnivian calendar

"That's enough, I get the idea."

A chortle came from Brucie. "Told ya it's freaky."

Somehow, James had the impression the muscle-bound man failed to grasp the actual reason for his discomfort. As he preferred avoiding such an awkward conversation, he mumbled, "Yeah, sure." Then they exchanged a few more pleasantries and James resumed his trip to the cafeteria.

Chapter 22

The mirror presented a smooth surface except for the crack near the bottom. When the incident had occurred, Rose had considered buying a replacement. However, she'd used this particular glass for her so-called divination séance since childhood and feared that replacing it might impede her. No reason to assume so. In fact, she employed others on occasion, including a pocket one she kept in her purse for emergencies. Still, in the end, she decided to keep it despite the blemish. At first the fissure distracted her, but she had grown accustomed to the damage. Why, then, did she stare at the crevice instead of asking for assistance?

In truth, she deduced the answer. Discussion with her double proved... uncomfortable at best, downright painful at worst. Oh, that hadn't always been the case. In the beginning, the cryptic conversations had confused her poor brain, but nothing unpleasant had happened. In later years, though, that'd changed. The reflection resembled Rose, but details were off. Something in the eyes; something in the eerie smile. Despite her apprehension, she decided she lacked alternatives.

A hard swallow and she said, "I need your help. This strike won't end. People on both sides are suffering. It seems we have run out of options."

"Run out of options?" The double giggled. "Oh, how silly. Are you kidding me? Life is a sea of possibilities, always plenty, though they are sometimes nasty."

"All right, would you prefer me to say that it seems we have run out of acceptable courses of action?"

The reflection's eyes glimmered in an unsettling manner. Her movement stopped. The smile vanished, replaced by a blank expression. With a gasp, Rose realized she'd loathe whatever came next. A headache assailed her.

"Acceptable? It's possible there are no acceptable ways. But you've never been able to accept that."

Prey to a sudden wave of exhaustion, Rose bent her head and rubbed her brow. "I'm... so tired. I can't think. Please, stop with the vagueness. Can't you tell me what I have to do?"

"What you have to do?" The image erupted in a maddening cackle. When she spoke again, the voice sounded distorted, and it became more garbled with every syllable. "What you have to do? You already know! You have to... kill yourself!"

Eyes wide and covered in sweat, Rose's breathing accelerated. Why? Why did her reflection say those horrible words? It had started not long before the war. "No! No! Stop, please!"

Puzzled, the image tilted her head and scratched the top of it. "But that would make things right! You should be dead. You were supposed to die years ago!"

Another cryptic message her twin had recited for a while. What did it mean? It had to be linked to that dreadful disease. Against all odds, she'd survived, and yet...

"If I committed suicide, I'd be banished into nothingness."

The instant she finished her sentence, the background reproduced in the mirror turned black. The reflection's irises vanished, replaced by pure white orbs interspersed with reddish veins. Lesions opened over her face. Blood dripped faster and faster from the gashes covering her whole body. Rose attempted to avert her gaze, but a morbid curiosity prevented her.

"Banished into nothingness... why deny the obvious truth? That is your greatest desire. What you have seen, what you have done! You can't stand it anymore." She clenched her fist. "You hate yourself so much, you want to be erased!"

A few tears dropped on Rose's cheeks. "No! No! You're wrong!"

"You... are correct, I apologize. You do not crave nothingness." Deducing the nightmare had concluded, Rose relaxed, but then the double burst into flames, charring her skin. "Nothingness is not enough... you want to burn for your sins!"

Rose screamed and jerked backward. The sudden motion rendered her chair unstable, and she fell down. On the floor, she covered her face, weeping.

"Stop it, go away!"

Thankfully, the glass returned to normal. Rather than utter nonsense, the reflection mimicked Rose's movements as intended. Rose got to her feet, collapsed on her desk and cried. The fact that her subconscious would claim such rubbish was atrocious in itself, but what if her followers were correct? What if she was the Melkar and Ulgorack spoke those horrible words? She failed to comprehend the implications but expected a negative connotation.

Chapter 23

Yushidor 9, 2134, on the Nirnivian calendar

The Good Doctor and I had matters to discuss. The logical meeting place was his office, but he was working on his Alcharia cure, so we met in the laboratory. I spoke to his back most of the time as he manipulated his vials and microscope. One might expect such a distraction would stop him from focusing on the conversation, but he never missed a detail.

—Thoughts of Evelyn Losier, Hocmar 28, 2134, on the Nirnivian calendar.

During a natural pause in the dialogue, the president lifted a test tube filled with a yellow liquid. In his other palm he clutched a dropper, which he positioned above the glass container. He achieved a perfectly steady hand. Tension gripped Evelyn, and her fingers caressed the front of her neck. By his demeanor, his current action required precision. One drop, two drops...

Then the wireless phone on the table rang. Evelyn was concentrating so hard on the Good Doctor's task that the chime made her jump. The cyborg, however, remained immobile, though the emoticon in his electronic eye changed to one with a surprised O-shaped mouth. Despite a lack of reaction, Evelyn sensed his disappointment at being interrupted at a critical point in his experience. Still, he rested the measuring cylinder and seized the receiver.

"Yes, yes, I see." There was a short silence as he listened to his interlocutor. "Then it is confirmed. Very well, you may proceed as planned."

The exchange ended and the mechanical man hung up, lowering his head. The smile on his infamous LED visage turned upside down. Then he glanced at Evelyn.

"It appears you and the cabinet will have your wish. Nirnivian blood will flow."

A pang in Evelyn's heart assailed her, and she covered her sternum with her palm. Did he truly think so badly of her?

"Good Doctor, I don't want this. None of us want this!" In her mind, she added, *Except maybe General Torn.* "But we've been caught in this artificial stalemate for years, and it has to be resolved eventually! Do you really believe we can manage that without casualties?"

"I suppose not, but one does hope." The president turned toward his tools and picked them up. In her brain, Evelyn imagined the resigned sigh his body denied. "Do not forget, Evelyn, that resorting to violence is not a show of strength, but rather a display of our failures."

***

A gust of wind blew a dust cloud in Catherine's face. Had this happened a month earlier, she would have erupted in a cough. But these proved a common occurrence in the Orontian desert, and she had soon grown used to them. Her only reaction was to move a strand of her auburn hair that the breeze had displaced. Then she glanced at the plans she held before looking at the incomplete structure born in large part from her design. A group of men and women toiled on the launchpad, no doubt covered in sweat due to the hard-hitting sun. A cacophony of yells, singing, and clattering tools engulfed the area, explaining the earplugs Catherine wore.

Several workers passed water bottles around. Hydration stood as a priority here. One of them had just offered Catherine such a beverage, and she'd snatched it. In a quick motion, she unscrewed the cap and swallowed over half the contents in a single gulp. As the cold liquid soothed her parched throat, she wondered how in the world she'd ended up here. When NISDA had presented her, a civilian engineer, with a military contract, her relatives and close friends had assumed she'd reject it. The day she'd announced that she'd accepted, she'd stunned everyone, most of all her husband, Ken. They'd immediately questioned her choice.

Why would she, a woman who had amassed a small fortune, take the risk? The fact that she'd earned a reputation as a scaredy-pissack only increased the confusion. Through her school years, how many pranks involving plastic insects and fake rodents had she endured? Too great a number to count, yet they always succeeded. Even as an adult, she fell for it more often than not, and Ken, as well as their son and daughter, teased her about it constantly. That someone so easily frightened was joining a mission in the neutral zone where her life would be in constant danger boggled their minds. The thing was, while she feared death, that outcome caused less dread than those disgusting critters. Same for the Ostarkirans they defied by their very presence in this restricted area. Sure, that didn't make sense as she cowered from the lesser threat, but Gorumars were weird like that.

Besides, how could she pass it up? NISDA had proposed an intriguing project the likes of which she'd never imagined participating in. From a professional perspective, it was the opportunity of a lifetime. Not only would it be her crowning achievement as an engineer, but she'd aid her country when it needed her the most. As a NISDA officer, Ken agreed she'd be contributing to a crucial program that might decide Nirnivia's fate, and so he respected her choice. Not that that meant he didn't worry. On the contrary, he'd tried to dissuade her.

A scowl formed on Catherine's brow as a low rumble reached her ears. The roar sounded like engines approaching their site, drowning out their own machinery orchestra. Curious, Catherine turned her head and scanned the area. There in the distance, shapes were flying through the sky. Were they... jets? Soon the figures grew closer, confirming her suspicion. Before she had a chance to swallow hard, someone grabbed her and pulled her toward cover. The would-be savior screamed words she failed to comprehend.

Once the planes reached their camps, they dropped their bombs. Gigantic explosions rocked the world as massive fireballs filled Catherine's view. The artificial quake threw her on the ground, and the tremors bounced her around. She lost any sense of direction. A dreadful pain assailed her whole body, and the attack left her covered in bruises. In the middle of the lunacy, she looked at the launchpad. A mere flaming wreck remained. The assault lasted less than a minute, but it might as well have been hours from her perspective.

Once the jets vanished, Catherine forced herself to sit up. The gesture demanded a lot of effort—every single bone ached. After she succeeded, her stomach twisted and she retched. As she puked, she witnessed the chaos surrounding her. Dead bodies everywhere. Surviving soldiers ran around the camp, helping the wounded. One of them rushed to her.

"Catherine, are you okay? Catherine, do you hear me?" Unable to speak, she nodded, causing her neck to complain in a most irritating manner. The man shoved his left hand right before her nose. "How many fingers do you see?"

Frustrated, Catherine almost pushed those six fingers out of her space, but then she detected footsteps. Troops walked toward the camp from every direction. Horrified, Catherine recognized their Ostarkiran uniforms and she wailed. The soldier at her side jumped to his feet and reached for his gun. A volley of bullets struck his head and torso, propelling him backward as his blood splashed on the sand.

Tears rolled down Catherine's cheeks as she crawled away from the coming horde, moaning. Impossible to escape; an enemy outpaced her and kicked her in the stomach. After several coughs brought by the impact, Catherine discovered she still had vomit left in her. The woman who hit her aimed her firearm and said, "Freaking BBR scum."

Chapter 24

Yushidor 10, 2134, on the Nirnivian calendar

Hunched over his desk and with his left hand covering his forehead, Daniel Ricdeau studied the golden fluid inside the shot glass. He picked it up and swirled the liquid within. A whiff of the sweet aroma caressed his nostrils. Priceless uisge—completely against regulation, as his Koporal often said. And he had a point. Should word reach the Council, they'd make a fuss. Then again, perhaps they'd understand that while intoxicating, in moderation, nothing steeled the nerves as effectively.

On that thought, Daniel gulped down his beverage. His lips contorted in a slight grimace at the strong flavor. Fruity, yet possessing a powerful kick, the uisge left his throat burning. Once the sensation passed, Daniel let out a satisfied grunt. That hit the spot. Tempted, he glanced at the bottle resting on his bureau, but he dismissed indulging in seconds. Courage would be useless if he was rendered drunk. Instead, he focused on the red videophone. Ten more minutes and it would ring. Where the freak was Tigh?

Though unassuming in appearance, except for the uncommon color, that phone served as the lone line of communication with Ostark. On the dawn of the uneasy peace, Doctor Death had insisted on its creation. The two countries needed to communicate for diplomacy and to avoid a potential crisis that might reignite the war. Along with the videophone, the system included a beeper with which Daniel and the president could exchange short twenty-character texts. In this manner, the cyborg had arranged an urgent meeting with Daniel and Ron Tigh, requesting to speak in an hour. Such a brief delay was unusual and implied an incoming serious discussion.

When Daniel had read the message, his spirits had sunk. Not surprising, considering it might spell Nirnivia's doom. Earlier this morning, they'd received reports that NISDA had lost contact with all their spies in Ostarkiran territory. With great effort, they'd infiltrated six undercover agents into the Ostark military, though they'd assumed minor positions, limiting their potential. Now they couldn't be reached, suggesting they had been discovered. Of course, the possibility of technical difficulties remained, but if the worst had happened... well, Ostark wouldn't be pleased.

The bad news kept on rolling. Soon after, they lost communication with the Orontian launchpad. Because of the neutral zone, Ostark stood out of the range of Nirnivia's missiles, a problem they had solved with this secret project. Given their technology failed to travel the desired distance, they'd built a launcher closer to their target without violating their agreement with Ostark. How to accomplish such a feat? Well, the old treaty defined a confined area as the neutral zone. They simply chose a location far enough to the west that it wasn't part of the forbidden land. After the war, radiation prevented anyone from attempting a visit there, but since then the situation improved. One could survive there with oral medication, no need for injections. Technically, NISDA broke no rules, but who could tell how Ostark would react. Nirnivia's defiance might trigger a new war. Then again, they didn't have a choice. Despite the relative calm, Ostark remained their enemy. Nirnivia found itself outclassed by their superior armaments. They needed a way to deal a devastating blow to the neighboring nation, for deterrence and as a bargaining chip. Besides, Ostark also adopted that same strategy, even if NISDA lacked proof.

To claim the idea behind the launchpad was controversial would be a major understatement. The Council and NISDA had debated the subject for months and the discussions had been uncivil at best. A smile appeared on Daniel's visage as he remembered how Rose had opposed the plot. She'd fought against it, claiming Doctor Death would notice the strange activity in the desert and then they'd be doomed. At one point, she'd even attempted to convince Doug Thomson to invoke the Tabarar measure, but he'd rejected her motion. By the end, his dearest daughter remained the lone opponent to their plan. She'd warned them they were making a terrible mistake and he should've listened. Why had he ignored the Voice of God's pleas? Perhaps because she had sworn her position had nothing to do with a vision or her being the Melkar. Still, he had been a foolish old man.

Of course, they'd prepared for the eventuality of Ostark learning of the launchpad's existence. The group in charge had dressed in BBR garb, and none of their possessions linked them to NISDA. On the surface, they appeared as terrorists building a weapon of mass destruction. But would Doctor Death be fooled by such an obvious illusion? Daniel doubted it. At that moment, his interphone beeped and his secretary informed him the Koporal had arrived. Seconds later, the door slid open and an out-of-breath Tigh stumbled into the office.

"Sorry I'm late, Dan." He huffed. "Nicky caught me at the last minute."

"Oh?" Intrigued, Daniel straightened and started rubbing his hands. "Did they contact the launchpad?"

A shake of the head and Daniel's spirits sank even lower. "Nope. Dead silence there, but they reached one of the spies. He's okay. He missed his last report because of unforeseen circumstances, but his cover is still intact."

Daniel caressed his cheek. "Excellent, but no sign of the rest. It doesn't look good for them."

"And there's more. Nicky told me there are signs of hacking at the weakest points in our system. It's how they discovered the spies and the launchpad. And, uh"—Ron scratched the back of his head—"listen, Dan, this is weird as balls. They hacked research centers too but only accessed data about weapons targeting the BBR founders."

"Strange. Surely there's more interesting things in there." Daniel dismissed the notion with a wave and sighed. "Never mind, it's the least of our concerns."

Ron groaned. "You bet your ass it is. We're screwed."

"Maybe not..." Thoughtful, Daniel tapped his chin. "I mean, if Doctor Death wanted to destroy us because of the spies and the launchpad, why would he set up a meeting? Why not just mount a surprise attack and ravage us? They could, no problem. But he doesn't want the uneasy peace to end, not yet. Don't ask me why. The bastard's playing with us."

The videophone rang, interrupting his musings. The two men stared at each other, swallowing hard. With a trembling index finger, Daniel pressed the answer button. The cyborg's image appeared on the screen, and a robotic tone echoed.

"Good day, Commander Ricdeau, and thank you for meeting me on such a short notice."

"Good day to you too, Mr. President." Stay calm. No sign of guilt, nor fright. Keep a steady voice, but not to the point where it sounded suspicious. When he'd endured military training, Daniel had suffered through acting lessons for these exact situations, and it had paid off.

"I apologize for the inconvenience, but there are matters we must discuss. Not long ago, we noticed activity in an irradiate desert outside what is considered the habitable zone. At first, we suspected BBR to be up to something and mounted an air raid. After the fact, we investigated the site and concluded that the installation there were beyond the terrorists' capabilities and so deduced that NISDA were the one responsible. It is the only possibility." He shrugged. "There is no point denying it. At any rate, I thought I should inform you of the death of your soldiers."

From the corner of his eye, Daniel spotted Tigh wiping the sweat off his brow. As for himself, he scowled. What would he give for a normal voice whose emotions he could analyze? "For the sake of argument, let's say hypothetically speaking that you're right and it was us." He raised a menacing eyebrow. "In that case, we were legally allowed to be there, and you slaughtered our men and women without just cause. That's an act of war."

The Doctor leaned forward. "Then, hypothetically, you were building a launch platform capable of striking the heart of our country, that could be construed as an act of war in itself. At any rate, Ostark has no intention of breaking the uneasy peace over this matter as long as NISDA agrees to two conditions. First, you must admit you were the ones behind the launchpad. We know it was the case; denying it would accomplish nothing. Second, Ostark believes the borders of the neutral zone must be redefined to avoid any future similar incidents." The cyborg crossed his arms and the emoji in his electronic eye switched from a smile to a glare. "And so you have the final word. Are these terms acceptable, or shall we prepare for war?"

With a grimace, Daniel aimed a discreet glance at Tigh, who nodded. In truth, he expected his Koporal to agree, and he was in charge to begin with, but he preferred consulting him regardless. "Fine. Yes, NISDA built that launchpad. I assure you we had no intention to attack. It was a precaution in case of future conflicts."

"For what it's worth, I believe you, but it was still a foolish endeavor."

"Yes, well, we all make mistakes. As for the neutral zone's border, I agree we should revise them. Things have changed a lot since the old war, the terms are no longer appropriate."

"Excellent! I suggest we organize an official meeting to draft the required documents. I will get in touch with you as to the exact date. Have a great rest of your day, Commander Ricdeau."

"Wait! Were there any survivors?"

"Alas, no, though I promise if there had been any, they would have been returned to Nirnivia without harm."

With that, the communication ended. All the tension accumulated in Daniel's muscles left at once and he exhaled. A slight tremble assailed his body. As for Ron, he caressed his brow and then chuckled. "Oh, Dan, we almost screwed ourselves. We dodged a bullet. Thank God the freak's committed to the uneasy peace."

"Yes, for now, but I don't like it." Daniel rubbed his chin. "If only we knew why he's so committed in the first place. There's something fishy going on."

"Yep! Ah well, at least we live another day."

***

Head resting against his bathtub's edge, the rest of Gareth's body lay submerged as he stared at the white ceiling. A bug crawled up there, defying gravity. While not a thrilling sight, he kept his eyes fixed at it as the floral smell from the perfumed ampson salt he'd mixed into the water tickled his nose. Before the war, he'd never bathed, instead preferring the swiftness of a hot shower. Since then, his therapist had suggested bathing might help him relax after stressful days. In addition, the shrink claimed using special ampson salt would enhance the calming effect.

Gareth's anxiety improved, and he hadn't bothered taking a bath for months. Then he'd heard about the Orontian launchpad. Struck by panic, he'd turned to every trick the doctor had shown him, keeping the bath for when he returned home.

Ever since the Chestnut War had ended, Gareth had believed that the conflict had never reached a proper conclusion. This uneasy peace was an exercise in delaying the inevitable. That Nirnivia prepared a plan to aim missiles at the heart of Ostark confirmed his suspicions. In fact, now that Doctor Death had discovered their ploy and destroyed the platform, he assumed they stood on the brink of annihilation. That in mind, he remembered when he'd told his friend Janice how he felt about the Chestnut War. She'd worried about him and said he had to continue therapy for his own sake. And she had been right. No matter the cost, he'd stick to it, and he'd ace his future psychological evaluations. He'd earn the privilege of returning to active duty and leave his current desk job behind. When Ostark struck, he'd be ready to finish it, like they should have done years ago.

Chapter 25

Rose lay on her mattress, staring at the ceiling and holding her doll, Ms. Penny, while caressing her hair. Multiple thoughts raced through her mind. For weeks, she'd discussed the strike's repercussions with the Council and others. The consequences ranged from minimal to drastic, the worst being an attack by Ostark resulting in Nirnivian victims. Those fears she'd dismissed, as she'd doubted he would go that far. And yet, here they were. To be fair, the targets posed a threat to Ostark, and she supposed, from his point of view, retaliation proved necessary. Still, she hadn't expected such coldness from him. If only that damned launchpad had never existed, most of the casualties would've been avoided. Alas, they'd ignored her. When her dad had announced the news, she'd almost snapped and screamed, "I told you so." Somehow, she'd resisted the temptation. The past was the past, and those accusations served little purpose now.

The major question lingered: What came next? Several courses of action branched before her. Which should she choose? Not taking sides caused destruction. Would intervening stop the madness? Would it be an abuse of her position? Would she edge closer to nothingness? Yesterday, she'd deemed the answer to those questions to be yes, but today, doubts assailed her. As Rose pondered the situation, she asked Ms. Penny for advice, a fantasy she'd often indulged in during childhood. The doll couldn't answer, but something could. That in mind, she sat up on her mattress and glanced at her looking glass. She took in a hard swallow, followed by shivers as she recalled her recent experience. She'd question her sanity if she reattempted this, yet what alternative option remained? With an impending sense of regret crushing her, she released Ms. Penny and walked toward the mirror.

"It's you again!" her double said once within reach. "I upset you last time. I apologize. I meant to help, I swear." There was a pause, followed by a tilt of the head. "Do you hear them sing? So beautiful, yet so sad. They sing the hymns of self-destruction." Another mystery Rose had failed to solve. The reversed image had begun speaking those words soon after the war had started. More precisely, about two years before Doctor Death had become president. She'd tried deciphering the riddle in the past but found no success. It remained as cryptic as ever. Exhausted, Rose ignored the strange speech.

"What should I do? What's the right choice?"

"Right and wrong; so confusing. The answer can be surprising. You seek an absolute truth, but I fear it is relative."

"You could have just said that you don't know," Rose mumbled as she massaged her temples. "Why are you always so tortuous? Can't you give a straight answer for once?"

"No matter what you choose, the future will determine whether you made the correct decision or not. Take the path you assume will be easiest for you to live with, regardless of the result."

Frowning and caressing her chin, Rose contemplated her reflection's suggestion. A minute or two later, she nodded twice. "Thanks." She sighed. A tightening sensation around her heart warned she would blame herself for this choice. And yet a bad conscience was a small price to pay if it saved several lives, wasn't it?

Chapter 26

Yushidor 13, 2134, on the Nirnivian calendar

While I didn't understand all the details, a tragedy hap-pened. Several Nirnivians died in an Ostarkiran raid, something about a secret project. NISDA organized a military funeral to honor their soldiers' sacrifice. As usual, Rose couldn't attend in person, and she invited me to join her in her office for a live viewing of the event. Apparently, she planned to address the crowd. Given I had nothing better to do, and I felt she wanted moral support for her upcoming speech, I ac-cepted. They lent me a fancy black suit for the occasion. Right when I finished putting it on, Rose arrived at my room along with Brucie and Kristina. We talked about what would hap-pen at the ceremony for a bit. The thing that surprised me the most was that Rose still wore her white dress. When I asked why, she said we were in a hurry and didn't have time for an explanation, but I received one later on.

—Thoughts of James Hunter, Hocmar 28, 2134, on the Nirnivian calendar.

The memorial took place outside, in a national park filled with greenery. A large crowd occupied the area. Many wore NISDA uniforms. James believed he spotted Janice Ricdeau among them on the screen. Others, in a dif-ferent section, dressed in civilian clothes—no doubt the deceased's friends and relations. After a proper religious service, several people addressed the group, praising the departed ones' virtues. Daniel Ricdeau had his turn, fol-lowed by Ron Tigh and others. Everyone spoke with such genuine emotion, James's heart ached and tears rolled down his cheeks. The same held true for both Rose and Kristina. Even Brucie suffered occasional cases of dust in his eyes and blinked frequently.

***

Though the ceremony lasted for over an hour, Rose soon found herself delivering her eulogy. A sickening sensation invaded her stomach as she stood before the camera. In the park, a large monitor displayed her image to the weeping attendees: friends and families, superiors and colleagues. An oblivious sun shone upon them.

The first half of her speech honored the victims, praised their bravery, and thanked them for their service. She expressed her sympathy for those mourning their loss. That part she managed without issue. How often did she perform this particular routine?

Then she reached the moment she dreaded. Worried, she took a deep breath and paused. Her lips moved, but no words materialized. The temptation of biting her nails proved stronger than it had in years, but she kept her fingers from her teeth. In a desperate effort at regaining her courage, she glanced at Kristina and Brucie. The blond assistant offered a small nod while Brucie presented a discreet thumbs-up. Or was that just her imagination attempting to soothe her nerves? Either way, she steeled herself.

"I want to be clear—Ostark is to blame for this tragedy. Nobody else is responsible for the deaths of our soldiers." She spoke with a tremor in her voice. "However, I must still consider the facts. Without the challenges imposed by the strike, this wouldn't have happened. I realize this was not the techs' intention. They had genuine grievances that needed to be addressed, and I applaud their temerity. Too often, we let powerful people abuse us and don't fight back. They did, and that deserves respect. Unfortunately, since these noble beginnings, the situation has escalated to an unacceptable level. NISDA presented a reasonable offer, yet it was refused. As a result, Gorumars died, and should this madness continue, they won't be the last. And that is why I implore the union to reconsider its position, not only for Nirnivia's well-being"—Rose's lips twitched as her inner conflict raged; she hoped no one noticed—"but also for your souls. I fear this horrifying event is a warning, and that if you don't stop now, you will step toward nothingness. Again, this wasn't your fault, but please don't let this tragedy repeat itself."

Chapter 27

Yushidor 14, 2134, on the Nirnivian calendar

With furious keystrokes, Jonathan Rivers pummeled his keyboard. The familiar ticks his typing produced had never resounded so loud nor so fast. As he wrote his letter, he grumbled curse words aimed at his colleagues. When he reached the halfway point, Brian entered his office and said, "Hi." Jonathan mumbled back a response without interrupting his work.

"You sure left quickly. Everything all right?"

"Yeah, I'm fine." He groaned. "I couldn't stand being around those morons anymore." His voice shifted pitch, producing a mocking tone. "Ooh, any salary cut is unreasonable. We have to keep on fighting! A secret project is attacked by Ostark, killing several Nirnivian soldiers? That's the price to pay for justice. Executed spies? Who cares!" Furious, Jonathan slapped his desk, resulting in a thud. "Oh, but now, our big bird in the sky is telling us we've gone too far." Mouth gaping, Jonathan rested his hands against his cheek in a display of mock horror. "What have we done? Dead people is one thing, but offending a fake prophet... that's unacceptable. Let's hold an emergency vote, reverse our decision"—his normal volume morphed into a shout—"and get our freaking asses to work!"

Shocked, Brian stepped back and shielded himself with his palms. "Whoa, that's why you're pissed?" He frowned. "But didn't you want to end the strike?"

"Yes, and I'm glad it's over, but apparently I'm the only one who has independent thoughts, and that bothers me." He gave a disappointed shake of the head. "Their own religious texts warn that the Melkar is only a person and can be wrong. Yet they must obey her without considering the implications." He threw his hands in the air. "For crying out loud, Nirnivia put her in power and she didn't even run for it. They made her into a dictator. She didn't have to try. Freak, maybe she didn't want to become one. This country is filled with fools, and I've had enough."

A grimace formed on Brian's lips. "Look, you have a point, but you're exaggerating."

Jonathan dismissed the suggestion with a wave and growled.

"Whatever, let's change the subject. What are you working on, anyway?"

"Be my guest." With that, Jonathan jumped to his feet and gestured for Brian to take his place and read.

Obeying, Brian sat in the chair. Less than a minute later, he stared at Jonathan, scowling. "Is that...?"

"Yep. I'm sending it tonight."

After a hard swallow, Brian rose and patted Jonathan on the shoulder. "How about you sleep on it and see how you feel in the morning?"

"Nah, I've made up my mind."

***

The instant the rumor reached her ears, Rose decided to intervene. That was why she waited for Jonathan at the door to his office, despite having a packed schedule. She'd tried contacting the Jonilan technician by phone, but either by chance or by design, her calls remained unanswered.

After fifteen minutes, Rose considered leaving, but then Jonathan arrived. The bewilderment caused by her presence increased when she asked to talk in his office, but he accepted. Now, sitting in his chair and swiveling, Jonathan studied her curiously.

"All right, Your Holiness"—as always, a dose of sarcasm tainted his words—"what can I do for you?"

"Nothing much. I've heard rumors about you quitting and I was wondering whether it's true or not."

Jonathan nodded and adjusted his glasses. "Yes, I'd like to stay home and take care of my son. I've barely seen the little bugger lately, and it will be good to reconnect."

"That sounds nice." Pensive, Rose caressed her cheek. "But I'm surprised you're leaving after negotiating a better contract."

He shrugged. "Oh, but I've been planning it for months. I preferred not to abandon everyone when they were counting on me, so I stayed until I"—Jonathan threw a few mock punches—"finished the fight." He scowled. "Why do you care, anyway? No offense intended, but it's none of your business."

Rose sighed. "Well, I was wondering if my sermon influenced your decision."

With a wave, Jonathan dismissed the comment and laughed. "Nah, why would it?" The way he scratched his nose and shifted his body away convinced Rose otherwise. Through years as a politician and alleged prophet, she'd dealt with various people—a large enough number to recognize the signs of lying. Instead of confronting Jonathan, Rose crossed her arms and kept staring in silence. "Okay, fine, it did, but not much. It's not your fault. It's my colleagues'. Listen, I'm glad the strike is finished and the new terms are satisfactory, but... sorry for being blunt, but I'm stuck with morons. They didn't care that people died, but the Melkar comes along and asks them to stop and suddenly they have a conscience. That's asinine!" He groaned. "I need a break from society."

Rose bent her neck and tapped her chin with her index finger. "That's true, but you're not being completely honest. I don't think you're angry. You're scared. Scared of my influence on people. Scared of the danger I represent." Though Jonathan stayed quiet, a twitch confirmed her suspicion. "Jonathan, I understand your point of view, but you're imagining things. When I addressed the techs, it wasn't some grand plan I masterminded like you accused me of. I didn't intend to, but the situation deteriorated. No one had figured out a solution. I meant to have the crisis solved without my intervention, but I lacked that luxury. Yes, I have a lot of authority, both as a prophet and a councillor, but I won't abuse it. Does that reassure you?"

Jonathan chuckled. "No."

"Good!" Rose fixated on him as her lips contorted in a devious smirk. "You should be afraid. I'm dangerous." The tone she adopted grew menacing. "With a snap of my fingers, I could destroy you. Screw up your life, lock you up, get you killed... same for your family. If I played my cards right, no one would question my actions. So, yes, be terrified. If I wished, I could convince the people to revolt, overthrow the Council, and make me their supreme leader. Some would resist, but in the end, either I'd succeed or Nirnivia would be devastated. Or both..." She shook her head. "You should fear me." Her voice, which had been so strong just seconds before, faltered. "Though I hope you understand." She let out a few tears. "I'm also scared. I never wanted these wings. Jonathan, I have no idea what I'm doing, I admit it. In the past, people suffered because of my mistakes, and the fact that it will probably happen again keeps me awake at night."

Furious, Jonathan slapped his armrest, producing a thud. Then he hopped to his feet and pointed a condemning index finger at Rose. "Fine, you didn't choose those wings, but you accepted the position on the Council!"

"Only after the election degenerated into a circus act."

"So what?" Jonathan threw his hands up in the air. "You still had a choice. It was still wrong. You say you don't want power, but when it was within reach, you snatched it. How the freak am I supposed to trust you?"

"From my perspective, I was a young fool who saw an opportunity to help Nirnivia's population, but I can't tell you whether you should agree or not. If you judge that I'm a monster because I accepted a seat on the Council, that's your right." Rose forced a giggle. "And I'm glad you're screaming at me. People are blinded by religion. No matter what, they deem me a prophet. Even if I deny it, somehow they end up with stronger beliefs. But you're different. You use your brain and facts to make up your mind. Of course, you can be mistaken, but at least you realize the danger the Voice of God poses. You don't assume I'm doing Ulgorack's bidding, and you are willing to criticize me. People like you are rare, Jonathan, and you give me hope. Hope that not everyone in the nation would follow a false prophet because that's easier than forging their own path. Hope that if I, or someone else, became a tyrant, there'd be a resistance rising. Thank you for that."

Shocked, Jonathan stood there immobile with his mouth gaping. Rose presented her hand, and he shook it. "Jonathan. Spending more time with your son sounds great, and if you'd rather quit in order to do so, that's up to you. That being said, don't quit because of me. I'm not worth it."

***

With the strike over, things returned to normal and Dylan organized the Rubarg tournament he promised. In fact, he decided to go bigger than just me, Janice, Patricia and him. Several people showed up, both as participants and spectators. Even Rose found time to come, though she didn't play. I tried, but I ended up beaten by Brucie in the first round. He gloated about his skills, but he really was great at Rubarg. Not good enough, though, as Dylan crushed him in the semifinal. The final pitted Janice against Dylan. It was incredibly close.

—Thoughts of James Hunter, Hocmar 28, 2134, on the Nirnivian calendar

Everyone sat on the edge of their seat as Janice prepared her shot. The gigantic woman bent over, aiming at the last ball. Despite the distance, James saw sweat on her brow. Should she succeed, she'd win; otherwise, Dylan would most likely claim victory on his next turn. After an agonizing wait, the cue made contact with the targeted sphere and it entered the pocket. The crowd erupted in cheers, with Rose, James, and Brucie demonstrating particularly strong enthusiasm. The three of them clapped; Rose even hopped in joy. Noticing Janice glance at him, James offered her a thumbs-up. She smiled and winked.

"Ain't no fair," the bodyguard said as he shook his head. "Dylan got me with a cheap trick, ya know. Shoulda won..."

Rose giggled. "Don't be a sore loser, Brucie. Hunter didn't complain when you eliminated him."

"Um, that's because I suck. I figure I'd lose, so it's easy to take it well."

"You're too hard on yourself, Hunter." The alleged prophet patted his shoulder. "You did far better than I would have."

James replied by shrugging and blushing. Then Dylan grabbed Janice's hand and lifted her arm in the air. "Here's Valardir's Rubarg champion!"

A familiar voice echoed from behind. James turned his head, confirming by sight that Daniel Ricdeau spoke. He hadn't spotted the Commander's presence. If he managed to be here, then the situation had truly returned to normal. "I object to that, my boy. How about giving an old man the chance to prove his skills, sweetie?"

Janice laughed and moved her fingers in a manner, suggesting for him to approach. "Bring it on!"

Sanctity of Life

Chapter 1

Yushidor 22, 2134, on the Nirnivian calendar

Another day, another bland lunch. It felt like routine, but this one turned out differently. Oh, at first, it was the same as usual, but then it happened... I was shocked. How did he dare do that when Rose was in the room?

—Thoughts of James Hunter, Hocmar 28, 2134, on the Nirnivian calendar

Once again, James, Rose, and Brucie shared a meal in the cafeteria. The trio enjoyed a conversation as they ate. James had almost finished cleaning his plate when he spotted a familiar silhouette in the distance. Closer inspection confirmed his suspicion, Daniel Ricdeau sat at a distant table. That in itself proved mundane enough—the Commander required food, of course. The first strange detail was that he chose not to acknowledge Rose's presence. However, his company might explain why.

An older lady dressed in military garb talked with him. Nothing special there; several women served in NISDA, and Daniel had plenty of reasons for discussion with a fellow officer. Except the way his hand rested on hers suggested a personal relationship, and a sense of discomfort seized James. He assumed his imagination played a trick on him. That was when both elders leaned forward. Daniel caressed the stranger's hair, and they kissed. Shocked, James's mouth gaped and he dropped his fork. The utensil hit the floor, producing a metallic clink.

Upon hearing the sound, Rose lifted her head. "What's wrong, Hunter? You're all freaked out," she asked with a touch of concern in her voice. Since her father was behind her, she failed to see him.

"Oh, um, I'm sorry, Rose. I... don't know how to say this."

Rose frowned and tilted her head. "What? Do I have something stuck in my teeth?" She giggled. "I thought you'd be conformable enough to tell me by now."

"Well, I... um... he... uh..." Without intending to, James pointed at Daniel.

Following the accusing finger, Rose turned around. Though her father appeared in her line of vision, she didn't show any reaction.

"I'm confused. I don't see anything special over there." Rose returned her focus to James and scratched her head. "What's so freaky? I don't get it."

Was she serious? She looked right at them. Was she blind? Didn't she care that he cheated? If I caught my dad with another woman, I'd be outraged. Yet it didn't bother her. I guess he wasn't her "real" father, but still.

—Thoughts of James Hunter, Hocmar 28, 2134, on the Nirnivian calendar

"Your dad!" a confused James blurted out after some effort. "Um, he's kissing that lady, can't you see them?"

"Sure." Unimpressed, Rose shrugged. "He's been involved with Ms. Jenkins for two years now. What's so wrong about that?"

James didn't understand how she could take it so casually. Perhaps after all this time, she had accepted his affair. If so, she displayed greater forgiveness than he could've managed.

"But what about your mom?"

With a laugh, Rose said, "Well, of course she doesn't kiss Ms. Jenkins. She doesn't like women."

I couldn't believe my ears. She joked about it!?

—Thoughts of James Hunter, Hocmar 28, 2134, on the Nirnivian calendar

Against his will, a touch of annoyance lingered in James's tone. "Don't you care that your dad cheats on your mom like that?"

That sentence obtained a reaction. Rose glared at him and aimed a furious finger in his direction. The alleged prophet rarely lost her temper, at least in James's presence, so he must've struck a nerve.

"Cheats? Hey, take that back! Dad would never date other women without her consent."

"You mean... you mean your mom knows?"

"Of course!" Rose crossed her arms. "He would be a pretty bad husband if she didn't. Same for her if she didn't tell him about Mr. Barrington."

As she said that, I realized marriage might be a little different in this universe.

—Thoughts of James Hunter, Hocmar 28, 2134, on the Nirnivian calendar

"Wait, your mom and dad both see other people? They're like an open couple? Doesn't that bother you from a religious point of view? I mean, you're the Melkar, and Madeleine's a priestess."

A puzzled expression formed on Rose's visage. "Why? Marriage doesn't have anything to do with religion." She paused for a second. "Hunter, why are you staring at me like I have two noses?"

Okay, so maybe a lot different.

—Thoughts of James Hunter, Hocmar 28, 2134, on the Nirnivian calendar

"Well, where I come from, marriage is a religious ceremony. Um, not always, but in many cases." He resisted a sigh. "It's complicated. It is in Christianity anyway."

Rose and Brucie exchanged a quick glance. No question the bodyguard stifled a snigger, probably to avoid a rebuke from his employer rather than out of politeness. As for the winged woman, she kept a straight face but still said, "That's so weird." Then she caught herself and covered her mouth. "Oh, I'm so sorry, Hunter. I don't mean to belittle your beliefs, but we have nothing of the sort, so it's unfamiliar to me."

James shrugged. "No worries, I only call myself a Christian so my grandparents don't freak out. I guess I'm more of an agnostic."

Not that I had any idea if they used that word in Nirnivia. Either way, she didn't bring it up.

    —Thoughts of James Hunter, Hocmar 28, 2134, on the Nirnivian calendar

Relieved, Rose continued, "For us, marriage is simply an agreement between two people that they will support each other until they die, or they decide to terminate the contract. It's not a requirement: some couples live together till death without being married. For the most part, it's a symbolic gesture, but it also provides legal advantages in some situations."

"Okay, I think I understand. Seems similar to our civil unions."

"Wait..." With a scowl, she rubbed her chin. "You implied I should be offended by Dad dating Ms. Jenkins. Your religion doesn't condone that?"

"Oh, yeah. In Christianity, you're not supposed to, um, get physical"—a blush reddened James's cheeks—"until you're married."

That broke Brucie's serious facade. He erupted in a chortle while slapping his knee. "Damn, bro, I'd have married at like fifteen tops. How do you guys do it?"

"Let's just say many take it more as a suggestion than a rule."

"Shit, I hope so." Brucie indulged in another burst of laughter. "I'd have over a hundred wives."

A scoff came from Rose. "That's an optimistic estimation."

"And you wouldn't be allowed to anyway, Brucie. Bigamy is illegal in my country."

"Wait a minute." A grimacing Brucie counted on his fingers as if performing a complex calculation. "Dude, only one person for your whole life?" His eyes widened. "Ain't no way fer a stud like me."

With a giggle, Rose shook her head. "Says the man who never married."

"Yeah, but I got laid plenty and I can list 'em if ya want proof."

"That won't be necessary." On that note, she smiled at James. "Before that guy makes you think Nirnivians sleep around with everyone, let me assure you that's not the case. Many couples are exclusive. For instance, Miguel and I were. Some, like my parents, prefer an open marriage. For others, it's inconceivable. In both cases, it's their choice and nobody will judge them. As the Melkar, it doesn't matter to me, and for good reason. Such personal choices are none of the clergy's business." She fell silent for a moment. "Of course, respecting your mate is important. Take Nadia—if she didn't want you to see someone else, and you agreed but did it anyway behind her back, you would be betraying her and that's wrong. Whether you are married or not, it's simply wrong and I wouldn't condone your actions. In fact, from an Ulgoronisoism perspective, you'd be sinning. Not because you were dating or even having sex, but rather because you deceived Nadia."

James acquiesced. "That makes a lot of sense, actually."

And after that, we talked about banalities. I must admit, the way marriage worked in Rose's society seemed logical to me, but I wasn't about to start an open relationship. That just never felt right, especially since I had Nadia back home. Even without her, I'm not that kind of guy. Not that I judged Daniel, Madeleine or Brucie. Okay, I judged Brucie, but hey... it's Brucie, so...

—Thoughts of James Hunter, Hocmar 28, 2134, on the Nirnivian calendar

Chapter 2

Yushidor 27, 2134, on the Nirnivian calendar

It took months, but at last, they installed a TV in my room. They had promised me one for a while, but there were technical problems. Something with the wires. Sounded weird to me, I mean, it's a high-tech military complex and they can't handle a television? Ah, whatever...

—Thoughts of James Hunter, Hocmar 28, 2134, on the Nirnivian calendar

With Brucie and Rose standing on each side, James held the remote control, about to perform the ultimate test. He gave a short pause for drama and then pointed it toward the monitor and pressed the power button. After a click echoed, white noise filled the screen before stabilizing into a discernible image. People chopped vegetables while surrounded by pots, pans, and other kitchen equipment. It seemed James had stumbled on a cooking show, which failed to thrill him, so he switched the channel and the TV showed a green field where large men chased a ball while wielding what reminded him of hockey sticks. Intrigued by the apparent sport, he brought his fingers to his chin and observed. Less than a minute later, they cut to a commercial break.

Annoyed, yet resisting a sigh, James changed the station again. This time, he spotted a small blue robot rolling around as an orator explained recent progress in artificial intelligence. The machine waved its short metal arms as it proceeded on its merry way. The overall effect proved amusing, and James couldn't stop himself from laughing.

"What a cute little guy," he said in the middle of his chuckles. Then he glanced at Rose. The prophet stared at the screen, frowning and gritting her teeth.

"Argh... is it okay if I change the channel?" Though he didn't understand why his friend made the request, James had no objection, so he nodded. "Thanks." Given permission, she seized the remote and pushed a button. Puzzled, James kept staring at her with a gaping mouth. Rose sighed. "I'm sorry, it's just AI and robots are abominations in my opinion."

The explanation failed to elucidate the matter, so he asked, "Why? It's not hurting anyone."

"Because life is sacred, and intellect is Ulgoron's gift to life." Rose groaned. "I'm fine with science and machines, but some things should not be done." Passion filled her voice. "Faking intelligence counts among them. Intelligence is for living beings, not poor imitations of people." Now she gesticulated, hands swaying in chaos. "Their existence is an affront to God and demeans the sanctity of life. Scientists shouldn't play God."

I didn't share her disgust for AI. I mean, as a guy who watched too many sci-fi movies, I feared the robot apocalypse, but I figured we were a long way from that. All joking aside, I didn't get why it upset her so much. Those scientists only tried to improve people's lives, not create monsters. Yeah, there were valid social concerns, but that didn't seem to be what bothered her. I guess I wasn't religious enough to understand. She had a strong opinion on the subject and I didn't want a fight, so I pretended to agree.

—Thoughts of James Hunter, Hocmar 28, 2134, on the Nirnivian calendar

"Um, yeah, you're right. We shouldn't play God."

Chapter 3

Yushidor 29, 2134, on the Nirnivian calendar

I was stuck in bed with a splitting headache and a sore throat thanks to some harmless but annoying Nirnivian virus. Actually, being human, it was hard to say how harmless it was in my case, but after a few days of rest, I ended up cured.

—Thoughts of James Hunter, Hocmar 28, 2134, on the Nirnivian calendar

James desired nothing but sleep. Exhaustion assailed him, yet his symptoms denied him the slumber he needed. Doctor Greenberg assured him he was fine, but he doubted the prognosis. After tossing and turning for an hour, James abandoned hope and turned on his TV. He browsed through the channels until he stumbled upon one of Rose's speeches and watched out of curiosity as she answered questions sent by her viewers.

"I received a letter from a thirteen-year-old. He finds himself confused by the multiverse. Given we have encountered visitors from other worlds, we can't deny its existence. This poses two problems for the young boy. First, he has never seen a religious text mentioning multiple universes, and he asks if some do. Having read everything, I can affirm that the answer is no. The second issue is that the rare visitors we could communicate with believed in different gods. The writer wonders how we can know we are right and they are wrong. He isn't alone. Many share his confusion. Ever since the discovery of the multiverse, there have been countless debates on the subject. Some denounce asking questions as heresy."

Rose sighed, then shook her head. "I feel this is terribly misguided. We are blessed with intelligent minds capable of rational thought. To think is to use our gift as intended. When our views are challenged, it can be unpleasant. It's easy to look the other way and ignore the objections, but if we acknowledge them and consider the implications, we can understand our religion better. Besides, if we forbid questions, that implies we lack faith in our beliefs and fear they won't hold up when scrutinized."

She paused. "This young boy has reached an age where he must choose his own path. I despise indoctrination, so instead I will educate him to the best of my ability. First, different religions aren't restricted to other universes. There are several religions in Nirnivia. Long ago, the Zargs had Taidism, the Perz had Win-Kui-Noi, and a vast number of Brigs followed Hynoist doctrine. While uncommon, practitioners of those faiths are present in modern times. Even followers of Ulgoronisoism split up into different branches due to disagreements. If Nirnivians can't agree, how can we prove we are right?"

Rose shrugged. "We can't. So far, proving Ulgorack's existence has been impossible, and it will likely be so forever. Some claim that the original Melkar, and me by extension, settles the score, but no. While I believe in the first holy prophet, there is the possibility it's a myth and the old war's real causes are forgotten. As for myself, well... I have wings, but considering I met a man with three eyes and four arms earlier today, I'd say there are alternative explanations. So again, we can't be certain. This is why we call it faith. We have faith that our beliefs are correct despite a lack of proof. Which leaves the question of other universes and why our sacred texts don't mention them. Unfortunately, we can only speculate. Some feel this means there is no God and that, when we die, we simply rot in the ground. I find this argument flawed. This world alone is so complex and beautiful, I cannot imagine how it could be without a superior form of intelligence creating it. When you add an unknown number of worlds, all different and wonderful in their own right, it makes the presence of a God more necessary.

"Now, for the believers' perspective, someone once suggested the multiverse was hidden from us on purpose as a simplification. In other words, it was just a detail we didn't need to concern ourselves with, so it was ignored. Simple idea, but it's often attacked because of that reason.

"Another theory proposes that each universe is ruled by a deity. At the top of the hierarchy rules an even greater being who oversees the multiverse. It helps if you compare it to our political system, where each region has representatives and the Council manages the country. There is a big difference, however: each god is unaware of the others. Because of this, no religion understands the scope of creation. This particular explanation raises several questions. Why did the god in charge hide the truth? Was the deception exposed when visitors appeared in Nirnivia? How did Ulgorack and Timagoron react? Because it is riddled with holes, this theory isn't popular.

"As another possible answer, some suggest that while there is a God, the multiverse proves that every faith is false, so the sacred texts we hold so dear are lies. I would advise the boy who wrote this letter to research further if he's interested. Then he can decide what he prefers for himself. In my heart, I have no doubt Ulgorack exists, but forcing my views on people is wrong. In the past, such attempts brought destruction, until the world itself faced annihilation. The important thing is not which god you worship, but rather that you strive to become the best person you can be."

I never considered it, but my religion didn't mention the multiverse either. Because of my experience, the subject intrigued me. I wondered how people back home would react if confronted with this fact. I had no idea then, but now I figure everyone would somehow convince themselves this new knowledge meant they were right all along. In general, we don't change our beliefs when they're proven wrong. It's easier to twist the proof so that it fits our point of view.

—Thoughts of James Hunter, Hocmar 28, 2134, on the Nirnivian calendar

Chapter 4

Yushidor 31, 2134, on the Nirnivian calendar

Tears rolled down Susan's cheeks as she walked toward the bed. On the mattress lay one of the worst cases of mutation in modern Nirnivian history. Every time she gazed upon the poor misshapen being, her heart broke. He looked closer to an animal than a Gorumar. An obese blob formed his body, along with small baby arms and twisted legs lacking feet. As for his face, two huge dark blue circles devoid of any white served as his eyes, while an amorphous gape stood for his mouth. When opened, it revealed sharp crooked teeth. Pointy ears and a round nose completed his visage. Not granting any mercy, nature had reserved a yellowish green for his complexion. The unfamiliar skin color suggested sickness and further exacerbated his abnormal appearance. If he had the ability to move and leave the house, Susan expected children would run away in fear, despite the fact that William was a gentle soul.

Susan had worked as William's nurse for years. The admission brought her shame, but when she'd started, the mutant had repulsed her. It had remained that way for several months, until she'd gotten to know him. Regardless of his monstrous outer shell, the soft-spoken man possessed great intelligence, kindness, and even charm once you grew used to him. Though many had mocked him in the past, he never wished them harm. Susan and William often enjoyed long conversations. They talked for hours. No one deserved his fate, least of all him.

"William, you have a visitor," Susan said in a whisper as she got near. On cue, a distinguished old woman approached.

"Councillor Carlson." William's lips contorted. While Susan recognized his smile, she wondered if the guest understood him. "Thank you for coming. I know you're busy and I appreciate your willingness to see me. For a few weeks, I've been meeting with those of your colleagues most likely to share my mindset. They all rejected my pleas. You're my last hope..."

***

Yushidor 33, 2134, on the Nirnivian calendar

That evening, I joined Brucie in the recreation room and we played Rubarg. Rose had no interest in that game, but she watched us anyway. She cheered me on. A nice, but futile gesture.

—Thoughts of James Hunter, Hocmar 28, 2134, on the Nirnivian calendar

Brucie aimed with his cue, considering every angle. Then he struck the white ball. In an impressive display, he pocketed the last two spheres in one shot, securing the victory. Thrilled by the outcome, the bodyguard erupted in laughter and pumped his fist.

"Yeah, freaking sweet! Ya can't beat the amazing Brucie, dude!"

James shrugged. "I never said I could."

The bodybuilder opened his mouth when a familiar female voice interrupted him. "Guys, can you stop talking for a minute, please? I must watch this."

Both hushed as requested. On the screen, a MegaNews journalist reported a story. "Euthanasia has always been a controversial issue. Most oppose it on religious grounds, and the law agrees. For years, a determined minority has wished to change this. So far, their efforts have failed. Of this group of dissidents, the most vocal is certainly Mr. William Adamant."

They showed us the picture of a guy. At least, I think it was a guy. I had seen mutants before, but dear God... yeah, they had deformities and extra body parts, but they still had a human silhouette. William didn't look like a person, but rather a monster from a bad horror movie. Um, I know we're not supposed to judge people by their appearance, but damn.

—Thoughts of James Hunter, Hocmar 28, 2134, on the Nirnivian calendar

"Mr. Adamant is the most mutated Gorumar in Nirnivia and has led a grueling life. Not only was he born heavily disfigured, he is paralyzed and thus spends all his time in bed. As if that's not enough, he endures constant pain that intensifies as he grows older. For years, he has yearned for death. However, in his state, he cannot commit suicide, and so he hopes to change the law."

Brucie leaned toward James and whispered in his ear: "Ah, dude, this ain't good. Maybe ya should get outta here before it's too late."

The comment puzzled James, but he chose not to heed the warning. The journalist continued, "Recently, Mr. Adamant found an unlikely ally. Councillor Jade Carlson announced she'd bring a motion proposing evaluating the possibility of legalizing euthanasia before her peers. Should it pass, it would be a historic event—for better or worse."

When Rose heard Jade's name, her eyes widened. She gasped and scowled. "Oh, Jade, this time you went too far," she murmured before proceeding at a normal volume. Rage and disdain tainted her tone. "This is a sacrilege! Life is precious. Life is sacred. It is not something to squander, no matter your suffering!" For a couple of seconds, she paced and then threw her arms upward. "Don't the fools realize suicide leads to nothingness? In the case of assisted suicide, two souls are lost forever." At that point, the prophet sat on the couch, grasped her head with both hands and sobbed. A minute later, she returned to her feet. Her expression hardened. "No, I won't let this happen. I'll do anything to stop them. I won't let them sacrifice Nirnivian souls in the name of false mercy!" She gazed at James. "Sorry, Hunter, I promised I'd spend the evening with you, but I must go. Come, Brucie!"

Though they left, I stayed in the recreation room, baffled by what had happened. Given her religious background, I guess I understand why euthanasia riled Rose up, but her reaction seemed overblown. She wasn't just angry or concerned, she was furious. There was this glimmer in her eyes... I can't explain it, but she didn't behave like the Rose I knew. I figured there was more to it than saving souls, but what?
—Thoughts of James Hunter, Hocmar 28, 2134, on the Nirnivian calendar

Chapter 5

Visited him. Often did. Got better. Facial scars gone. Got new eye. Hand almost grown back. Was amazing...

—Thoughts of Wrathchild, Hocmar 28, 2134, on the Nirnivian calendar

When Melissa arrived at Diabo's side, the huge mutant slept. Not wanting to wake him up, she considered leaving, but then she noted a twitch on his face. Soon, the crimson beast groaned, opened his eyes and rubbed them.

"Wrathchild, you keeping in touch?" he said in a voice far weaker than usual. When healthy, his words resounded with power, but in his current state, they barely registered above a whisper.

Wrathchild smiled and leaned forward. "Eh, normal. You're getting better. Should be out soon."

"Yeah, I ain't too bad." Diabo lifted his hand and flexed his new fingers. While the movement caused a slight grimace, he had regained his full range of motion. "This body that Doctor Death gave me ain't pretty, but it's tough as shit, and luckily fo' me, it grows back. That explosion messed me up. I almost... I was a dumbass. I can't get injured like this again."

Wrathchild hoped the near-death experience had taught Diabo the value of caution. Both Plague and Stalker believed they should hide in the shadows until Ostark and Nirnivia calmed down. She definitively agreed with their point of view, but they all feared Diabo wouldn't be receptive.

"Yes. Must be careful. Been attracting too much attention. Time lay low."

Diabo frowned. "Am I surrounded by a bunch o' idiots? What happened back then is 'cause we're too soft. We ain't done enough. We forgot our goal. BBR exists fo' one thing, killing Doctor Death. Yeah, we hunt his troops, but he's safe in Ostark. We gotta take him down. The sooner the better."

"What?" In disbelief, Melissa's mouth gaped. "How? Inaccessible..."

"Ain't got no idea." Diabo shrugged. "We'll figure somethin' out. I need rest. In a few days, I'll be ready. That mechanical freak better watch his back. I'm coming fo' him."

"Can't rush or all dead!" Wrathchild gritted her teeth. "Better slow win than lose. Must be reasonable—"

"Only reasonable thing is killing that son o' a bitch!"

Swallowed hard. Bad sign. Might cool down later, doubted it. Knew Stalker and Plague wouldn't be happy. Wasn't either.

—Thoughts of Wrathchild, Hocmar 28, 2134, on the Nirnivian calendar

Chapter 6

As soon as Rose left the recreation room, she headed for her office. Once inside, she picked up the phone and dialed Jade's personal number, but her butler explained the councillor was stuck in a late meeting. After leaving a message, Rose hung up and groaned. She started pacing around her quarters massaging her temples.

About ten minutes had passed and despite the improbability of Jade having returned already, she called again. The butler confirmed that indeed wasn't the case. Though his tone remained serene, Rose suspected the poor soul wondered if the holy prophet would keep calling at such frequent intervals. Of course, her status as the Melkar guaranteed he would never dare show any sign of annoyance over her insistence.

Regardless, Rose had research to perform for a sermon. Figuring she might as well accomplish that task, she headed for her library. Still, apprehension grabbed her in fear Jade would attempt contacting her. Valardir's standard "phones" were wireless, but they only reached other similar devices within the complex for security purposes. To circumvent the issue, Rose possessed an "outside" phone in her office, but it was wired, so she couldn't bring it with her. In addition, it lacked the video capability of the Valardir's transmitters.

For all her efforts, Rose failed to keep the horrors of euthanasia from her mind. Nevertheless, she eventually finished her work and returned to her quarters. By then, she learned she had missed Jade's attempt at reaching her and resisted a Brucie-inspired curse word. Rose contacted Jade again, and after confirming his employer's presence, the butler went to fetch her. Several minutes passed and she was still waiting for Jade to arrive. Exasperated, she tapped on the desk with her fingers. Soon, however, the clicking sound vanished as Rose interrupted the motion in order to bring her nails to her teeth. Thank God she stopped herself before the first nibble. Given that vanquishing the bad habit had taken years, she'd rather not undo that achievement. Fortunately, Jade's voice reached her ear before she succumbed to the temptation.

"Your Holiness, I expect you want to talk about William Adamant. Am I right in assuming you're against my proposal?"

"Of course I am! Jade, we've had our differences, but nothing like this. Euthanasia? What are you thinking? You must stop this at once. Revoke the motion, I beg you. If the law changes, so many souls will be condemned to nothingness. We may have different opinions, but you are a religious person. You've consulted me often on such matters, and you know I speak the truth. You can't agree with Mr. Adamant. It's impossible!"

"No, I don't." Perplexed, Rose tilted her neck and scowled. A sad laugh escaped Jade. "Yes, I understand your confusion. Rose, this isn't my world anymore." The senior sighed. "I've lived my life, and now I'm an old lady waiting for the end."

"That's not true. You have so much more to offer."

"The mind wants to agree, but the body... it can't follow anymore. This will be my last term on the Council. I'll be retiring once it's done. Don't ask me why, but many younger folks are favorable to legalizing assisted suicide. To me, it's madness, but in the end, it's up to the next generation to take over. It's their world now. They're the ones who'll live in it, so it's only fair they decide what rules will govern it." A groan came from Jade. "Besides, it's how it's meant to be. Politicians serve the people and not themselves. The electors are our bosses, not the other way around. We enact and reject laws based on Nirnivian values, not our own. Values change over time, and the law must do the same so it reflects the public's opinion."

At that instant, Jade indulged in a humorless chuckle. "Oh, those idealistic notions have long been abandoned. Politicians aren't public servants, they are there for their own interests. They ignore the people they represent and fatten their pockets with bribes from corporations. Even I may have strayed on occasion, but I won't anymore. Don't think I'm deluding myself—the motion won't pass. The other councillors, you included, aren't fond of euthanasia. They are older folks with old values, much like me. But even if it's futile, at least my conscience will know I did the right thing."

The speech left Rose breathless. While she pondered Jade's argument, she returned to her seat and rubbed her forehead. There was logic there, no question, and yet some topics trumped logic. "Jade, please, I implore you: don't do this."

"Or what? I'll risk being condemned into nothingness?" The elder exhaled. "I've made my peace with that."

"But what about the others who will suffer such a fate should the law change?"

"Anyone who commits the sin of euthanasia will doom themselves by their own choice, as it is for almost everything else. I'm sorry, Rose, but I won't budge on this, and I'm tired. There's nothing more to say on the issue."

Chapter 7

Yushidor 35 2134, on the Nirnivian calendar

With a groan, Susan lifted William's body and slid his arm into his shirtsleeve. His weight proved considerable, a fact she was already aware of, but through the years, her muscles had learned to handle it. Still, a few pearls of sweat formed on her brow. No doubt the task would be easier with a partner. She'd once had one, but funding cuts to the various government programs and charities had forced William to reduce his staff.

Most days, William didn't require fancy clothes and instead remained nude except for underwear. That served his purposes well enough. Only on rare occasions did he leave his house in a wheelchair pushed by Susan, and he entertained few visitors. Those who did visit grew used to his condition and understood his attire.

Today, however, William had an appointment with an important person. She couldn't meet him face-to-face, so he'd join her in a video conference. Assuming she was on time, it should begin soon, and Susan stood by for moral support. Besides, he might require medical assistance during the conversation.

After a sigh, she said, "I don't see why you have to talk to her." Susan noted the perhaps undeserved bitterness in her own tone.

"Because Her Holiness is not only an esteemed figure in our society but also a wonderful woman who has sacrificed so much for Nirnivia." His soft voice contrasted with her resentment. Despite the suffering the Melkar's stance had brought him, he understood and accepted her position on the issue. That was William—refusing to judge others on a single aspect, focusing instead on their whole personalities. Maybe the derision he'd endured due to his physical appearance had taught him that approach. "If she wishes to speak to me, I must oblige out of respect."

"But you already know what she'll say..."

"Yes, but speaking with her is an honor."

***

When William's image appeared on Rose's monitor, she resisted a gasp. Though they'd met in person before her incarceration in Valardir and she had seen several pictures since, the ravages caused by his mutation always shocked her. The sight of the poor man broke her heart. A while back, she'd mentioned to Max Kenneth that William was a level three on the Rockter scale and that, in the past, level six mutants had been common. What cruel torture such an existence must be...

The conversation started on a positive note. Then again, that was the easy part, since they merely exchanged greetings and standard pleasantries. Now came the moment where the discussion turned serious.

"William, I realize you bear a heavy burden. Many Nirnivians suffer from mutations, illnesses and other ailments. We try hard to ease their suffering. The government has instituted special programs for this purpose. While you received financial aid, it's clear your wish to end your life means we haven't done enough. That's why both the Melkar Funds for the Needy and the Kenneth

Foundation plan on joining forces to offer greater assistance."

A cough came from William. "Thank you, Your Holiness, but I receive beyond adequate treatments." The soft-spoken man insisted Rose use his first name, so she proposed he do the same. So far, he'd failed to oblige and employed her religious title. Rose had grown used to this kind of behavior over the years. For most, addressing the Melkar informally proved an insurmountable challenge. "Nothing can be done at this point. You can't cure my paralysis. My eyesight is waning. TV was one of my few hobbies; now I can't see the screen even inches away. More importantly, you can't stop the ever-increasing pain." His lips twisted. "There's this sensation in my bones like someone is sawing through every single one. Whenever I breathe, my lungs are on fire. I'm already on several pain-killers, which don't help. The doctors said something stronger would dull my mind. That's unacceptable; my mind is all I have left. I appreciate your willingness to offer more assistance, but what would it accomplish?" William indulged in a short pause for dramatic effect. "Besides, I fear I'm not only bearing a burden but also have become one for society. Many resources are wasted on my well-being. I'm a hopeless case, Your Holiness. I won't get better, but there are people who will if treated properly. Once I'm gone, the money spent on my care can go to them and—"

"No, stop!" a furious Rose yelled, thus interrupting the mutant. Without quite realizing it, she stood up with her hands resting on her hips. "Don't use twisted logic to justify suicide! You're wrong! You—" She sighed and forced herself to relax. Scolding William wouldn't achieve her goal, but sympathy and comprehension might. "William, never assume you are worth less than others because of your disability. That's not the case. All life is sacred, including yours!" Rose's voice broke as she proceeded. "What you're suggesting sullies the sanctity of life. If you kill yourself using the hand of another, you'll condemn your soul to nothingness. Don't do that, William. Don't deny yourself the afterlife. There, we'll finally be happy, and you deserve happiness. If extra care can save a soul, then it is money well spent."

"Your Holiness, that you worry about my fate touches my heart." A glimmer of gratitude shone in his eyes. "However, I am tired. I do not want another life, not even if it's perfect." William sighed. "In one of your sermons, you said that we choose the hardships we face, though we don't realize it, and that we do this because pain teaches us. If that's the case, then here's what I've learned: nothingness suits me. Why can't I decide to damn my own soul when others are permitted to do it through lying, cheating and any number of legal sins?"

Rose swallowed hard as tears rolled down her cheeks. Her hands trembled, encouraged by the implications behind William's words. Still, she took a deep breath and steeled herself. "Except we're not just talking about your own soul. With euthanasia, the person who commits the act is also damned. I barely know you, but I'm convinced you aren't selfish. Are you really willing to pay that price?"

The mutation rendered William's expressions difficult to read, but Rose noted what she believed to be a scowl forming on his brow. "I would never ask someone to sacrifice their soul for my sake. However, if I can find a person who decides to help me of their own volition, then it's their choice. Whatever fate comes for them will be of their own making, much like mine." He groaned. "Your Holiness, I realize my stance on the issue is due to my specific circumstances, and I don't expect you to understand."

"The thing is"—Rose sobbed as recollections from the past invaded her mind, weakening her muscles—"I understand more than you think. The main difference between you and me is that my pain is emotional while yours is physical. Didn't our wisest minds write that emotional torments are worse than the ailments inflicting our bodies?"

William burst out laughing. "In my experience, people who say that nonsense are blessed with general good health. A bump on the head might sting less than a broken heart, but what I have... oh, you have no idea. Like most Nirnivians, I'm aware of the nightmare you went through, and I don't mean to belittle your pain. However, despite everything, you still have the possibility of a better future. That's a luxury I don't have. Your Holiness, I am stuck in this bed. I can debate with you all day; in fact, I'd love to. I'll listen to you for as long as you speak, but no matter how hard you try, you can't change my mind."

Rose ignored the warning and kept trying. She fired argument after argument and William shot them down. Two hours passed before she abandoned hope.

Chapter 8

Lacdor 2, 2134, on the Nirnivian calendar

Rose usually ate her meals with me, but sometimes that wasn't possible. When that happened, I found an isolated spot where I could be on my own. That was my plan on that particular day, but fate decided otherwise.

—Thoughts of James Hunter, Hocmar 28, 2134, on the Nirnivian calendar

As James navigated around the area, his mind complained about how crowded the cafeteria was. Despite the fact that he'd waited until past noon in hopes of avoiding the rush hour, finding a free table proved a challenge. After exploring the whole room without locating a seat, he considered giving up and bringing the food to his chamber when he heard a voice calling his name. For a second, he thought his imagination played a trick on him, but he still turned toward the source and noticed a hand waving for him to approach.

Puzzled, James contemplated the burly stranger gesturing at him. Then he recognized Charlie, a soldier he'd met through Janice. Back when they had watched Daniel reveal his mutation on TV, James had introduced him to Rose. That had been a dream come true for Charlie, though the Melkar's presence had ended up intimidating him. Four others shared a meal with Charlie—the Perz woman named Patricia, Dylan, who'd recently organized a Rubarg tournament, a scarred soldier James recognized as Gareth, a friend of Janice and a bearded man James had never seen.

The unfamiliar face displayed the same bronzed skin tone as Rose and most people here. If James had learned his lessons on Nirnivian races correctly, that made him a Brig.

Perhaps mistaking his confusion for hesitation, Charlie's companion joined him in motioning for James to sit with them. Since accepting the invitation seemed a better option than retreating to his quarters, James walked toward the group. When he arrived, he dropped his tray on the table and a *plock* echoed.

Before he pulled out his chair, Charlie presented an open palm and said, "Hey, James, long time no see!"

James high-fived him as requested. "Um, yeah."

Both Patricia and Dylan then offered their greetings while Gareth settled for a nod. After, Charlie pointed at the Brig James had never encountered. "This fellow here's Nathan."

In addition to sporting facial hair, James noticed that Nathan wore an eyepatch on the left side, presumably due to an injury sustained during the war. While James attempted to ignore it, he found his attention drawn to it and hoped his curiosity didn't show. Except, of course, it did and with a laugh, Nathan touched the piece of fabric.

"When your parents tell you not to run with scissors, listen to them."

Patricia giggled and leaned forward. "You thought it was a war injury, huh?" She dismissed the notion with a wave. "Nah, that lazy bastard spent the whole time breaking code while we three risked our butts in battle."

"Oh, please! You guys are jealous 'cause you didn't pay attention in math class. Anyway, at least I'm not the only disfigured guy around." Nathan slapped Gareth's shoulder. "This is Gareth Stevenson by the way."

"Actually, we met." With that, Gareth extended his hand and James shook it. "Nice to see you again."

At that moment, the conversation turned to various subjects, like rumors spreading through Valardir and their daily lives. I mostly stayed silent. Once in a while, one of them asked me a question, so I'd somewhat participate. I appreciated the effort. Soon, the discussion switched to a darker topic.

—Thoughts of James Hunter, Hocmar 28, 2134, on the Nirnivian calendar

After a lull in the banter, Patricia paused between two bites and scowled. "Have you guys heard of the latest kidnapping? It's the third in a month, and I'm getting paranoid. Just thinking someone might take Darren away is driving me crazy."

Dylan nodded. "Yeah, I can't help but worry about my daughters too, but it'll be fine. There was some custody battle. My bet is the dad took him. It's usually how it turns out."

Unconvinced, Patricia shook her head. "No, that'd only explain the third case. What if the mobs are behind it? That kind of bullshit happened before."

"Nah, gal, you're panicking for nothing," Charlie said. "They're probably unrelated crimes."

Then Patricia swallowed hard. "Yeah, but what if they aren't?"

A chuckle came from Nathan. "You guys give me shit because I didn't fight in the war, but you're a bunch of pussies. Like, none of those goddamn kidnappings happened near here."

Patricia fired him a dark glare. "You freaking bastard, I can't wait until you become a parent."

"Yeah, I don't plan to." He winked. "I don't want to become a nervous wreck like you."

Patricia replied with a deserved middle finger. I understand Nathan wasn't serious, but joking about kidnappings seemed cruel. I mean, I'm not a parent, so I wasn't as concerned as Patricia or Dylan, but I have a deep hatred for the bastards who do such things. Ah well, it's not like I was about to confront Nathan about it.

—Thoughts of James Hunter, Hocmar 28, 2134, on the Nirnivian calendar

Chapter 9

Lacdor 4, 2134, on the Nirnivian calendar

Rose had a rough day. She contacted Jade again, but like with her first attempt, she failed to convince her. She also talked to William, without any luck. They just wouldn't see things Rose's way, and she grew frustrated. I guess she visited me because she needed to unwind.

—Thoughts of James Hunter, Hocmar 28, 2134, on the Nirnivian calendar

"Jade is a dead end. She made it clear she won't change her mind," Rose mumbled while pacing around the room. Both James and Brucie sat on the bed and listened in silence. "William is just as stubborn and said he wants to die. When I offered help, he declined." The prophet stopped walking and rubbed her brow. The image conveyed a touch of despair. "They don't understand. I reminded them both about the sanctity of life, to no avail. William doesn't care about condemning his soul to nothingness, and he's willing to bring another soul with him." Upset, she grunted and resumed her striding. "Why can't they realize this is wrong? It's obvious!"

After a moment of hesitation, James frowned. "Um... well, William has lived his whole life stuck in bed. If you were paralyzed and always in pain, you might have a different point of view too." As he mumbled this sentence, the bodyguard panicked. Brucie didn't dare voice his concern, but he gestured a slashing motion against his throat, suggesting James should drop the subject. Too late, but

James nevertheless heeded the warning and added, "Not that assisted suicide is right; it's wrong, I'm just trying to see William's perspective."

Enraged, Rose turned toward James and glared, though he sensed the fury was not aimed at him, but rather the general situation. The Melkar rested her hands on her hips, her classic angry posture.

"Listen, I'm very sorry for William. I'm not an uncaring monster. That's why I proposed more help. He refused. The fact that William suffers saddens me, but it's not an excuse for throwing away his sacred life!" she yelled. Then she threw her fists in the air and proceeded at a manic pace. "We all suffer. We bring our own pain, and by overcoming it, we learn. William decided to accelerate the process by taking a lot of hardships at once. In theory, he'd access the afterlife faster. Except it was too much, and now he can't handle it. I feel bad, I swear! If he'd let me, I'd do everything in my power to get him through this. He'll damn his soul. The soul is the most important part of our being! Our doctrine says so! And it's not only William's own soul—he'll doom another one. And also—"

One and a half hours. She lectured me about the evil of euthanasia for one and a half hours. It was counterproductive: by the time she finished, I wanted to shoot myself. Again, I get that, with her background, Rose felt strongly about the issue. Me, I could've gone either way since I understood both sides, but I wasn't ready to pick one yet. Thing is, there was something strange about Rose. I mean, in the past, she'd welcomed different religious opinions. During her sermons, she always said she could be wrong and that people should respect others' beliefs. But with assisted suicide, her tolerance vanished. I figured there was more to it. That it wasn't just religion or souls that bothered her. At any rate, a speech as long as an hour and a half was overkill. And even then, she only stopped because Kristina "saved" me.

—Thoughts of James Hunter, Hocmar 28, 2134, on the Nirnivian calendar

The prophet still showed no signs of relenting when a beep interrupted her. Someone was at the door. Through the speaker, a female voice said, "Rose, are you there?"

Eager to be free from Rose's tirade, James went and opened the door, revealing Kristina Dupree. The blond assistant stepped inside, standing beside James's shelves thus keeping some distance from the others.

"Rose, Madeleine has been waiting for you in the office for fifteen minutes."

The winged woman gasped and brought her palm to her cheek. "Oh, that's right. Thanks, Kristina, I'll be right there. Why didn't you call?"

Puzzled, Kristina tilted her head sideways. "Um, I did. You didn't answer, so I figured you forgot your phone. It happens often enough."

Rose rubbed her chin. "Well, I'm guilty as charged on that, but I did bring it for once. Though I put it on vibrate. I guess I didn't notice. Sorry." On that note, Rose began to leave, waving to James. "Bye, Hunter, I'll see you later."

"Um, yeah, sure!"

And so Rose exited the room, trailed by Kristina and Brucie. After the door closed, James exhaled in relief, sat on the mattress and massaged his temples.

***

When Rose stepped into her office, Madeleine sat at the desk, reading a book. The second she heard the door slide open, the head priestess closed her volume, swiveled her chair in order to face Rose, and smiled. Rose rubbed her hands while her fingers interlaced. "Mom, I'm so sorry."

A dismissive wave came from Madeleine. "Oh, do not be concerned, my dear." She pointed at her tome. "When one enjoys the words of Priest Sarabra, waiting is a blessing."

Rose rushed toward her bureau and joined her mother while Kristina followed. As for Brucie, he remained outside as ordered. While this was not a secret meeting, the chamber proved smallish and felt crowded when four people or more assembled. "How are our plans proceeding?"

"I am pleased to announce Head Priest Galan and Conival have both agreed to cooperate in order to fight the heresy Councillor Carlson has brought upon us."

With her palm on her heart, Rose exhaled in relief. As she'd explained to Hunter before, the Ulgoronisoism faith wasn't a united front. Through the years, disciples had come to different interpretations of sacred texts and the original Melkar's prophecies. Since they'd failed to reach a compromise, the religion had eventually broken into three branches. Madeleine headed the progressive branch, and Galan the centrist branch. The instant Rose and her mom had proposed that the three branches unite to protest Jade Carlson's proposal, Galan had pledged his support. Conival, the orthodox, however, had shown reticence, as expected.

Despite the fact that Rose obeyed the rules forbidding her from endorsing a specific branch, her beliefs spilled out through her lectures. It'd be impossible to conceal her opinion with one hundred percent accuracy. Soon it became clear she couldn't be an orthodox. Why, even Hunter, a stranger to their land, had come to this conclusion. That the head priestess of the progressives served as her adoptive mother only increased the chances that Rose would share Madeleine's views. Thus, most assumed her to be a progressive, or perhaps a centrist.

Due to this unwilling endorsement, many people had switched to the progressives. While the centrists had suffered losses, the exodus had mostly affected the orthodox. At this point, they made up less than a tenth of the population. Instead of softening their doctrine as their church crumbled, Conival had doubled down, catering to their most fervent devotees.

This situation put the orthodox in a strange dilemma. On one hand, Rose was the reason for their fall. On the other, they had no choice but to venerate the Melkar, prophet to their god, Ulgorack. In theory, they could've claimed Rose a fake—and a few had tried this approach, but it had backfired, causing more to leave. So the orthodox had accepted Rose as the Melkar and instead blamed the centrists and progressives for spreading false rumors concerning her leanings. This discord rendered any cooperation between the three branches almost impossible.

"What a relief! I feared Conival would be too stubborn to accept joining us."

Madeleine allowed herself a distinguished laugh. "Oh, my child, Conival is a proud fool blinded by his hatred of the progressives. However, enough sense remains in him to understand the danger Jade brings. If anything, as an orthodox, he despises euthanasia more than us. With everyone on board, we must plan our protests. Time is limited, so maximizing effectiveness is paramount."

For hours, Rose and Madeleine discussed where the manifestations should occur and other arrangements. For every word they pronounced, Kristina jotted down notes so details wouldn't be forgotten. Though she didn't complain, Rose caught a glimpse of her scowling and grimacing.

"Is everything all right, Kristina?"

"Oh, yes!" She rubbed her neck. "Um, of course!"

"Because, if there's something you wish to say, I'd like to hear it. I value your opinion."

"It's just"—the blond woman bit her lip—"um, I'm not convinced we're on the right side of history. I mean, Jade Carlson is only doing her job." Rose glared at her, and Kristina twitched. "Don't get me wrong, I'm against euthanasia, but Jade has a point." Perhaps due to being intimidated by the focus imposed on her, the assistant's cheeks reddened. "Laws are to be revised from time to time, and assisted suicide is gaining popularity with the younger generation. As public servants, the councillors are supposed to listen to the population's opinion, which is what Jade proposed they do. She's not talking about legalizing euthanasia, only opening the question for debate. There's no need to panic yet. Besides, it's a matter of policy, not religion. State and church are separated for a reason. I'm uncomfortable with this."

Then Rose jumped to her feet and slapped her brow. "Oh my God, you too? Why don't you guys understand how serious this is!" She rested her hands on her hips. "Yes, your words are true, Kristina, but when it concerns suicide, even condoning it can steer you toward nothingness." Her stare intensified, and Kristina recoiled, bowing her head. "I'm all for debates and respecting others' beliefs, but when doing so may damn souls—"

That was when Madeleine caressed Rose's shoulder in an attempt to calm her down. "Now, my dear child, I understand this is a sore subject for you, but do not put the blame on poor Kristina, for she is correct." The elder turned toward the assistant and smiled. "Ideally, the church should not interfere with politics, but there are circumstances where it cannot be avoided. I concede that Jade is merely acting as a councillor should. That is why, though we are obliged to condemn her proposal through our protest, we shall not demonize her. Where it gets complicated is that Rose and I share the same situation as Jade. Both the head priestess and the Melkar must denounce any course of action facilitating euthanasia. It is part of our duties, and we would be failing our obligations otherwise." She paused. "That being said, Kristina, I am certain there are other tasks Rose can appoint you to, and I have access to plenty of resources. If you prefer not to get involved, I am confident that can be arranged."

Frowning, Rose opened her mouth but then took a deep breath. "Yes, I suppose so."

Kristina exhaled and lifted her neck to look at them. "No, that won't be necessary. Rose hired me as her assistant and I'll do my job. Sorry, I shouldn't have brought it up."

With a sensation of guilt rising in her, Rose approached Kristina and patted her upper arm. "No, I should apologize. I asked for your opinion when I couldn't handle it. I'm on edge and..." She sighed. "Anyway, I do value your input, even if I don't always agree."

The blond woman beamed. "I know."

***

Once Rose left, I needed a break. I had received enough anti-euthanasia arguments for a lifetime. Luckily for me, that evening I bumped into Janice, and she proposed a game of Rubarg. I appreciated the offer and figured it'd be a good chance to forget about William and Rose. Still, for whatever reason, I couldn't help but bring it up.

—Thoughts of James Hunter, Hocmar 28, 2134, on the Nirnivian calendar

As James rubbed his chin, he studied the table. Two balls for him to pocket while one remained for Janice. No question he stood at a disadvantage, but he'd give his best effort. Still, he failed to decide which orb to target. His eyes switched from one potential candidate to the other in search of any detail that might provide guidance. Perhaps sensing his torment, Janice pointed her finger toward number eight. "Go with that one, it's the easiest."

The suggestion made sense, but James wanted to keep it until last. A success would get his hopes up, only for them to be crushed when he missed the second shot. Should he manage the miracle of sinking number six, however, number eight would provide an easy first win.

"Um, have you heard about that mutant who wants to legalize euthanasia?" James asked as he aimed. Janice nodded. "Rose is up in arms. She's really, really angry. Um, I mean, it's fine that she's against it, I understand why, but she's so annoying lately."

Despite his best effort, James missed and consoled himself with the thought that at least he'd avoided dashed expectations. Janice giggled and extended a playful tongue.

"Told you!" Then she approached the table and, in a master stroke, seized victory.

"Congratulations!" James said, clapping.

As a reply, Janice mocked a bow. "Thanks! Oh, but what were you saying about Rose?"

"Oh yeah, earlier today, Rose lectured me about assisted suicide for an hour and a half. Why? What did I do? It's not my fault. I've got nothing to do with it!" He sighed. "I guess she needed to unwind, and that's fine, but it was a bit much. And she's so obsessed. It's not like her, you know what I mean? She's always babbling about the sanctity of life. I don't get it."

With a grimace, Janice scowled. Was that a tear James noticed in her eye? Before he could tell, she turned her head to conceal her face from his sight.

"Maybe it's because, for Rose, the sanctity of life is more than some text in a book." Though she remained calm, a hard edge seeped from her tone. James noticed the tension in her muscles. "Buddy, to her, it's not just a debate. It's not even about saving souls. Rose needs to believe life is so important. If she didn't..." Janice grunted and dismissed the matter with a wave. "Ah, forget it, bud. Hang in there, it'll be over soon. Rose is worried for nothing. Trust me, they won't change the law."

I was confused. Why the hell did people keep bringing things up, only to drop them before it made sense?

—Thoughts of James Hunter, Hocmar 28, 2134, on the Nirnivian calendar

"Anyway, I'm tired." Janice faced him again and smiled. "I'll be going home now. It was fun, thanks."

"Janice, did I, uh, say something I shouldn't have? I'm sorry I—"

She laughed and slapped his shoulder in a comforting gesture. "Nah, nothing like that. Just a long day."

Chapter 10

Lacdor 6, 2134, on the Nirnivian calendar

As Daniel shuffled the deck, Ron gulped druikinaka juice, the fruit's sweetness tickling his tongue. The sound of cards rubbing each other reached Tigh's ears. Though soft, the noise gave him goose bumps, much like nails on a chalkboard would, except to a lesser extent.

Once his friend finished, he dealt the cards, alternating between Ron and himself. Tigh grabbed each one and studied them. What a terrible hand. The red and green circles formed a pair, but the rest proved useless. With a groan, he discarded the three other cards, and Daniel offered replacements as dictated by the rules. Again, disappointment gripped Tigh. He almost gritted his teeth but resisted the temptation. Bluffing proved his only option, and he attempted a confident smile. However, thanks to the good old Commander's magic vision, he doubted his deception ended up successful. Daniel returned four cards of his own, and as he did, the song playing on the radio stopped, replaced by the news. The broadcast mentioned how Her Holiness and the head priestess had denounced Councillor Jade Carlson's recent actions, and Ron half-listened.

"Hey, Dan, you're stuck right in the middle of that thing, ain't you?" He chuckled. "Must be a pain in the ass."

"Yes, I guess you could say that." The Commander shrugged. "Madeleine is always babbling on about it. We can't talk about anything else. And Rose is worse, believe it or not. I saw her today. She's really upset." Daniel snickered and snapped his fingers as if remembering a detail he had forgotten. "Actually, I got off easy. I ran into James, who told me Rose lectured him for over an hour."

"Poor bastard!" On that note, Ron studied his hand. With this crap, it'd take a miracle to pull off a victory. A last chance remained—the exchange rule. Once in a match, a player could ask the other if he had a specific card type in his possession. If so, he would give it to his opponent, who then surrendered a card of his choosing. Ron considered his options.

He could request a circle and turn his pair into a three of a kind, but the odds that Daniel would have one were low. He'd have a better chance at obtaining a double of his other shapes. That would give him a second pair. Should he go for broke or choose the less risky approach?

Luck had failed him so far, so he asked, "Got any lozenges?" As demanded, Daniel passed two cards to Ron.

Impressed, Tigh whistled. He had made the correct choice. Then he said, "People like Rose and Madeleine, the hard-core religious type—they don't get it. They take a high-and-mighty attitude and condemn every damn thing. Like William; they can't understand why he'd want to die." Tigh then adopted a mocking tone and said, "Life is sacred. Suicide is the ultimate sin. Your soul will vanish into nothingness because you're an immoral bastard, you son of a bitch." After a grunt, he shook his head and returned to his normal voice. "It's easy to judge when you haven't seen real pain. Shit, you're a soldier too. You freaking know what I mean. All the guys who were almost killed and ended up disfigured—some called 'em the lucky ones. They weren't." He stared at Daniel. "You can't deny that."

"You're right, I can't." Daniel raised a contrarian eyebrow. "But as a religious person, I can't condone what

William is doing, even if I understand where he's coming from."

"Fine, don't condone it. I'm not sure I do either. It's just, to me, if someone wants to damn his soul, that's his freaking business. You know, free will and all that shit."

"Free will is important, and in most cases, I share your philosophy." The Commander reordered his cards and licked his lips. "The problem is that euthanasia is different. It's not only your soul, it's—"

"Yeah, yeah, please spare me that cliché." A groan came from Tigh as he waved the argument away. "Ah, look, I'm not saying we should change the law or anything, just that we shouldn't judge William. We're not in his shoes. Anyway, this is getting too heavy. We're supposed to relax, for crying out loud." After that comment, they dropped the subject as well as the cards on the table, revealing their hands. Three of a kind against two pairs in Ron's favor. After he enjoyed some lighthearted bragging and Daniel congratulated his victory, they started another round.

***

After Daniel left, Ron walked upstairs to his room. The conversation on euthanasia had shaken him more than he wanted to admit, and it weighed on his mind. Soon, he found himself sitting on his bed and staring at the night table. His lip quivered as he pondered his next action. No question it would hurt; it always did. Still, he reached for the drawer and opened it, revealing the dozens of photos inside—some framed, some not. With a whimper, he grasped the one on top, his wedding picture.

On the right side, he stood beaming and wearing a tuxedo, far younger, though already balding. However, his earlier self failed to interest him. Instead, he fixated on the other figure, his now-deceased wife. Between her long auburn hair, elegant blue dress, and smooth bronzed skin, she radiated with beauty. Eyes watering, Tigh caressed her visage with the tip of his index finger.

"Myriam... I'm sorry."

A heaviness weighted on his heart, and soon, Ron sobbed in the dark. Even if they didn't voice their concern, the fact that he didn't have any pictures of his family in the office shocked people. In truth, he had a photo of Myriam there, concealed in his desk, much like those in his home. Whenever he gazed upon her image, he fell prey to sorrow and cried.

Filled with regret, Tigh remembered that fateful day. He'd arrived at the hospital with flowers even though he'd understood Myriam was too far gone to appreciate the gesture. When he'd entered her chamber, she had lain in bed alone. That was pre-budget cuts, back when patients might expect privacy from a hospital room. A breather rested on her face, the only reason for her survival. While awake, she remained mostly silent, and when she spoke, it consisted of nonsense. Despite this, Ron stayed and talked to her, describing what happened in daily life and how much everyone missed her.

It'd be a lie to claim their relationship had gone well. In truth, they'd fought a lot, to the point where they'd almost divorced. Marriage counseling had kept them afloat, but none could tell for how long. Still, she was the only woman Tigh had ever loved, and he'd pay any price for her to regain her health.

For several hours, Ron stayed by Myriam's side, recalling anecdotes from their years together. Soon, he reminisced about their first date and caressed her hand. When he mentioned a particular incident involving a snobbish waiter at a restaurant, he looked into Myriam's eyes. There he saw a spark, a lucidity that rarely showed itself. On occasion, his wife regained her senses and became able to form coherent sentences. These events were rare, however, and the more time passed, the less they occurred.

Myriam opened her mouth, and Ron leaned forward. They hadn't shared a real conversation in so long. Tingles of anticipation ran through his spine. Then Myriam's pupils darted toward the respirator's plug as she said, "Ron, please..."

At first, the statement confused Tigh. He blinked twice, considering the words. Finally, he understood, and after a gasp, he hopped to his feet and took a few steps back. "But that'd kill you!"

"Honey, you know as well as I do that I'm dead anyway. Please, I can't take it anymore. I don't want to live like this."

A gulp came from Ron. "I can't. I'm sorry, I can't do that."

She fired a pleading gaze at him, the same that had often won arguments in the past. "Can't this old lady have some agency before the end?"

For months, Myriam had lain there, both body and brain degenerating. Ron had witnessed it all. He was present when Myriam lost her strength until lifting a fork required too much effort. He was present when her lungs failed little by little. He was present when her mind deteriorated until her mental faculties rested below those of a young child. After swallowing hard, he reached for the plug, his hand trembling. Before he managed to touch it, a scream echoed, stopping his motion. A nurse had arrived to check on Myriam and caught him in the act. He denied the accusations and nothing came of it, except they wouldn't let him visit Myriam alone from then on, preventing him from fulfilling her wish.

Four long months of agony Myriam endured before she passed away. Four months of Tigh watching her suffer, wondering if he'd have spared her the torment had he not hesitated. Rose knew nothing of William's ordeal. Neither did he, but he had a better idea than most...

Chapter 11

Lacdor 9, 2134, on the Nirnivian calendar

People crowded the observation walkway, mostly medicine students eager to witness the Good Doctor's amazing talents. Evelyn stood among them. She'd cleared her afternoon in order to assist. Though her presence was unnecessary, she enjoyed watching him perform. Below in the operation room, the cyborg grabbed a scalpel and made the first incision. Then he seized a different tool, one unfamiliar to Evelyn, and performed complex motions requiring a dexterity she lacked.

The president was such an amazing surgeon, his movements so graceful he made it an art form. He rarely lost a patient; even the direst cases usually survived. Of course, his new mechanical body helped. It was much more precise than one of flesh and blood, and it never tired. Still, according to rumors, he was almost as great before.

—Thoughts of Evelyn Losier, Hocmar 28, 2134, on the Nirnivian calendar

The patient was a mother of two young children. She suffered from a rare cardiac disease. While an operation capable of curing her condition existed, it possessed a limited success rate. No doctor dared risk their stats to save her. The president had learned about the sad story by pure coincidence. He'd heard of those poor kids who cried themselves to sleep every night fearing they'd lose their mommy. Without delay, he'd made the necessary arrangements, and now he was attempting a miracle.

Next to Evelyn, a young man dressed in white scrubs observed the scene with his mouth gaping. Enthralled by the performance, he leaned forward until his nose touched the glass. Every so often, he shook his head in disbelief.

"He's incredible... most surgeons would take over twice as long."

Evelyn stifled a giggled in case her laughter might offend him. That was slow by the Good Doctor's standards. No doubt he adopted a deliberate pace in order to minimize the possibility of error given the complexity of his current task.

"You've never seen him operate before?"

"N-no. I've never seen anything like it."

"He's passionate about saving lives. That body helps too. It gives him the precision of a machine, yet he still has the intuition of a living man."

"Sure, but people with automated limbs can't wield them to their maximum capacity. The brain never adapts. But the Good Doctor's did, and quickly. How did he manage?"

The boy raised a valid question, but Evelyn couldn't provide a satisfactory answer. Nobody understood how the president had accomplished the feat.

"I don't know." She paused and contemplated the possibilities. "My guess is he was simply more motivated than most."

The operation succeeded. I wasn't surprised, but the family was another story. When the Good Doctor announced in his monotone voice that the most important woman in their lives would live, the kids jumped around laughing, and the dad cried tears of joy. They hugged the president. He remained there, expressionless. To a normal viewer, he appeared indif-

ferent, but I knew that, as a cyborg, he had lost his capacity for both tears and smiles.

—Thoughts of Evelyn Losier, Hocmar 28, 2134, on the Nirnivian calendar

After the operation, everyone eventually left and the Good Doctor returned to his lab. Evelyn followed him. He toiled on an experiment as he often did.

"Congratulations. You were amazing as always, Mr. President."

"I thank you for the kind compliment, Evelyn. I was merely doing my part to make Ostark a better place." He paused as he grabbed a beaker. "Personally, I prefer not to live in a world where no one dares to save a dying mother for selfish reasons."

Filled with admiration, Evelyn beamed. "Spoken like a true hero. We should celebrate your accomplishment!"

"Celebrate?" The cyborg shook his head. "Please, feel free to indulge if you wish. In my case, I believe my time is better spent in other ways. Besides, this body does not allow me many pleasures."

He was dedicated to his people and cared about our fate so much. As president, he had several obligations, yet he still operated on patients who needed him and helped develop cures for diseases. Of course, he didn't sleep anymore, which made him far more efficient than a normal person. Still, he didn't need to work so hard for our sake. That the Nirnivians called such a hero Doctor Death sickened me.

—Thoughts of Evelyn Losier, Hocmar 28, 2134, on the Nirnivian calendar

Chapter 12

Lacdor 14, 2134, on the Nirnivian calendar

I ate lunch with Rose and Brucie as I often did. Rose's mood had improved a lot. She was unusually happy, and she whistled as she ate her meal. While that made me glad, I wondered why she was so cheerful, and I didn't have to wait long for an explanation.

—Thoughts of James Hunter, Hocmar 28, 2134, on the Nirnivian calendar

"They haven't announced it on the news yet, but it's official: the Council rejected Jade's motion," Rose said after sampling her food. "Jade and William failed. Morality prevailed and I'm glad it's over."

"That's great!" Since Rose cared about this issue more than he did, James forced a touch of enthusiasm into his tone. However, the risk of the prophet noticing and embarking on another anti-euthanasia speech gave him shivers. "But, uh, I doubt William is so thrilled about it."

"He's probably not." Rose sighed and then shrugged. "That's okay. Now our job is to relieve him of his pain and improve his quality of life. With time, he'll understand why suicide would've been a mistake, and he will thank us. Trust me."

***

On the TV screen, the journalist uttered the words Susan dreaded to hear. Despite Jade's efforts, the Council refused to study the possibility of legalizing euthanasia.

The news failed to surprise her or William, but still, there had been a glimmer of hope, and now it was dashed. If anything, William took it better than Susan. When the announcement echoed through the speakers, he closed his eyes, let out a resigned moan and said it was the expected outcome.

While William appeared to have accepted his fate, denials and protests invaded Susan's mind. Those bastard politicians didn't care about his plights. And Her Holiness... though it might be blasphemy, Susan cursed her name in silence. What a hypocrite. She spoke about compassion and helping your fellow Gorumar but condemned William to suffering. The mere thought boiled Susan's blood, and she gritted her teeth.

Poor William remained stuck in bed each day, unable to even feed himself. How often did he endure the humiliation of having Susan clean up vomit or other bodily secretions from his body? How often did he stay awake during the night, assailed by excruciating pain while all she could offer were drugs that failed to quell his torments? Let Rose take care of him and see with her own eyes the torture she'd doomed him to. Maybe then she'd understand why he wished to end it all. Perhaps she'd come to question the principle of sanctity of life she valued so much. Except it would never happen... Rose would never experience Susan's daily life. With that realization, Susan approached William's bed, grasped the railing and bent her neck, granting her a full view of the mutant's face.

"William, I..." She sobbed. "You remember the promise I made? I'll do it."

"As much as I appreciate the offer, I can't accept. You will be demonized. They won't show any mercy."

"I know. It's okay, it's my choice to make." Despite her sorrow, Susan smiled. "It's the least I can do for the one I love." Then she kissed him for the last time.

Chapter 13

Lacdor 15, 2134, on the Nirnivian calendar

What a boring day. Nothing on TV, no one in the rec room. Hell, so little happened, I had nothing to tell Nadia's photo. It would've been the perfect time to play games on the minicomp Janice had given me, but I couldn't find it. Actually, I hadn't seen it for a while. From what I remembered, I'd left it on the shelves, but nope. I searched everywhere, from the drawers to the closet and even the fridge, but no luck.

—Thoughts of James Hunter, Hocmar 28, 2134, on the Nirnivian calendar

Though he'd checked there earlier, James slithered under the bed to locate the missing device. Many dust bunnies, but no electronics. Disappointed, he moaned. As he was crawling back out, the doorbell echoed, causing him to raise his head in surprise. With a shout of pain, he hit the top of his head. James winced and stifled a curse while he continued his trip to freedom. Once he emerged from underneath the bed, he caressed his hair and a sharp ache spiked, confirming a bump. Then the ringer beeped again.

"Please open up, James," a female voice said over the intercom. "It's Kristina."

That sounded like her, but why visit him? She had shown little interest in James and in fact seemed to dislike his presence. As a sense of dread filled James, he forgot his injury and opened the door. Indeed, Kristina waited there, fists clenched and eyes watering. The poor woman's skin tone had turned a shade paler than usual. She stepped inside the chamber and James swallowed hard.

"Kristina, are you okay? What's wrong?"

"Oh, it's not me, it's Rose." A sob came from the assistant. "William Adamant's health care provider poisoned him. He died, and she's been arrested. The police assume she euthanized him since Jade's proposal was refused. When Rose heard, she locked herself in her room. I tried talking to her, but she ignored me. Please go to her," Kristina whimpered, lowering her gaze and grimacing. "Um, I'm no good with these kinds of things—"

I rushed out before she finished. Maybe that was impolite, but I had a bad feeling.

—Thoughts of James Hunter, Hocmar 28, 2134, on the Nirnivian calendar

***

When James arrived, Brucie blocked the door, cross-armed and frowning. James wished to reach for the interphone to ask Rose to let him in, but the bodyguard barred his access. "Um, Brucie, can I..." With a trembling hand, he pointed at the intercom.

A shake of the head came from Brucie. "Can't let ya do that. Ain't nothing personal. She wanna be alone."

"Um, I think she needs me." James scratched the back of his head. "Kristina is worried, and she wants me to check on Rose."

"Yeah, well, Kristina ain't my boss. Listen, bro, sorry, but she ordered me. Ain't putting my ass on the line fo' that blond iceberg. Almost got me fired 'cause I'm a funny guy."

James straightened and gathered his courage. "Then do it for Rose." As James hoped, those words had an impact.

Brucie grimaced and averted his gaze. Taking the opportunity, James reached for the interphone's button, but with impressive reflexes, the bodyguard snatched his wrist. Though James whimpered, the touch proved gentle and caused no pain.

With a laugh, Brucie released James. "Yer lucky I'm worried too." He waggled a menacing finger. "Don't ya dare try that again."

"Um, yes, sir!"

With a groan, the large man rifled in his pocket and produced a key card. "I got this to open the door in case of emergency—bodyguard stuff. Dude, I'm gonna let ya in, but ya better appreciate it. Might lose my job over this."

James exhaled in relief. "Thanks. If I had money, I'd buy you a beer."

A wink came from Brucie. "How 'bout getting a job, then?"

"I'll consider it."

As promised, Brucie opened the door and I stepped inside. Rose lay facedown on the mattress, holding a framed picture in one hand and hugging her doll in the other. Even from the entrance, I heard her sobs and walked toward the bed. When Rose noticed, she turned her head and sat up. Her eyes were red from crying.

—Thoughts of James Hunter, Hocmar 28, 2134, on the Nirnivian calendar

James joined her on the bed. "Rose, are you okay?"

"No." The alleged prophet's voice sounded hoarse, as if she had wept for hours, yet that'd be impossible. "Hunter, why are you here?"

"Um, Kristina told me about William and his nurse."

Rose whimpered. "The poor fools. I only met them once, but they were good people, and now... William condemned himself to nothingness and so did Susan. This is her last life and she'll spend it in jail. I tried to avoid this! I offered assistance, but he refused. When I talked to him, William said he'd listen the whole day if I wanted. I gave up after two hours. To me, a sacred life is worth two lousy hours. I should've tried harder. Then maybe he'd still be alive!" The winged woman burst into tears, and James patted her shoulder.

When I realized that I had touched Rose, I panicked and removed my hand, but then she forced a smile. I sensed she appreciated the gesture.

—Thoughts of James Hunter, Hocmar 28, 2134, on the Nirnivian calendar

"No, Rose, it's, not like that at all. It's not your fault. William wanted to stop the pain. When people want something bad enough, they'll do whatever it takes, no matter how wrong it is."

As I looked at her, something clicked in my mind. I fitted the last piece of the puzzle. Everything made sense. Why Rose was so against euthanasia. Janice's cryptic message while we played Rubarg. Why she didn't want to talk about it. Rose worried about souls, but like I expected, there was far more to it.

—Thoughts of James Hunter, Hocmar 28, 2134, on the Nirnivian calendar

"Rose, I, uh, probably shouldn't mention this, but"— James wavered—"you attempted suicide, didn't you?"
"Yes."

***

She couldn't keep on going this way. Something had to be done. Time passed in isolation. Though her family and friends tried comforting her, Rose pushed them away. Any act of compassion proved too good for her. She didn't deserve their support. Most days, she remained in bed, immobile and replaying the tragic events in her mind. Her memory always forced the images on her. She failed to stop them.

On the rare occasion Rose managed to get up in the morning, more often than not, she ended up dropping on the sofa and lying there. Her appetite abandoned her. The mere thought of lifting a fork and bringing it to her mouth caused exhaustion. More than once, she endured a whole day without food. When she did eat, her energy only allowed the preparation of frozen meals. Soon, she'd run out of those, and heading to the grocery store to buy more seemed an impossible challenge. Then again, what did it matter? She made her choice.

With a whimper, Rose grasped the orange bottle and poured the viscous liquid into her glass. Then she reached for a green jug and added its contents to the mixture. She continued combining the various ingredients. The flasks did not contain juice or alcohol or even water, but rather cleaning products. Each of these substances might kill her on their own, but there was a chance she'd survive. By mixing them, she guaranteed her death. She'd located the recipe in the darkest recesses of the GlobalNet. Finding it had required considerable effort. A gun to her head might've provided a simpler alternative, but she lacked a firearm, and besides, that sounded too messy. Poison, however, spilled no blood, and the pages she'd consulted promised the concoction acted quickly.

A couple of minutes later, Rose finished her blend. She seized the glass and lifted it, her hand trembling. Midway, she wavered and almost rested it on the table again, but she continued. A putrid smell burned her nasal canal and throat. She coughed, spilling a few drops as a result, and assumed the potent odor confirmed the cocktail's lethality. After a sob, Rose gathered her resolve. The goblet touched her lips...

Then a strong force impacted her from behind. With a gasp, Rose collapsed on the floor, and a bang echoed. Pain raced through her on impact, and she lost her grasp on her glass. It shattered. The liquid spilled, staining the floor as the stench spread across the chamber.

"No!" Rose yelled. Torrents of tears flowed down her cheeks. Powerful arms wrapped around her torso, and she fought against the grip. Despite her wriggling, the assailant held strong. Though she didn't reveal her identity, her moaning confirmed the attacker to be a woman. Beyond that, Rose caught a few details that hinted at who assaulted her. She saw black hair during their fight, and those large muscles were familiar. "Janice, let me go! I was so close!" On that note, she elbowed her sister, but the blow caused no reaction.

"Are you freaking insane?" The older sibling tightened her hold. "If you drank that crap, you'd be dead meat! I saved your freaking life. Stop hitting me!"

"I didn't want to be saved!" As if to stress this point, Rose struck Janice once more. This time, the soldier groaned.

"Rose, you can't kill yourself! You'll be condemned to nothingness. You're the one who's always babbling on about that stuff!"

"That's fine with me! I can't... I can't go on like this! You don't understand. You can't understand..."

"Oh, I understand all right." A chill of comprehension tainted her tone. "Listen: don't do this over a man. Not over a goddamn man! They're not worth it."

***

As Rose turned a page of the book, she sensed someone watching. Since the incident, her parents had insisted she come to live with them so they could keep an eye on her. As such, she guessed the visitor to be Madeleine, but when Rose spun, she instead faced Janice. Contrary to her usual outgoing self, the soldier stayed outside the room with an averted gaze—no doubt the fury Rose had unleashed when they'd last met had left Janice reticent.

"Janice, hi!" Rose smiled. "I'm so sorry. I said horrible things when I should've been thankful."

The older sibling shrugged. "Eh, no worries, I get it." The gigantic woman stepped forward until she stood beside Rose. "You look better now."

"I am, after a fashion." With an exhale, Rose gestured toward her tome. "Mom's forcing me to reread a bunch of texts on the sanctity of life so I remember why I shouldn't have done what I did. Surprisingly, it's helping. I guess I forgot about that stuff..."

Janice giggled and hugged Rose. "Yeah, I guess you did!"

***

"Janice saved me and Mom forced me to read scripture." Rose closed her eyes and scowled. "The sanctity of life kept me going. That's why it's so important to me. If I lose my faith, I'll..." A sigh escaped the prophet. "Don't tell anyone. It's a family secret. If it spreads, there'll be a scandal. Even Brucie doesn't know."

"I swear I won't say a word."

Then without providing an explanation, Rose offered him the picture she held. The metallic frame proved cold on James's flesh as he studied it. The photo depicted a couple embracing on a park bench. On the left, James recognized a smiling Rose. He had never seen the winged woman so filled with joy. As for the man she hugged, he guessed him to be her deceased husband. Piercing blue eyes graced his face along with medium-length blond hair. While he wasn't as ridiculously huge as Brucie, an impressive physique lay under his dark gray suit. No question, he was the kind of person James might envy should they cross paths on the street.

"When Miguel died, something in me broke, and I never recovered." Rose sobbed. "I was depressed and decided to end this life and all life after, like William, so I attempted suicide. Even now, every day is a challenge. It's been years. I should let go, but... it's so complicated."

Poor thing never got over her deceased husband. Rose was stuck in the past. In a way, I could relate: I felt the same about my relationship with Nadia. Sure, she wasn't dead, but it wasn't working anymore, and yet I couldn't bring myself to end it.

—Thoughts of James Hunter, Hocmar 28, 2134, on the Nirnivian calendar

The tears kept rolling down her soft cheeks, and nothing suggested they'd stop soon. The sobs distressed James but, unsure how to console her, he bit his lip. Without consciously intending to, he slanted toward Rose, inviting her to lean on his shoulder. James gasped in surprise when she hugged him for comfort, but quickly recovered and wrapped his arms around her body, patting her back.

***

The next book, The Cyborg's Riddle, is available for preorder and releases on January 8, 2024.

Do you want a free short story that serves as a prequel to The Cyborg's Crusade? Then, join the cyborg's fan club on my website,
https://thecyborgscrusade.com/fanclub.html

Please consider leaving a review. Those help a lot. Note that you can buy books, and follow me on social media with this link:
https://thecyborgscrusade.com/hub.html

Thank you for reading, I hope with all my heart you enjoyed The Cyborg's Warning.

ABOUT THE AUTHOR

My name is Benoit Lanteigne and I'm a French Canadian (outside of Quebec) who's trying to write in English. That can be tricky. I'm a computer programmer and I enjoy it. I see many inspiring writers who hate their day jobs and hope to quit someday, but that's not my case. Mostly, I've worked on websites and web applications.

Back in school, I enjoyed writing and according to my teachers and classmates; I had a talent for it. Well, not so much for grammar and spelling, but they liked my stories. Once I went to university, I dropped writing as a hobby. There were other things I wanted to focus on, such as my career. Then, in the early 2000s, around 2006 I'd say, I had a flash of inspiration. At first, it was a single character: a winged woman with red hair. I didn't even know who she was, but the image stuck with me. From there, I began figuring out details about her origins and her world, but I only started writing for real in 2009. After over ten years of hard work, books of The Cyborg's Crusade are finally ready for release.

9 781777 900281